"Seems to me friends help each other."

Neither of them broke from staring at the other. Neither of them relented from their position.

"You got an objection to being friends with me?" Ward asked.

Red sniffed. "Seems to me friends don't push at each other, making impossible demands."

"Push? Impossible demands? Red, I have no idea what you are talking about. All I've done is rescue you and Belle from Thorton, bring you to a safe place and make sure you're taken care of. How is that pushing and making demands?"

She sniffed again and gave him a look dripping with disdain. "I guess it meant nothing to you, but I recall a kiss or two."

He gave her a look rife with disbelief. "Didn't see you resisting."

"Maybe," she said with annoyance _____ syllable, "I was just _____

This was not going _____ planned. Red was s_____ offer of friendship, a_____ was appropriate, see_____ to help was genuinely generous. Maybe even confess to liking, to even a small degree, that she liked having him around....

Books by Linda Ford

Love Inspired Historical

The Road to Love
The Journey Home
The Path to Her Heart
Dakota Child
The Cowboy's Baby
Dakota Cowboy
Christmas Under
Western Skies
   "A Cowboy's Christmas"
Dakota Father
Prairie Cowboy
Klondike Medicine Woman
*The Cowboy Tutor

*The Cowboy Father
*The Cowboy Comes Home
The Gift of Family
   "Merry Christmas, Cowboy"
†*The Cowboy's Surprise Bride*
†*The Cowboy's Unexpected Family*
†*The Cowboy's Convenient Proposal*

*Three Brides for Three Cowboys
†Cowboys of Eden Valley

LINDA FORD

lives on a ranch in Alberta, Canada. Growing up on the prairie and learning to notice the small details it hides gave her an appreciation for watching God at work in His creation. Her upbringing also included being taught to trust God in everything and through everything—a theme that resonates in her stories. Threads of another part of her life are found in her stories—her concern for children and their future. She and her husband raised fourteen children—four homemade, ten adopted. She currently shares her home and life with her husband, a grown son, a live-in paraplegic client and a continual (and welcome) stream of kids, kids-in-law, grandkids and assorted friends and relatives.

The Cowboy's Convenient Proposal

LINDA FORD

HARLEQUIN® LOVE INSPIRED® HISTORICAL

If you purchased this book without a cover you should be aware
that this book is stolen property. It was reported as "unsold and
destroyed" to the publisher, and neither the author nor the
publisher has received any payment for this "stripped book."

Recycling programs
for this product may
not exist in your area.

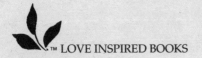 ™ LOVE INSPIRED BOOKS

ISBN-13: 978-0-373-82963-7

THE COWBOY'S CONVENIENT PROPOSAL

Copyright © 2013 by Linda Ford

All rights reserved. Except for use in any review, the reproduction
or utilization of this work in whole or in part in any form by any
electronic, mechanical or other means, now known or hereafter
invented, including xerography, photocopying and recording, or in
any information storage or retrieval system, is forbidden without
the written permission of the editorial office, Love Inspired Books,
233 Broadway, New York, NY 10279 U.S.A.

This is a work of fiction. Names, characters, places and incidents are
either the product of the author's imagination or are used fictitiously, and
any resemblance to actual persons, living or dead, business establishments,
events or locales is entirely coincidental.

This edition published by arrangement with Love Inspired Books.

® and TM are trademarks of Love Inspired Books, used under license.
Trademarks indicated with ® are registered in the United States Patent
and Trademark Office, the Canadian Trade Marks Office and in other
countries.

www.LoveInspiredBooks.com

Printed in U.S.A.

In him we have redemption through his blood, the forgiveness of sins, in accordance with the riches of God's grace that he lavished on us with all wisdom and understanding.

—*Ephesians* 1:7

Don't we all need God's grace in our lives?
This book is dedicated to those I love
who are in need of a special awareness
of God's grace and love and forgiveness.
I won't name names, but you know who you are.

Chapter One

Eden Valley, Alberta
July 1882

Ward Walker wanted nothing more than to get back to the ranch. He'd spent the better part of three days locating a man and delivering a message from his boss about purchasing a prize stallion.

With no interest in the men crowding the saloon nor what they were so concerned about, he sat back waiting to get something hot to eat before he headed back.

"I perceive you are all anxious to see Red." The man to his right lifted a bowler hat from his pomaded hair and held it out. "You willing to pay?"

Each hand dropped in a coin.

He waved the hat toward Ward.

"Ain't interested," Ward said, not bothering to keep a growl out of his voice.

The man roared with harsh laughter. "You'll change your mind soon enough."

"Doubt it. I'm just waiting for a dish of stew." In his

twenty-three years he had learned to stay away from trouble as best he could.

As if summoned by Ward's words, the barkeep swung from the back room with a bowlful of steaming food. Ward turned his attention to his meal.

The man shook the coins from his hat into his palm and pocketed them. Grinning widely, he bellowed, "Red."

The silent expectation in the room held Ward's interest despite his vow that he cared only about eating.

"Aw, Thorton, she ain't coming," one disgruntled cowboy murmured. "I want my money back."

"She'll come. She knows what to expect if she don't." The way the man smacked his fist into his palm sent tension crawling up Ward's spine, the words bringing with them memories of another time, another man who said similar things and followed through with fists or boots, or anything he could lay his hands on.

"Red. Get out here. Now." The harsh voice practically stole Ward's appetite. But he had to eat to survive so he took a scoop of the succulent stew.

The gray blanket hanging crookedly in the doorway on one side of the room full of crowded tables fluttered. The men cheered and from behind the curtain stepped a woman with flaming-red hair in a mane of curls down her back. Her blue-green eyes flashed rebellion, as did the set of her mouth. She pulled a man's shirt closed across her front.

"Girl, shed that shirt."

The girl scowled fiercely.

"Need I remind you …?" The man's chair squawked back.

The girl shuddered.

Ward's fists curled as she shrugged out of the shirt to expose a red dress with a bodice that was far too revealing. Her skin flared bright pink.

"That's better. Now give us a little dance. And smile."

Red speared the man with a look so full of heat that when Ward jerked toward him, he thought he'd see scorch marks on his face. Instead, all he saw was a leer. Ward couldn't decide the man's age. Somewhere between his own and already worn out. The man had a clean-shaven face and wore a black coat that looked as if it might have belonged to a preacher, but the narrow set of his eyes and the humorless smile convinced Ward that the man was no preacher.

Red turned, revealing pale shoulders. Her dress didn't quite cover a red streak the width of a belt in the center of her back.

He didn't need such evidence to know that man named Thorton beat the woman, but seeing the bruise filled Ward with rage. He jerked to his feet, sending his chair skidding away. He'd walked away from this kind of abuse once before. He'd regretted it every day since. He would not walk away again. Not even from people he didn't know and who were none of his business.

Thorton jerked about at the noise of Ward's sudden rise. "Something bothering you, boy?"

"You beat this woman."

Thorton laughed. "Only way I can get her to do what I say. She's a bit headstrong, you might say. Ain't that right, fellas?"

The raucous laughter of the men fueled Ward's anger until it burned like an out-of-control forest fire. He was long past being reasonable and keeping his nose out of trouble. "I don't aim to stand back and allow some poor woman to be used as a punching bag."

"Is that a fact?" Thorton grinned. "Now ain't he a feisty little rooster?"

Ward caught Red's startled look, then she shook her head hard. As if telling him to leave it alone.

But he could not. Would not. "I'm telling you to let her go."

Thorton grabbed Red's arm. She cringed, then straightened and faced him squarely, defiance blaring from her eyes. But Ward knew it was only a defensive gesture. One he had grown familiar with. *You can beat me all you want but you can't control my mind.*

"She's mine," Thorton said. "I do with her as I please. Besides, I have a duty to control her. The good book says—" The man puffed up his chest as if expounding words of utmost importance "'—A man should rule his own household.' I aim to do exactly that."

Ward stepped closer. He had no plan. He didn't know if Red was the man's lawful wife or not. He only knew he would not allow the abuse to continue.

From somewhere a gun appeared in the hand of a man to Ward's left, leveled at Ward. "We paid to see her dance."

Ward hesitated, his gaze slowly shifting from the gun back to Red.

"This the way you want it, boy?" Thorton shoved Red away. She stumbled. Ward reached to stop her fall but she spun about as smooth as a fox and pushed the tipped chair of the nearest man, sending him crashing to the floor. Several men tumbled like dominos. The gun went off. Bedlam erupted.

Ward glanced down at himself. Saw no blood. He looked for Red. She was sprawled flat-out, a bright pink stain on her skirt.

"That'll bring the Mountie," a man near the door bellowed.

Men scattered, bursting through the door. Ward figured they must have about bowled over anyone approaching the saloon. Horses pounded away. Thorton had slipped into the back room. Only Ward and the saloonkeeper remained. And Red.

"Best get her out of here," the saloonkeeper said.

Ward didn't pause to ask questions or wonder. He scooped Red off the floor and beat it out the door. He scrambled to the back of his horse, Miss Red in his arms. No one asked him what he was doing or challenged his actions. Without a backward look he headed for home.

The bloodstain on Red's dress spread but his sense of decency forbade him checking it. Unless her life seemed threatened, and it didn't. He explored her scalp with his fingers, found a knot the size of an egg and discovered her tangled curls felt all springy and satiny under his fingers.

"I'll take you home and turn you over to Linette," he said. Linette was his boss's wife and she took in strays and injured people, fixed them up and made sure they had a safe place to continue their lives. "What with Eddie—that's the boss—and the other cowboys, I don't expect you'll be bothered by Thorton again. Sure hope you're not married to that man or we'll have to deal with the law."

He urged the horse to a trot. He longed for a cool breeze, but the heat of midsummer beat down on them.

If he rode steady he could reach the ranch by the evening. At least with the long summer days there would still be some light. Not that he feared getting lost. 'Sides, if he did, the horse knew his way home.

Red moaned and clutched her head. She'd be confused when she came to, so he tightened his arms around her waist to prevent her from falling.

He knew the precise moment her senses returned. She stiffened like a rod. If he hadn't expected some sort of reaction, she'd have shimmied right out of his arms and likely landed on her head again, or under the horse's hooves.

"Relax. You're safe. Got a little gunshot wound, but I think it'll wait till we reach the ranch." He realized she hadn't heard his earlier words about Linette and Eddie, and repeated them, then gave his name.

She squirmed about to direct those green eyes at him. None of her defiance had faded. "Put me down right this minute."

"Ma'am…miss…you don't have to worry anymore. 'Less you're married to that—" Best not call him a beast just in case "—that man." He realized women married scoundrels. Usually because the man in question tricked them with words of love. Love? He snorted softly, hoping she wouldn't notice. Love made a person do foolish things. Made them regret decisions. Sort of messed up a man's or woman's thinking. He'd long ago decided it wasn't for him. Nope. He'd accept responsibility, work and do anything for people he cared about. But he would not allow his heart to rule his head.

She made an unladylike noise. "We are most certainly not married."

"Then you're safe. I'll take you to the ranch."

"I do not want to go to your ranch."

"It's not mine—"

"Put me down this instant. Or better yet, take me back."

"You're safe with me."

She exploded into a ball of flailing legs and arms. Managed to scratch his cheek before he could corral her arms. She kicked the horse, sending him into a panicked bolt.

"Whoa. Whoa." Ward had to turn his attention to getting the horse under control before they both ended up on the ground miles from home. It should have been easy, but Red made sure it wasn't. He couldn't hold both her and the horse with only one set of hands, and she slipped under his arm and jolted to the ground.

"Ooh."

No doubt she'd felt the pain of her wound, but he didn't have time to give her more than a passing thought as he fought to calm the horse. "Settle down. You're okay." Free of Red's vicious kicks, his mount settled.

Ward turned to see how Red fared. Her skin had turned pale as a sheet. Yet she flashed him continued defiance. He was beginning to understand the peculiar frustration of dealing with Red. He rode to her side and offered a hand. "Come on, get on and I'll take you—"

She slapped him away. "I'm going back." She slapped the horse on his withers.

Ward held the horse under control. "Look, lady. You'll be safe from Thorton where I'm taking you."

She took a step, wavered. He kind of figured she was a little dizzy and probably her leg hurt some.

"Leave me alone."

"Yes, ma'am." He kept pace at her side as she took another step and another, continuing to sway like a tree before a brisk north wind. Only difference being a tree had roots that anchored it to the ground. Red had no roots, no anchor. Nothing to keep her from toppling.

He figured he'd be there when she went down.

She paused, sucked in air, pressed a palm to her eyes and slowly folded to the ground.

Ward jumped down and scooped her up. "Here we go again."

She moaned. Her eyes fluttered and she sank against his chest. She'd be a whole lot less trouble this way, but for all he knew she was bleeding to death under that crimson-stained dress.

He kicked the horse into a gallop. "Let's get home as fast as we can."

Red struggled briefly and ineffectively twice more before he topped the last hill. Thankfully the little town of Cross Bar wasn't any farther away. But at least it was far enough to discourage frequent visits. Maybe far enough to keep Thorton from riding after him.

He sauntered past the empty winter pens, thudded over the bridge and passed the new house where the foreman, Roper, lived with his new wife and the four children they'd rescued and adopted. Through the kitchen window, Roper saw him pass, lifted a hand in greeting, then saw Ward had his arms full and leaned closer.

The bunkhouse lay in darkness. The men would be out with the cows or sleeping.

He glimpsed the empty table in the cookhouse as he passed. His stomach growled. He hadn't eaten more than a mouthful of that stew back at the saloon. Maybe Cookie would rustle up something for him.

He continued up the hill toward the big house. As he drew closer, he saw Linette and Eddie through the window. Eddie glanced up as he'd heard the sound of Ward's approach, and went to the window. Ward waved and motioned toward the woman in his arms.

Eddie turned away and strode from the room, Linette in his wake. By the time Ward reached the door, they had flung it open.

"What do you have there?" Eddie called.

"Woman named Red. She's been shot."

Linette sprang forward. "How bad?"

"Haven't had a look. It's her leg."

"She's unconscious?"

"Off and on."

Linette reached for Red, but Ward didn't release her until Eddie took her and strode into the house. Ward leaped from his mount and followed.

"I ought to warn you. She's a little feisty."

Eddie chuckled. "Seems pretty standard behavior around here."

Linette's look held both denial and affection. "Let's get her into a bed so I can see how badly hurt she is."

Ward followed as far as the hallway leading to several bedrooms. He plucked his hat from his head and watched Eddie duck into the doorway Linette indicated. "She's in good hands now. I'm going to see if Cookie has anything for me to eat."

Linette turned. "Wait. Who is she? Where did you find her?"

He twisted his hat. He knew nothing about her except her name and he wasn't even sure "Red" was her real name. He'd simply rescued her from a man who ruled with his fists or a belt…likely both and other things as well. "All I know is her name's Red and she was in a bad situation."

Linette studied him a moment, then nodded. "She'll get the attention she needs here."

Ward slapped his hat to his head and headed out the door. He cared for his horse, then went to the cookhouse to seek something to fill the hollows of his hungry stomach.

Only as he ate the generous plate of mashed potatoes and gravy and thick slices of beef, raised right on the ranch, the food failed to satisfy the emptiness around his heart that he seldom acknowledged…that he'd carried since he'd walked away from his brothers and left them to deal with a situation that mirrored the one he'd found Red in. Sure he'd done it for the right reason, figuring the beatings would stop if he left.

But how could he be certain they did? Would he ever see his brothers again? Or his mother? Love had made her blind to the faults of the man she'd married a few years ago as a widow. The man who became Ward's cruel stepfather. Again he reminded himself, love made a person unable to see the facts.

He pushed the plate away and bolted from the table.

* * *

Red sat upright so fast her head spun and pain shot clear through her brain. "Oww." She pressed her palms to her head. "That hurts."

"Take it easy." Cool hands touched hers. "You're safe here."

Safe? Was it possible? "Where am I?" She glanced around the unfamiliar room. She lay on a bed with a small table across her knees. This certainly wasn't a room she'd been in before. Dark green drapes hung at the sides of a window. Brilliant sunlight spilled into the room. The bed was covered in a bright quilt full of swirls of color. She stole a glance at the woman before her. "Who are you?" The woman had plain brown hair. Oh, how Red wished her hair was brown and straight and would stay in a tidy bun. The woman smiling at her had the gentlest eyes she'd seen anywhere since Mother died. Red's throat clamped at a rush of regrets sweeping over her.

"I'm Linette Gardiner. You are safe in my home. I'm guessing you have your memory back. Perhaps you can tell me a bit about yourself now." She removed the bed tray on which rested a half-full cup of tea. Red had no recollection of having drunk the top half but it seemed she must have.

"My memory back? How long have I been here?"

"Two days."

Two days. Her blood burned through her veins with desperate urgency. She tried to swing her feet to the floor and fell back as pain ripped through her head and leg.

Linette caught her hand. "Sit back and relax. You're injured."

"Am I alone?" She moved her head gingerly, ignoring the pain, as she checked out every corner of the room.

"You are alone and safe. I know your first name is Red, though I suspect it is a nickname. Can you tell me your full name?"

"It's—" She paused.

"Don't push it if you can't remember. I'm sure your memory will return in good time."

Her memories were intact. She was Grace Eileen Henderson, eighteen years of age. But her name no longer fit. "Red Henderson." She had a little sister, Belle, who was eight years old. Her lungs spasmed. She couldn't get her breath.

"No need to be afraid." Linette rubbed her shoulder and soothed her with a sweet voice. But the panic would not ease.

"I have to get back." Without Red's protection, what would be happening to Belle?

Linette sat back and studied her. "But why? Ward told us how that man treated you."

She couldn't tell the real reason. They wouldn't understand. No one would. Her situation would only make good people like Linette view her with even more alarm than she did now. "Where's my dress?"

"You're welcome to keep the one you're wearing."

Red rubbed the soft cotton of the muted brown dress. No doubt the color would also mute her coloring, stealing some of the red from her hair, turning her complexion muddy. More than enough reason to wish for many more dresses the same. But she could just imagine how

Thorton Winch would react to her wearing an outfit that covered her from neck to wrists to ankles. A great lump of longing swelled within her. If only she could own a dozen such dresses. "I would like my own gown back, if you please."

Linette hesitated a moment, then nodded. "Very well. I shall get it." She slipped from the room.

As soon as she was gone, Red pushed carefully to her feet and waited for the dizziness to pass. Ignoring the pain in her leg, she made her way to the window. The scene spun crazily. But she squinted to focus. She was in the second story of a house that sat on a hill overlooking a large collection of other buildings. This must be the ranch that cowboy had talked about. She eyed the barn and the horses corralled outside it. A cowboy with a rolling gait moved among the horses. She studied him. Was it the man who had kidnapped her? She'd tried to escape his clutches on the way here. Would he likewise try to prevent her from leaving?

She could not allow it.

"Here it is." Linette stepped into the room. "Oh, you're up. You shouldn't be."

Red cautiously turned to face her. The red satin dress hung over her arm. "I'm fine."

"I regret I couldn't get all the stain out." She showed the dress with a faded brown stain on one side.

"Thank you." She clutched the dress to her as if it were something treasured. But it wasn't that she cared about the dress. Only about not provoking Thorton. Bile rose in her throat. Oh, how she regretted her gullibility. She'd trusted the man when he said he was a preacher and could take her and Belle to his sister. They'd be safe, he promised.

He'd lied. She'd never again trust a man.

She shuddered. Two days. What had happened to Belle? She must leave.

"I heard she was feeling better."

A man's voice pulled her attention to the doorway and her cowboy rescuer. He'd given his name as Ward Walker. He was solid-looking with a thick thatch of black hair.

"You." She managed not to spit the word out.

He grinned. "Yup. Me. Glad to see you have your memory back."

For two heartbeats she wished she didn't, but the alternative was unthinkable. "Don't expect me to thank you."

He chuckled. "Yup. I see you're back to normal. You were mellow when you didn't remember your name." He shot a triumphant look toward Linette. "I told you she was feisty."

Feisty? He had no idea how quickly she'd learned to keep her opinions and objections to herself. She had to return to Thorton. There was no alternative. She would demand transportation back this moment, but the room suddenly tipped to the right and black folded inward from the corners.

Ward rushed forward and caught her before she hit the floor. "You're too weak to be up." He carried her to the bed and eased her down on the pillows.

For some reason her fingers refused to release him. She clutched his shoulders, finding strength and steadiness there. That was all it was, she reassured herself. Holding on to him kept the world from spinning.

"You're safe here. No one will hurt you." His intensely blue eyes drilled straight through her, invading her mind, probing her heart. If only she could accept his words, allow herself to settle back and feel safe.

But she had Belle to consider. Besides, no decent man would ever look at her without judgment or lust in his eyes. She'd performed dances that made her grateful her mother couldn't see. And men touched her, their hands soiling her soul every bit as much as Thorton's belt damaged her body.

"I can't stay," she murmured, unable to break from his promising gaze. "Please take me back."

He straightened. "Never." His eyes blazed. "I saw how that man treated you."

She lowered her gaze. "I can take it."

He perched on the edge of the bed. "I understand how you fear him, but there is no need. He can no longer harm you. No one here will let him."

Linette murmured agreement.

"So you rest and get better. Things will sort themselves out. You'll see." He patted her hand.

She nodded. Obviously she was going to get no help from him or likely anyone here. They all saw themselves as noble rescuers. But she would find her way back. She must.

Ward watched her closely. "Your coloring is coming back. That's good."

Self-consciously she brushed her hands over her hair. For half a wooden nickel she would shave off that offensive red hair. Wouldn't Thorton find that idea just lovely? "I'd like to get up now."

Ward shook his head. "Think you better give your head a chance to get back to normal."

"For all you know, this is normal." He knew nothing about her or her circumstances and she was happy to leave it that way.

Ward's eyes crinkled with amusement. "You forget I saw how nimble you are on your feet."

He was too close, too big, practically blocking everything else from view. "I still am. Let me show you." She shoved him aside and swung her feet to the floor, feeling the blood drain from her face. Her skin grew clammy. No way could she stand up without clutching support. For sure she couldn't do anything nimble. But he didn't need to know it. She pulled in a breath, sucked strength from it and forced her legs to hold her upright. "See? I'm fine."

But by the way Ward hovered at her side and the anxious look on Linette's face, she knew she had not convinced them.

"I'll just sit a moment on that chair." She indicated the hardback chair a few feet away.

Ward jerked it closer. She didn't know if she should be annoyed that he didn't think she could walk that far or grateful that she didn't have to prove she could. Her knees waited until she reached the chair before they buckled. Still she sat straight, trying hard to convince everyone in the room she was okay. It was hard to say if either of the others thought she was fine. She knew she wasn't.

She could not make it back to the saloon without help.

Help was not to be found from Ward or Linette.

Where would she find it?

"I'll let you handle her." Ward nodded toward Linette and headed for the door. He paused, turned to consider Red. "I'm glad you're on the mend and hope you'll soon feel safe here."

She scowled at him with all the strength she could summon from her uncooperative body. What right did he have to come into her life and complicate matters? He knew absolutely nothing about what was at stake.

She could not continue staring at him. It made her head hurt like fury. She settled for simply nodding—let him think what he wanted from that—then lowered her gaze and studied her fingers, noting how they twisted together until there were spots of white and red. Let them think what they wanted about that, too. Put it down to tension or pain. They would never guess how worried she was.

Ward finally left, his footsteps echoing down the hall.

Determination filled her, giving her strength to remain sitting upright. "I'm fine," she insisted.

She had to get her strength back. But with Linette hovering, she couldn't move. "I think I'd like to rest now."

Linette hurried to her side and held her elbow.

She let Linette ease her to the inviting bed, and snuggled down like she meant to have a long sleep. Linette spread an afghan over her, then tiptoed from the room. Red sighed. It was tempting to close her eyes and give in to the lethargy of her body.

But that would not get her back to Belle.

She remained tense, waiting for Linette's footsteps to fade, then she pushed herself to the side of the bed and took deep breaths to stop the dizziness. Holding carefully to the frame on the foot of the bed, she again made her way to the window and rested her forehead on the glass. Men went back and forth outside. Too many for her to slip away unnoticed. Even if she had the strength.

But she must find the strength somewhere. Somehow.

Too bad she no longer believed God would help her or she would pray for His intervention.

Chapter Two

"Boys." Eddie stepped into the cookhouse as the cowboys ate their breakfast. "Red is missing."

Ward dropped his fork and stared. Yesterday she could barely stand. Now she was gone?

Eddie continued. "Her room was empty when we got up this morning. I'm telling you, Linette is some concerned about her. Figures she's lost her memory again and is wandering about, lost and alone. Or worse, passed out somewhere." He scrubbed at his neck. "Boys, we have to find her before Linette gets it into her head to go looking. We can't have that. Especially in her condition." Linette was in the family way, and Eddie worried constantly about her.

Ward was already on his feet. "I'll check the barn." He was out the door while Eddie ordered men to various corners of the yard to search for the missing woman.

Ward raced to the barn. Had she wandered out in the dark? Fallen in the river? He shuddered as he imagined her alone. Further injured. Suffering. He'd rescued her from a harmful situation. He could only pray she hadn't fallen into a worse one. The door squawked a protest as he pushed it open and stepped into the warm, dusty interior. "Red," he yelled, wondering if she could hear his voice. Would she respond even if she did? He headed down the alley, paused at the first stall. It was empty. The horse that should be there was gone.

Gone? Had the animal let himself out? Probably not, since it was Moon that should have been in that stall and Moon liked the comforts of the barn too much to wander.

Suspicion crept into Ward's thoughts. Red kept saying she wanted to go back. He went to the tack room and counted the saddles. Sure enough. One missing.

His jaw clenched. Even though he knew it was useless to search the rest of the barn, he did so. More out of wishing she was here than thinking she was. Then he headed back to the cookhouse. Eddie paced the floor, waiting for someone to return with good news to ease his wife's worry.

"'Fraid I have bad news," Ward said. "There's a horse missing. And a saddle." Even though Eddie looked ready to chew nails, he might as well tell it all. "There were small footprints in the dust. Lady-sized."

Eddie groaned. "She stole a horse? Don't hardly call that gratitude. Do you?"

Ward didn't say one way or the other. "I'll ride after her and get the horse."

"You do that."

Ward hesitated. Did Eddie want him to turn Red over to the Mountie as a horse thief? Though Ward was beginning to think the only place Red would be safe was behind bars.

"Just get the horse back." Eddie spun about and

paced to the far side of the room. He stared out the window as Ward waited. With a gut-deep sigh, Eddie turned. "And bring her back, too, or Linette will have both our hides."

"Boss, you expect me to tie her to the saddle?"

Eddie grinned. "Ward, charm her into coming back."

"Yeah, right." So far neither charm nor superior strength had convinced Red she didn't need to go back to that man Thorton. "Why in the name of all that's right would she want to return?"

"I don't know. Doesn't make sense. He must have some hold on her, though I can't imagine what it could be."

Ward turned and headed back to the barn. Whatever Red's reason, he intended to stop her. No way he could stand by and see a person subjected to the abuse he knew she received. As he saddled up, he prayed for a way to convince her. *And, Lord, keep her safe.* In her condition she could have fallen from the horse and received further injury.

Following her tracks presented no challenge and he galloped down the trail. The sun rose higher in the east, bringing with it the promise of heat.

Was Red in that silly dress she clutched in her arms yesterday? If so, she'd soon be burnt a matching color. Though anyone riding back into her situation deserved to suffer some misery. Might make her reconsider her decision.

But worry soon replaced his annoyance. And a large dose of confusion. He knew firsthand the pain and fear of living with someone who controlled with fists to the flesh and a belt across the back…or anywhere it landed.

Why would she return to such a situation? Eddie said the man must have a hold on her. But Ward couldn't imagine what that could be.

He settled into a lope. An hour later he glimpsed her in the distance and urged his horse to a gallop.

As he closed the distance, she turned, saw him and kicked poor old Moon into a jarring trot. Ward knew from experience how rough a ride Moon was and almost felt sorry for her.

He easily overtook her, grabbed the bridle and pulled them to a standstill. "What do you think you're doing?" At least she'd chosen to wear the brown dress rather than the revealing red one.

"I'm going back where I belong." Her green eyes blazed with defiance.

"You know the kind of trouble you can get into for stealing a horse?"

"About the same you will be in for kidnapping me."

"Kidnapping!" She had to be joshing. "I rescued you."

"Don't recall saying I needed rescuing."

He reached out and touched her back where he'd seen the red welts and knew a fleeting sense of triumph when she flinched. "You planning to tell me you like that kind of treatment?"

"Wasn't planning to tell you anything."

"I know what it's like to have a belt used on me. I know what it does to your mind."

Her eyes darkened. She pressed her lips together. For a moment he thought she might soften. Admit the pain. Relent. But then her shoulders went back and her chin went up and he knew she wouldn't give in.

"Nothing touches my mind."

Ward shrugged. "You'll never convince me, 'cause I know better. Not only does it affect your mind, it affects your heart. Teaches you to build guards around it so no one can get in."

"Speak for yourself." She jerked away and urged the horse forward.

He grabbed the bridle again. "You ain't going anywhere."

She yanked at the reins, trying to get free. When that didn't work, she slapped his hands, tried to kick his horse.

"Stop it."

"Let me go."

They stared at each other, both breathing hard. He knew his eyes were as hard and unyielding as hers, which blared brittle, green shards. "Why would you want to go back to such a situation?"

He could feel her measuring him, trying to gauge him. He could see her throat work as if she struggled to swallow.

Finally she nodded. "He has my little sister. Belle's only eight."

The words thundered through him. A person would do anything to protect a little sister...or brother. Hank was only six when Ward left, Travers, thirteen. He did a little mental arithmetic. That was seven years ago. How had time passed so quickly, silently...sadly?

He wished he could know if leaving had made it better for Hank and Travers.

"Has he hurt her?" Each word ripped a piece of flesh from his heart.

All the starch left Red and she sank forward. "You talk about how cruel treatment touches the mind and heart. I see it in her. But so far I've protected her from worse." She scrubbed at her eyes. "I have to get back to her."

He understood that there were other kinds of torture, especially for a little girl. He nodded and together they rode onward. "We need to get her out of there. You, too." Though technically Red was out of the situation, he now understood why she would return. Why she felt compelled to.

"He will never let us go."

He heard the resignation in her voice. But he wasn't about to accept defeat. This time he would fight to make sure a man like Thorton could not continue to rule by the power of his fists. "Have you ever considered going to the Mountie?"

"Thorton never lets us out together unless he's with us. If I ever went to the Mountie on my own, I fear what would happen to Belle."

"I figured as much." He considered the situation for the next few miles. "Here's the plan. I'll go with you to the Mountie and he'll make Thorton release your sister."

Red didn't answer for a moment as she studied his suggestion. Finally she nodded.

He considered her from under the brim of his hat, wondering if she only pretended to agree. He was learning she didn't easily go along with plans others suggested. More than that, he understood why she would agree to something with her mouth while dissenting with her mind.

The sun reached its zenith as they neared town.

It blared down on them without pity. One of the first buildings was the Mountie station. A horse stood patiently at the front. Hopefully it belonged to the lawman. Their whole plan rested on him being there.

Ward swung from his saddle and hustled over to help Red dismount. He guessed from the way she pursed her lips she might have protested but reconsidered and allowed it with barely a hesitation and likely only because her leg hurt. But after she gained her feet she pulled away so they marched side by side toward the door. Ward fell back to let her step in first.

The Mountie sat behind a desk, writing in some sort of ledger. He glanced up at their arrival. Ward got the feeling he saw them both in detail but his eyes lighted on Red and he slowly rose to his feet. "Thorton said you'd been kidnapped. This man the one responsible?"

Ward's neck tingled. His plan didn't include getting arrested and maybe hung.

"He didn't seem particularly worried about it, I might add. Said you'd be back soon enough." The Mountie considered Ward from head to toe, no doubt silently examining him for a weapon.

Ward could assure him he carried no hidden pistol or knife. In fact, he kind of counted on the Mountie's authority to accomplish what they needed. "I didn't kidnap her. She was injured. I took her to a friend to be doctored."

"That right, miss?"

Red dismissed his question with a wave of her hand. "I'm here to tell you the truth."

"Always interested in the truth."

"Thorton's got my little sister under lock and key. That's how he knew I'd be back."

The Mountie came to rigid attention. "That's a serious charge. One I intend to follow up on."

"We're counting on it."

He grabbed his wide-brimmed Stetson. "Let's go talk to Thorton Winch."

Ward and Red trotted after the Mountie. Red would have burst into the saloon ahead of him but he pressed her back. "I'll deal with this."

Ward could feel Red's hot impatience as they followed the Mountie inside. Mr. Winch jolted his chair to all fours when he saw the three of them. "Told you she'd be back."

"She tells me you have her little sister locked up here."

Thorton chuckled loudly. "She's addled. Don't know why I keep her." But Ward saw the evil glint in the man's eyes and knew he would beat Red unmercifully if he got his hands on her.

Ward didn't intend he should get the chance.

"Have a look, Constable." Thorton waved his arm to indicate the whole place was open to him.

"I'll show you where she is." Red stomped past Thorton, being sure to stay out of arm's reach.

Ward and the Mountie followed.

Red threw open the door to a tiny room with a narrow bed against one wall. But the place was as clean and tidy as an unused manger. "She's gone." Before either man could think, she dashed back to the grinning Thorton and tried to claw his eyes out. "What have you done with her? Tell me."

The Mountie peeled her off the man. "Sorry to bother you," he murmured to Thorton.

Red broke from the Mountie's grasp and raced outside.

Ward noted that Thorton appeared totally unconcerned. The man knew he had Red in his clutches.

Without a doubt his ace was Belle, Red's little sister.

Where had he hidden her?

Red swallowed back a yard-wide wail as she stood in the center of the street. She stared the full length one way. Where was Belle?

She turned slowly and studied the other side of town. Slowly her thoughts settled. Thorton would not let Belle go if for no other reason than it forced Red to dance for the despicable creature who considered himself her owner. Belle was around here somewhere. Close enough that Thorton could mock Red's frustration. She shuddered. He delighted as much in tormenting Red as in anything else.

Where would he hide Belle? Likely any number of men would help him. Men of the same quality as he. Like Mr. Shack, who ran the feed store. Or dirty Old Mike Morton, who worked at the livery barn. Mike had a little cabin behind the barn where the owner allowed him to live.

The perfect place to lock up a little girl.

Without a backward glance or a considering thought, she steamed down the street, crossed behind the store to avoid being seen approaching the livery barn. She reached the tiny cabin. Sure enough, it was locked solid and the windows were boarded up tight as a drum. She tapped the door. "Belle?"

Did she hear a rustling? "Belle?" She dare not call loudly and alert any of Thorton's willing cohorts, but she was certain something—or likely someone—moved inside.

The padlock was solid. No way she could hope to break it.

The wood on the windows was thick and nailed to last eternity.

No willing tool stood ready for her use. She glanced toward the sky, her frustration longing to escape in a scream. But she bit back any sound.

She looked to the right and the left. Saw the woodpile behind the store. Where there was wood, there was an ax. Exactly what she needed. She clambered over the debris between the yards, found the ax with its head buried in a log, wriggled it loose and stomped back to the shack. Gritting her teeth, she swung the ax with all her might against the padlock. When it refused to give, she attacked the door. Chips flew but the door did not give way. Again and again she swung. If only she was stronger she could inflict real damage.

The racket brought Old Mike from the barn. "Whatcha' think you're doin'? That's my house. Get away."

When he tried to drive her off, she swung the ax at him.

He wisely backed off.

The storekeeper and several other men joined him in a knot.

"Someone fetch Thorton. He'll put a stop to this."

"Yeah. Seems he's the only one who can make her behave herself."

Their words lent power to her arms and she swung harder. Now she could see inside. "Belle, keep back. I'm going to free you."

"Who's she talking to?"

"She's strange. Just like Thorton says."

A whole section of the door gave way. Holding the ax ready to use as a weapon, Red poked her head through the opening. Belle sat shivering on a crude bed. "Belle, honey. It's me. Come here." She held out her arms.

Belle's eyes were wide and staring.

What had these men done to her in the three days that Red had been missing? She swung about and faced them, the ax lifted like a sword. "Anyone touch either of us and I'll leave you in pieces."

The men kept back a safe distance.

She turned back to her sister. "Belle, come here. I'll look after you. Just like I always do."

Whimpering, Belle slipped from the bed.

"What's going on here?"

Red slowly turned to face the Mountie with Thorton on one side and Ward on the other.

"She's trashed my house." Mike pointed. "Arrest her, I say."

"Red, what are you doing? Give me the ax." The Mountie gingerly reached for her weapon.

Red didn't budge. Didn't offer to release it. Nor would she until Belle was safe and sound. "Have a look for yourself." She stepped aside and indicated the Mountie should look in the hole.

He watched her carefully as he edged forward. She

kept her back to the shack as she watched the circle of men for any threat, but she knew the moment the Mountie saw Belle because of his indrawn breath. "Come on, child. You're safe now."

Red kept her eyes on Thorton. She saw his intention to escape and sprang forward, waving the ax.

Ward also saw his intention and grabbed an arm and twisted it behind Thorton's back.

The Mountie lifted Belle through the opening. She glanced about at all the men and pressed her back to the shack.

Red dropped the ax and held her arms out. Belle hesitated a moment, then raced to her sister.

"Thorton Winch," the Mountie said, "I'm arresting you for kidnapping and a number of other charges. Take a good look at the sky. You won't get many more chances."

As he was led away, Thorton turned to Red. "Don't think this is the end. I'll get away and I'll find you."

The Mountie jerked his arms. "You aren't going anywhere.

"Mike Morton, you are under arrest, too. Ward, would you bring him along?"

Thorton gave Ward a look fit to cure leather. "I'll find you, too, and make you regret your part in this."

The Mountie pushed him along.

The men shrank away, muttering they didn't know about a child. She expected most of them told the truth.

In a few minutes Red and Belle were alone.

"What are we going to do?" Belle whispered.

"We'll be fine."

"Who's going to take care of us?"

"We'll take care of ourselves." She spoke so reassuringly she almost believed her words. But she had no money. No clothing except the dress on her back and grateful she was for the brown one Linette had given her. But they had their freedom.

"Let's go." She took Belle's hand and headed out of town, a different direction than the one that had brought her back a few hours ago.

"Where we going?"

"To a new life." One, she vowed, where she would never again depend on a man. Or trust one.

They marched bravely onward until Belle dropped to the edge of the trail.

"We're lost. And I'm hungry." Silent tears trailed down her pale cheeks.

Red hated those tears and that silent cry, even though she felt like sitting at Belle's side and joining her in a good wail. Her leg hurt even though she'd looked at it closely when Linette changed the dressing last night and knew it was a minor injury. Her head pounded like a thousand horses kicking to be released. "We'll be okay."

Belle shook her head. Not that Red blamed her for not believing. She had no plan. No options. "Come on. We can't sit at the side of the road feeling sorry for ourselves."

Belle didn't move.

Red dried her sister's tears on the skirt of the brown cotton dress. "Something will work out. It always does, doesn't it?" Even though she said the words, she could think of too many times when things had gone wrong to be convincing.

"Can I call you Grace now?"

Red looked past Belle to the low bushes beside the trail. "I'll never be Grace again. Continue calling me Red." She yanked on a lock of hair. Why had she been cursed with hair that drew unwanted attention?

Belle sprang to her feet. Her eyes widened as she stared down the road. "Someone's coming." She bolted for the bushes.

"Belle, wait." But Belle didn't slow until she was well out of sight.

Red shared her sense of panic. Had Thorton escaped? She squinted at the approaching rider. He led a second horse. That fact alone sent shivers up and down Red's spine. Slowly she backed away, aiming for the opposite side of the trail as Belle. That way if Red was caught, Belle might hope to escape.

To what? Starvation in the wilds?

She spun about. Her head did not like the sudden movement and dizziness made her stumble and fall to her knees.

"Red. Hold up. It's me."

She recognized the voice. Ward. Interfering again.

But her annoyance was laced liberally with relief. Surely he'd give her a ride.

To where? She had no place to go.

Ward was too far away to do anything but kick his horse to a gallop, and watch helplessly as Red fell to the ground. The woman seemed to have a knack for getting into trouble. But right now he didn't have time to analyze that observation. He had to take care of Red and her little sister. Where had Belle disappeared to?

He jumped from his horse and trotted over to Red

who now sat on the ground, her legs drawn up, her face buried in her knees. He squatted at her side. "Are you okay?"

"I'm fine. Just turned too fast and fell." She eyed him with squinting disfavor. "Could happen to anyone."

He chuckled. "Yup. Happens to me all the time."

She snorted. "Sure it does."

"Well it does every time I have a blow to my head that leaves a lump the size of a turkey egg."

She stared away.

He looked in the same direction. Saw nothing of interest. Some scraggly bushes along the trail, poplars with their lacy leaves dancing in the breeze, and further off, dark green spruce and pine. In the distance, the blue-gray Rockies. "Where you going?" Seemed to be nothing much out there for her to aim for.

"To freedom."

"Yeah, sure. But where will you hang your hat?"

"No hat to hang."

He guessed she had little of anything to hang. She'd left without pausing to collect her belongings. All she took with her was her little sister. Who—if he had to guess—hid from the sight of a man. No doubt men represented danger in her young mind. Maybe in Red's not-so-young mind as well. "Even without a hat, you need a place. You can't survive out in the open. Do you have any family?"

She didn't shift her gaze. "Just Belle."

"Uh-huh. Friends? Anyone who would give you a home?"

The look she gave him dripped disbelief. "Do you

think if we did, we would have fallen into the clutches
of a man like Thorton?"

"Guess it was a stupid question."

"It sure was."

He sank to his backside and drew his knees up in a
pose that mirrored hers. Together they stared down the
trail. "I got a place. Ain't much. Just a tiny cabin. Someday it's going to be more. Got plans for a big house."

"What you want with a big house? You got a girl?"

"I got a mother and two brothers. It's for them."

"No pa?"

"He died."

"Where are they now?"

Her question unleashed a tornado of memories, in-
filtrated with regrets and pain. "Back in New Bruns-
wick. Travers is three years younger than me..." When
he and Travers said goodbye, Travers swore he would
come and join Ward when he thought Hank could take
care of himself. The Travers he remembered never went
back on his word. "Hank is ten years younger," he continued. "He'd be thirteen by now. I ain't seen him since
he was six."

She shifted to see his face. "How come?"

"I left."

"Who is taking care of them?"

"My stepfather." The man had vowed he loved Ma
and the boys. *Love!* A word easily spoken. It meant
nothing. Taking care of others was all that counted.
That and kindness.

"Oh." Her voice was small, tight. "That why you
left?"

Something in her tone drew him. He met her probing gaze. "He didn't care for me. Just me being there made him angry."

Understanding flickered through her gaze. "He used a belt? Fists?"

He nodded, and in that moment they formed a bond—one based on the shared experience of abuse. He looked deep into her hurting soul, found a reflection of his own. He knew then what he must do. "I'll take you to my cabin. You can stay there as long as you need."

"What about your family? Aren't you expecting them?"

He closed his eyes, shutting out her gaze, as a newer, fresher pain surfaced. "They aren't answering my letters." He'd had but three letters in the years since he left—two from Ma and one from Travers. Nothing in almost three years.

"Oh. I'm sorry." A cool hand touched the back of his, and he jerked his eyes open. She pulled her hand to her knee and looked into the distance, but she'd touched him. Offered comfort. That tiny gesture slipped into his troubled heart and mind like a warm summer breeze full of sweet scents.

"So you'll accept my offer?" He hoped she'd agree willingly. Let him help her and Belle.

She developed a keen interest in the blade of grass plucked from nearby. Her hesitation gave him plenty of time to reconsider, but rather than withdraw his offer, he silently begged her to accept it.

Slowly she turned and faced him. "What would you expect in return?"

The question sliced through him like she'd used the ax she'd threatened the circle of men with. Then the meaning of her words hit him with peculiar force. He sprang to his feet and backed away three steps. "I am not that sort of a man. I made an offer out of concern for you and Belle. I have no ulterior, despicable motives." What had Thorton demanded of her? His cheeks burned to think of the sort of things that went on in the back rooms of a saloon. Some would see Red as soiled, ruined. But all he saw was a woman who needed help to escape a bad situation. He could offer that.

She didn't lower her gaze, nor did her silent demand ease.

"If you accept my offer, it will be clearly understood that I—" he could think of no gentle way to say it "—I do not want repayment of any sort. My only concern is making sure you and Belle are safe from the kind of treatment you received at Thorton's hands and that you have a place to live."

Still she considered him, looking up from her seated position. He felt her careful examination of his words. Of him. As if she probed his thoughts, his heart. His very soul.

He met her gaze without once blinking. She would find him reliable, trustworthy, perhaps even noble so far as he was able.

Finally she spoke. "Very well. I will accept your offer until I can find something suitable that allows me my freedom and independence."

Her answer was less than satisfactory. After all, he had no intention of infringing on her freedom, though she'd had none whatsoever until he intervened. She might remember that. And how much independence did she expect? She had neither means nor opportunity to pursue such. "I'm not asking to own you, only help you." But at least she had agreed to use his cabin. "Then let's get on our way. Where's Belle?"

"Belle, come."

Nothing.

"She's afraid of you."

"Now, that hurts. If you'd said she's afraid of men, I'd understand, but you make it sound like it's only me."

"That's because you're the only man here. So at this point she's only afraid of you."

"Do you always have to win every argument?"

He might as well have accused her of some heinous crime the way she glowered at him. "I most certainly do not. Do you turn everything into a confrontation?"

"A what?"

"Yes. See, a simple comment about Belle being afraid of you becomes a—a—"

"Yeah. What?"

"A challenge. That's what."

He slapped his forehead. "I can see this is going to be a fun time."

She slowly rose to her feet, planted her hands on her hips and stuck out her chin as she faced him. "Do you mean to say you will be residing in this cabin? Because I did not understand that part. If that is so, then I change my mind. We'll find some other place."

He groaned. "I will be living at the ranch. That's where I work. But unless you have a means of getting supplies, filling the wood box, bringing in meat... Well, do you?"

She squinted without answering.

"I thought not. So I expect you'll be happy enough to

let me do that. Which—if you can bear the thought—means I will occasionally come by to perform those necessary tasks." Suddenly the idea held a lot less appeal than it did just a few minutes ago.

"Just so long as we understand each other."

"Oh, I think we do."

"Fine."

"Fine."

Her gaze slid past him and her scowl vanished. "Belle?" Her voice grew soft, gentle, inviting.

Ward's first instinct was to spin around, but remembering Red's words that Belle was afraid of him—the way she'd said it still irritated—he stepped aside so he wasn't blocking Belle's view of Red and slowly, cautiously turned about.

Belle stood at the far edge of the road.

"It's okay. He won't hurt you." Red's words were as much warning to Ward as encouragement to Belle, and irritation scratched at his decision to help.

Ward let Belle assess him. Though the wariness never left her eyes, she crossed the road to take Red's outstretched hand. She carefully kept Red between herself and Ward.

"He has a cabin we can use until we sort ourselves out."

If not for Belle's presence, Ward would have pointed out how she made it sound as if accepting his offer was a last resort. She gave no account of the fact it was a generous offer made from a concerned person. After all, he was preparing a place for his mother and brothers. Having Red and Belle there would be inconvenient should they arrive. But he already knew the frustration and folly of pointing out flaws in her words. Still, he couldn't keep from murmuring, "I'm only trying to help."

"You think that will be okay, Belle?" Red asked.

"I guess so."

No one acknowledged his generosity, so Ward had to settle for feeling like poor-quality chicken feed. "Then let's ride."

He made his way back to the horses and left them to follow. Or not. Whatever they decided. He had done his best. Not much else he could do. But he knew he would not ride away and leave them at the side of the road even if the pair got it in their minds to turn all prickly.

Shoot. They were already more prickly than he cared to deal with.

He reached the horses and turned back to them, standing exactly where they were when he left. "You coming or not?"

Their hesitation was palpable. "I get it. You don't want to come with me. But you don't have a lot of options. And I don't aim to leave you here. So let's get moving."

They sure did know how to look less than enthusiastic as they picked their way across the grass to his side. He cupped his hands to help Red mount.

Belle drew back, her fear as thick as stew.

"I have to lift you up to sit behind your sister," he said, wanting to warn her before he touched her.

She nodded but her eyes flooded with wariness.

He grabbed her about the waist, heard her indrawn breath, felt her stiffen, but before she could reconsider he had her perched behind Red.

He swung into his own saddle and led the way.

"How far?" Belle whispered, likely meaning only for Red to hear.

"It will be almost dark before we get there."

The sooner she learned that Ward meant her no harm nor posed a threat, the better for them all. How long before either of them felt comfortable with him?

Chapter Three

Belle's arms clutched about Red's waist. Feeling the fear and desperation in her little sister, she almost forgot the way her head pounded, the pain driving deeper with each thud of her mount's hooves. She shivered, though the sun beat down with enough heat to bake biscuits on the dirt trail. Where were they going? She took some comfort in the fact it was the same direction as the ranch. She could always flee there for protection should the need arise. Of course that depended on how far Ward's cabin was from the ranch. He rode a few feet ahead, leading the way. Why had he offered his cabin? Did he have an ulterior motive? Or was it born from knowing what it was like to receive the blows of fists?

She urged the horse forward until she rode at Ward's side. "Where is your cabin?"

He pointed in the general direction of the ranch. Some help that was. Would it hurt the man to give exact directions?

"It's nothing like Eden Valley Ranch. For one thing it doesn't have the backing of a rich family back in England. Nor does it have the thousands of acres of the

Eden Valley land grant. But I'll be able to run enough cows and horses to make a good living." He sat easy in the saddle as only a cowboy used to long hours on the back of a horse could.

Red shifted, wishing she could be half as comfortable. But her leg hurt almost as much as her head. She was tired and admittedly, a tad cranky. She didn't need a cowboy to point it out to her.

Ward continued talking as if his cabin was the most important thing in the world. Maybe it was to him. For her, it was only a place she would go to because she had no other option. Resolve drove away a great deal of her discomfort. She would find a place as soon as possible. She allowed herself to dream a little. Wouldn't it be nice if Belle could attend school and later, they could celebrate Christmas together in their own home? She'd trim the tree with red ribbons tied in bows of various sizes. There would be gifts. Nothing extravagant. Perhaps a new dress for each of them. Warm mittens. Woolen coats. Maybe she could splurge for one extravagance. A storybook for Belle and a book of poetry for herself.

Poetry? She mocked her dreams. How foolish. That pleasure belonged to the past. As did such dreams. She couldn't afford half a penny candy let alone frivolous things. With every ounce of self-control she could muster, she jerked her attention back to Ward, who still talked about his place.

"I wanted to get a simple cabin built first in the hopes of persuading my family to join me. Once they're here, I figured there would be plenty of hands to help make it larger. Next spring, I hope to buy enough cows to start my own herd." His voice rang with hope and pride.

Red accepted that she had neither hope nor pride left. Nor was she bitter about it. Not with Belle safely behind her, Thorton locked up and a chance to make a better life for them.

"Red," Belle whispered. "When did you eat last?"

She let the horse drop back and spoke low, hoping Belle would be the only one who heard. "Been a while. But we'll manage. You and me, we're survivors, remember? Nobody and nothing can defeat us. Especially not a little bit of hunger."

"I have an awful big hunger."

No doubt Old Mike never thought to feed a little girl. Red was glad Belle couldn't see her face or she might guess at her anger. She could take all sorts of mistreatment, but it made her boil inside that people seemed to forget Belle was a child. Children should be protected, guarded, treated as gifts from God. They should never know anything but trust. "We'll be okay. You'll see."

Ward slowed until he rode beside her. "We'll rustle up some food soon." He'd overheard them.

Seems the man was determined to stick his nose into everything she did. However, she was grateful for his help. Or was she? She gave a humorless smile. Not really. She didn't want him or any man extending favors. If she never again saw another man or had to accept anything from a man's hand, it would suit her just fine.

They continued on the worn trail. Grass whispered as the wind passed over it. Birds scolded the intruders. The gentle scent of pine trees filled the air. They climbed a hill, the Rockies rising up in the distance.

Belle leaned over to get a better view. "Are we going to live in the mountains?" Awe rounded her words.

Red thought of all the places a person could hide in that rugged expanse. She'd heard men tell tales of treacherous cliffs and impassable barriers, but they'd also spoke reverently of roomy caves, rushing water and ideal camping spots. *Where a man could live forever in peace with a boundless supply of fish to eat and fresh water to drink.* It sounded ideal to Red's ears. Ward shifted in the saddle to answer Belle's question. "We'll be pretty close to the mountains. Some mornings it feels like you can reach out and touch them right outside the window. But the distances are deceiving. It would take a hard day's ride to get to the foot of one of those giants."

Despite her resistance to anything he might offer, he made the view from his cabin sound appealing. And the way his eyes flashed blue as if reflecting the sky back, Red found herself drawn into his description.

"Every time I see them out the window, I think of a portion in the Bible, one of the Psalms, 'They that trust in the Lord shall be as mount Zion which cannot be removed, but abideth for ever. As the mountains are round about Jerusalem, so the Lord is round about his people from henceforth and forever.' Reminds me that God doesn't change."

Belle sighed heavily. "Red says we don't trust God anymore, even though Mama and Papa said we always should." The accusation in her voice brought a choking argument to Red's throat, but she would not list all her reasons in front of Ward.

Ward pushed his hat back and gave Red an unblinking look. But rather than accusation or disapproval, she thought she saw sympathy. "Sometimes it's hard to trust. Awfully hard."

She couldn't jerk from his gaze and, as it deepened, something warm and gentle seemed to brush against a dark and angry spot buried deep within.

With an effort, she shifted in her saddle, keeping her attention on things close by, ignoring the mountains. But again and again her gaze was drawn to the distance. If she could escape to the mountains. Find safety.

Resignation sighed into her soul. Ward's cabin would have to do. For now.

If they ever reached this cabin.

She'd been half slouching in the saddle, weary from too much riding, too much struggle, too much life, but now she straightened and stared ahead, though she saw neither the mountains nor the narrow trail. What if there wasn't a cabin? What if it was all a trick? Had she, in her desperation to escape Thorton's clutches, fallen into a worse situation? She began to shake and sucked in air. She could not let Belle know of her concern. Whatever came, wherever this man led her, her first and foremost thought was to protect Belle.

Perhaps she should get Belle to slip from the horse now and hide in the trees. Then when she knew what lay ahead she could come back for her, either to take her to a real cabin or to escape into hiding. But the idea of abandoning Belle for any reason did not rest easy in Red's mind. Instead, she would be attentive and prepared to take evasive action if things turned sour.

The sun ducked behind the mountains, sending rays of light upward into the sky.

"Look," Belle said. "God is sending out fiery arrows to show us the way."

Despite the knot of disbelief in her heart, Red couldn't

help thinking that's exactly what it looked like. For half a second she let herself think her life could be different, that God was directing her to a place where she could forget the past.

But reality could not be wished away or fancied out of existence. She was headed into an uncertain future. Moreover she was Red. A woman who would forever be known as a saloon dancer. Many would question if dancing had been the only thing she did. It had been, though few would believe it. Seems Thorton wasn't interested in anything more than forcing her to dance for others so he could collect the money he demanded before each performance. That and controlling her, humiliating her.

He'd never allowed any other man to go beyond touching. She shuddered at the memory of those harsh fingers feeling her. Then she forced herself to sit motionless so as not to alarm Belle.

"There's the ranch." Ward pointed.

Red pulled back on the reins. The horse stopped moving and Red stared. "You said we were going to your place." It was the Eden Valley Ranch. The place she'd ridden away from before daylight. Had he tricked her?

He didn't turn toward her, which was probably for the best. He might not like the suspicion and anger tightening her face. "Have to let the boss know I got his horse and saddle back."

"What is he going to do?"

"Horse thieves aren't treated kindly around here."

"I have firsthand knowledge of not being treated kindly."

He turned to consider her. "They're usually hung."

She pressed her hand to her throat. "So you're really turning me over to a hangman? This was all just a ruse to get me to come along." Belle's hands dug into Red's ribs. She shouldn't let her anger make her forget to guard her words. "It's okay, Belle. I'm not going to hang. Now or ever." She yanked on the reins and jabbed her heels into her mount's ribs. The animal jerked so hard, Red almost came unseated, and then it took off in a bone-pounding trot. She kicked again. "Faster, you lazy animal."

But faster wasn't something this horse understood. She'd do better to try to escape into the trees, and she pulled the horse off the trail. It went reluctantly, crashing through the brush. Red ducked to avoid branches. Belle clung to her, a high-pitched sound whistling from her.

The horse jerked to a halt and stood quivering, surrounded by trees. Despite Red's urging, it refused to take another step.

"Get down, Belle. Hurry." She held out an arm to help Belle to the ground, then dropped down beside her, grabbed her hand and raced into the trees. They were making too much noise. Ward would have no trouble tracking them. She stopped. "We have to be quiet." To their right was a thicket of bushes. "There. Crawl in out of sight."

Belle clung to her. "Me?"

"I'm coming, too. Hurry up." They fought through the tangles and crouched on the ground. She wrapped her arms about Belle and held her tight. Red panted, the sound ragged and loud. She forced herself to breathe slow, deep.

The soft thud of horse hooves approached. The leather of a saddle squeaked.

Red didn't move, didn't release the air in her lungs.

No sound came from the horse or the cowboy. How long could she hold her breath? Her head felt funny.

"I know you're in there and I'm not leaving." Ward sounded so sure of himself that she wanted to jump out screaming and scare his horse so Ward would get dumped off.

She let the air whoosh out of her lungs. Stupid man probably wouldn't get thrown no matter what she did.

"I'm not about to get myself hanged."

Belle twitched and turned toward Red, her blue eyes big and full of fear.

"Nobody is hanging me," she assured her little sister.

"I doubt Eddie will want to hang you." Ward didn't need to sound so regretful.

"You might as well come right out and say you consider it foolish for him to show any leniency."

"Yeah, well, he hasn't had to fight you every mile of the ride."

"You tricked me."

He groaned. "I thought you might like a meal. There's little in way of supplies at the cabin."

"I'm awful hungry," Belle whispered.

Red considered her options. They were pretty unappealing. Either hide in the bushes while Ward waited, determined to take her to the ranch, or admit defeat. Either way, she was destined to go to the ranch.

"Let's get out of here," she whispered to Belle, and

they scrambled from the bushes. She drew herself up tall and straight. She'd go to the gallows, she'd face her punishment. But no one would see a shadow of fear on her face.

"We're ready." She marched back to the trail where the horse munched on grass. Stupid animal. If it had run like a horse was supposed to, they would be far away now.

Ward swung to the ground and came to assist her back to the saddle.

She grabbed the saddle horn and pulled herself up without assistance, but as she reached for Belle, Ward swung her up. Red didn't wait for Ward, but headed straight for Eden Valley Ranch and whatever justice Mr. Gardiner would mete out.

She kept her attention on the trail as they edged downward, passed empty corrals, clattered over a wooden bridge and turned toward the big house. But with each step forward her enthusiasm and determination weakened.

Ward drew abreast of her. "He isn't going to let you hang."

"I guess not. Who would look after Belle if he did?" Did she manage to keep a defensive note in her voice?

"I expect Linette would give her a home. She's given Grady one."

Red had seen a little boy previously but assumed he was Linette and Eddie's son. "Good to know someone would show my sister some Christian charity."

Ward sighed long and loud. "Linette is a very sweet, patient woman."

He didn't need to say what he really meant. That

Red wasn't. But before she could point out that it was hard to be sweet and patient under her particular circumstances, the cowboys poured from the building she knew to be the cookhouse. They didn't make a sound.

"They're staring." Belle sounded scared.

"Guess their mamas didn't teach them it was rude." She kept her attention fixed straight ahead.

The door in the house up the hill opened and Eddie stepped out, Linette on one side and a little boy on the other. They waited as Ward escorted her toward them. They stopped ten feet from the watchful trio.

Ward swung from his horse. Red would have dismounted on her own, but her skirts made it awkward at best and with Belle pressed to her back, impossible. So she allowed Ward to grasp her by the waist and assist her. It meant nothing that his hands were steady, and his shoulders where she was forced to rest her hands, solid. As soon as her feet touched the ground she sprang away, brushing her skirt clear up to her waist trying to flick away the feel of his touch.

Ward's eyes narrowed as if realizing what she did. Then he quirked one eyebrow and lifted Belle down so quickly she didn't have time to protest. But she skittered over and grabbed Red's hand, burying her face in the brown cotton of Red's borrowed dress.

"It's okay, honey. You're safe with me," Red assured her.

"With me, too," Ward said, his voice so quiet she could almost persuade herself she didn't hear. Just like she could almost believe he wasn't more than a bit offended that she tended to put him in the same category as a man like Thorton. Not that she really thought he was. But still, he was a man and she and Belle were at his mercy and that of his boss. She intended to be cautious around them.

"I see you found them," Eddie said.

"You have a child." Linette sounded every bit as sweet and patient as Ward said she was and it almost made Red want to weep.

Ward turned to his boss. "This is Belle, Red's sister. They both need a home. You have your horse and saddle back so if you're okay with that, I plan to take them to my cabin."

Linette sprang forward and grabbed his arm to shake it. "You'll do no such thing. It's isolated up there. They'll stay here with us." She reached for Red's arm, but Red backed away.

Isolated sounded about right to her. "That's very generous of you, but we've already accepted Ward's offer." Once Linette heard where Red had spent the last few months, she'd want her as far away as possible.

"I won't hear of it." Her eyes flashed determination.

Ward neglected to say his sweet, patient boss's wife was every bit as stubborn as Red. Red allowed herself a moment of admiration for the woman before she rallied her arguments.

"Belle's been through a difficult time. I think she needs some time alone to get over it."

Linette studied Belle, who buried her face in Red's skirts. Each breath released on a shudder. "The poor child." She nodded as if she'd made up her mind. "If you think she needs time alone, then you can live in the little cabin across from the cookhouse." She pointed to the place.

In the dusky shadows, Red saw a tiny log cabin facing the roadway that ran through the midst of the ranch buildings but tucked into a cluster of trees that went on and on to the river. It was almost tempting to live where she could dream of finding friends. But once they knew the truth, no one would accept her. Better to be isolated.

Linette, guessing at Red's resistance, spoke to Ward. "I won't hear of her living alone in your cabin."

Red turned to Ward as well. "We had an agreement." She kept her voice low, but knew from the flash in his eyes that he understood she wanted to jerk every word from her mouth and spear him with them.

Linette appealed to her husband. "Eddie?"

Eddie cleared his throat and spoke to Red. "I don't know what your circumstances are, but in the future if you are in trouble and need help, I hope you will come and ask rather than steal a horse."

She'd forgotten the threat of hanging. "I apologize. But I had to rescue my sister."

"In that case…" He seemed to consider his next words. "I won't seek justice, seeing as the horse and saddle have been returned, but I think you owe it to Linette and I to accept our offer."

Linette grinned like the decision had been made.

Red sent a silent appeal to Ward, who shrugged.

"Can't argue with the boss's wife," he said.

Red seemed to have little choice in the matter. But she vowed it would be temporary. Only until she found something else. "Thank you," she murmured, managing, she hoped, to sound grateful as no doubt they all thought she should.

"I'll show them the way," Ward offered. "And make sure they have food."

Linette thanked him, then turned back to Red. "I'll check on you in the morning and see if you need anything. In the meantime, get settled, make yourself at home and have a good night's sleep."

Red allowed Ward to take the reins of her horse and struggled down the hill with Belle still glued to her skirt. Evening had crept in and filled the hollows, so she felt as she and Belle were alone with Ward.

A cowboy stepped from the cookhouse and Ward handed him the horses. Ward signaled Red and Belle to follow him to the cabin, where he opened the door and indicated they should enter.

Red took a step forward. She paused at the doorway, unable to make out the interior in the darkness.

Belle whimpered and pulled on Red's skirt, hampering any further progress. Red extricated Belle from the material and tipped her face up. Even in the growing dusk, Red could make out Belle's eyes—so wide they practically swallowed her face.

Red's heart burned. Why should her little sister know such insecurity, such terror? Had Thorton's treatment of the past few months, and before that, the death of their parents and Red's attempts to support them, robbed this child of any childhood innocence and faith? "Belle, honey, what's wrong?"

Her hand still clutching Red's skirts, Belle lifted one finger toward the cabin. "It's dark. Like that other place." Her voice shook.

Red straightened, silently cursing herself for not taking into consideration where Belle had spent the past three days. In almost total darkness in an unfamiliar cabin. Not unlike the one they now faced.

Ward must have had the same realization as he sprang forward. "Wait there while I light a lamp." His footsteps thudded into the darkness of the cabin.

Belle shuddered. "He's disappeared."

Red knelt and pulled her little sister into her arms. "No, honey. He's only inside."

A yellow light flickered and grew stronger. It shifted, making Ward's shadow lurch like something alive. Belle squeaked in terror. Red feared Belle would shred the brown skirt as she squeezed her little fists tighter and burrowed closer.

"It's a lamp, honey, so we don't have to go into a dark room."

The light steadied, grew larger as Ward headed for the door. He stepped out, the lamp before him. The yellow light filled his nostrils and highlighted his eyebrows, giving him a wild appearance.

Red swallowed a nervous giggle. "It's okay—" She meant to reassure Belle but Belle didn't hear her as she tore from Red's side with a piercing scream and ran into the dark.

"Belle!" Red called, racing after her. "Belle, come back."

But Belle continued her headlong flight.

Ward stared past the golden lamplight, trying to see where Red and Belle had gone. But the light effectively narrowed his vision to a tiny circle. Not that he needed to see to know what happened. His ears proved more than sufficient.

Belle had run screaming into the woods, Red in her wake.

Birds exploded from the trees at the noisy disturbance.

Belle's fear of him, and Red's distrust, were starting to wear his patience a might thin. He only wanted to help them. Get them away from men like Thorton Winch and that creepy guy with the boarded-up shack. Two or three times he'd considered he might have taken on more than he anticipated. His already tense jaw tightened further, making his teeth hurt. He would not abandon this pair, no matter how difficult they proved to be. One thing he'd learned…walking away was not the answer, even if he'd done so with the best of intentions.

He lowered the lamp and hurried after Red. She stood at the back of the cabin, calling into the darkness.

"What happened?"

"You."

That was it. One word, chewed up and spit out like something dirty. "What did I do this time?" He didn't care that he sounded put out.

"You looked like a monster the way the lamp flared on your face." She gave a brief, humorless chuckle.

"Thanks." He'd about had his fill of insults.

"Well, it's true. You scared her whether you meant to or not."

"Whether?" His frustrations of the day were about to boil over. "You think I might have intended to frighten her? What kind of a man do you take me for?" He held up one hand. "Don't tell me. I don't think I want to hear."

"Good, because I don't want to say something I might regret."

He snorted. Not something he usually did around ladies. But seeing as she wasn't acting like a lady, he didn't think it counted. "Do you mean to say you sometimes regret what you say?" He expected she caught the way he emphasized *sometimes* and the way doubt dripped from his voice, but he was beyond caring what he said to this woman.

"Not often." She gave him a look of pure defiance. "Now are we going to look for Belle or not?" She stomped away without waiting for his reply.

Great. Now the pair of them was going to wander around in the dark. If he'd known how much aggravation they would turn out to be…

Who was he fooling? He would still have done the same thing. He would have rescued Red even if she accused him of kidnapping. He would have followed her back to the saloon, confronted Thorton and, yes, offered them his cabin. Having her in Eddie's cabin suited him even better. He'd be able to make sure she and Belle were safe.

He'd not done well on that front so far.

He had to find Belle. Chasing after her would serve no purpose. She'd just hide. But he recalled she'd complained of hunger. "I have an idea."

"I hope it's better than your last one."

He wondered which idea that was, because so far he thought his ideas had been good. "What idea do you mean?"

"Holding the lamp to your face and scaring a little girl half to death."

"That wasn't— I didn't— Oh, what's the use? You're determined to twist every word and action of mine into some sort of attack."

She stepped back into the circle of light to glower at him. "I most certainly do not."

"Uh-huh, you do. Now can you keep quiet long enough to hear my plan?" He paused for good measure. "Unless you've thought of one?"

Her glower deepened as she was forced to acknowledge she had not. "Go ahead. Talk."

He chuckled. "Knew you wouldn't admit you had no plan."

"You gonna tell me this wonderful plan or flap your jaws?"

He grinned at her. "Like I asked before, you ever lose an argument? No, wait. What I mean—" He leaned closer until they were almost nose to nose. "Do you ever admit it?" The lamplight reflected in her eyes, filling them with something he hadn't seen before—wasn't sure what to call it. Perhaps fear. Or loneliness? Even though it was barely a shadow, hardly a hint, he knew it was there, and knowing, all resentment left him.

He straightened. "Belle is hungry."

"So what? We've been hungry before. Expect we will be again."

He decided it wise to refrain from saying they would not go hungry while they lived in this cabin. "I'm going to build a nice fire over there." He pointed to where Eddie had dug a fire pit, lined it with rocks and placed logs around it at a safe distance to use as benches. "And start cooking up a meal. I'm guessing she'll soon come out of hiding when she smells the great food I cook."

He grinned, meaning it as teasing. After all, he was a cowboy and only cooked out of necessity, and even then it was the simplest of fare. But at the way her eyes widened and the loudness of her swallow, he guessed she was as hungry as Belle. Right then and there he vowed to make the best meal he'd ever made.

He led the way to the fire pit and soon had a roaring fire going. Red reached out her hands to the flames. For the first time he considered she wore only a brown dress. Belle had on a shapeless gray thing that had seen better days. That observation coming from a cowboy who spent weeks in the same clothes indicated a large degree of wear and tear. Good thing he could count on Linette to help him on that score.

"You stay here. Maybe she'll come back when I leave."

Red's gaze jerked from staring at the flames to look at him. "You're going?"

"Just to get supplies."

He dashed across the road to the cookhouse. "Cookie, quick, lend me a bottle of that meat you put up."

Cookie crossed her arms and looked at him like he'd suddenly sprung a second head. "What for? My cooking not good enough for you?"

He jerked to a halt and swallowed hard. He had no desire to offend Cookie. "I've got two hungry females over there." He gave a wave in the general direction of the cabin.

"Didn't the boss send you out to bring back his horse and saddle? Instead, you come back with two women?" She sniffed her disdain.

"The horse and saddle are in the barn. Red and her sister are going to stay in the cabin."

"A horse thief! Whose idea was that?"

"Linette's."

Cookie's scowl disappeared in a wreath of confusion.

"They understand why she had to do it." As quickly as he could, Ward explained how Red had to rescue her little sister. "And now she's out in the trees, hiding in fear." Before he finished, Cookie started filling a basket with jars of meat, bottles of preserved vegetables, fresh produce and some biscuits.

"You tell her to come over in the morning and I'll have freshly baked cinnamon rolls."

"I'll tell her." He grabbed the supplies and hurried back to the cabin. He dumped meat and vegetables into a cast-iron pot. As he worked, he thought of how Red looked and sounded scared when he said he was going. She'd unwittingly allowed him to see that she liked having him there, though she would deny it with every breath she had. Not that he intended to mention it. He would simply accept it as a step forward. Balancing the lamp in one hand and the makings of a meal in the other, he made his way back to the fire. No one sat beside Red or anywhere around the fire. "She hasn't come back yet?"

Red shook her head. "Belle?" she called. "Come on, honey. It's nice and warm here."

"She do this often?" Ward asked as he fashioned a spit over the fire and hung the pot. He dug a hole nearby and dropped in several hot stones, put a pan of potatoes still in their jackets on top and left them to bake.

"Do what often?" He doubted Red tried to keep the challenge out of her voice.

"Run away."

"Did you see the little room in the saloon? Well, that's where she's spent the last four months. Apart from when Thorton thought to take us out for a walk, and he made plenty sure to hold tight to her hand. So, no, she doesn't do this often."

"I'm sorry. I never realized, though I suppose I should have." He'd seen the little room, even noticed how the window was barred, allowing only slits of light to enter. "She'll have lots of chance to roam free out here."

"Hope she doesn't get lost."

Ward thought it best to not echo his worry along the same line. After a bit the stew bubbled, and he moved it down the spit to simmer while the potatoes cooked. The smell of food was enough to flood his mouth with saliva. He'd eaten a fair-sized breakfast but nothing since. He guessed Red hadn't eaten since the day before, and who could guess when Belle had last eaten. He hoped the aromas floating from the pot should soon bring her in. "How's your leg feeling?"

"It's fine."

"I suppose your head is fine, too?"

"Yup."

"Would you admit if it hurt like fury and your leg pained clear to your eyeballs?"

She laughed, a sound that startled him, expecting, as he was, another fierce argument. "I'll admit it hurts some, but seeing as there's nothing for it but to endure, doesn't seem much point in bemoaning the fact."

He'd told himself the same thing many times so couldn't argue. Somehow hearing her say it made him like her just a little. "You will keep an eye on your leg and make sure it doesn't get infected? If you see any sign of it, let me know. Linette will have ways of treating it."

"I can manage on my own."

"I was only being helpful." He felt her wariness and recalled her earlier words. "And I don't expect any form of repayment in return."

"I would pay cash for the use of the cabin if I had any. I don't. Nor do I aim to repay favors with favors."

He sighed loud and long. "I would not take either." He tested the potatoes with a fork. They were cooked. He trotted back to the cabin for dishes, paused to fill a bucket of water at the well. Back at the fire, he handed her two plates, forks and cups.

"Thank you," she said.

He chomped down on his teeth to keep from saying it was good to see she had a measure of manners. "Call out and tell Belle the food is ready."

"Belle. There's food. It smells mighty good. Can you smell it?"

They both waited silently for a sound of the little girl. To his right, the grass rustled.

"She's coming," he whispered.

"Ward made lots of stew and there's baked potatoes. When was the last time you had a whole potato?"

The grass rustled some more, then Belle hovered at the edge of the darkness.

"Come on, honey," Red urged.

Belle darted glances at Ward as she made her way to

Red's side, going the long way around the fire to avoid having to pass him.

He tried not to let it bother him and failed miserably. Instead, he had to be content with handing them a heaping plate of food. He handed Red a potato. She took it. But when he held out one toward Belle, she shrank back. Red reached for it but Ward withdrew. He wanted Belle to trust him enough to take it from him. After all, he had provided the food. Besides, he was getting tired of being treated like one of the bad guys.

Belle's fear was palpable, but so was her hunger. He offered her a towel. "It's hot. Hold it with this."

She snatched the towel, took another moment to consider the potato carefully, then, doing her best not to touch his hand, took it.

It was a start. Satisfied, he sat down with his own food. "I'll say grace."

He didn't need to look at Red to feel her resistance. But Belle met his eyes steadily a moment before she bowed her head.

He prayed, and then they ate in silence. When he saw they'd cleaned their plate, he offered them another helping, which they didn't refuse.

The evening deepened. Despite the warmth of the fire, he felt coolness moving in. "I need to do my chores." Though likely Slim or Roper had seen to them by now.

Red sprang to her feet. "You go. We'll be fine."

Ward picked up his hat from beside him and slammed it on his head. "What's your hurry?"

"I didn't mean…"

"Don't bother backpeddling. But if you don't mind,

I'll see that you're settled in the cabin and the fire is dowsed before I leave." He grabbed the lamp and strode back to the cabin. He set the lamp on the tiny table.

Red slipped into the room. "Guess you can't blame me for being leery. I want to make it on my own. Owe no man anything."

"I could carve it in the log by the table so you don't forget."

"What are you talking about?"

"Lady, my stepfather made no secret that my presence set his teeth on edge. So I walked away from my family because I figured if I left they'd be better off. But I've never known if it was so or not. Instead I wonder. And I regret leaving. My only reason for helping you is to make up for leaving my family. It's nothing to do with you. So don't think I plan to take advantage of you. You mention it again and I will carve 'I want nothing in return' in that there log." He slapped the chosen place.

"Well, fine then. Just so long as we understand each other."

"I'm pretty sure we do. There's the bedroom." He pointed toward the door. "There's the stove. I can light it now if you think it's too chilly in here, though likely you would then roast like trussed chickens. There's food in the cupboard. Not much. I'll be back with more in the morning. The place is yours."

He headed for the door, which was all of three steps away, and Red bolted out of his way. He stopped to give her a long, steady look.

She lowered her head and mumbled something that sounded vaguely like "thank you."

He nodded briskly and stepped outside. "Call your sister. I'm going to put out the fire."

At her call, Belle dashed past him to join Red.

He carried the dishes to the cabin and set them in a pot without any comment, then grabbed a shovel from the corner.

Smacking out the lingering flames and covering the embers with dirt allowed him take care of most of his frustration.

He wondered if rescuing this pair would in any way ease his guilt about having left his own family, or if he had bitten off more than he cared to chew.

Chapter Four

Red and Belle stood silent and motionless as Ward called from outside, "Goodbye. Be safe."

Red knew Belle didn't breathe any louder than she did as they listened to him stomp away from the cabin. As the sound faded she strained, but couldn't tell if she still heard his footsteps in the distance or if it was the pounding of her blood against her eardrums. So she waited, not daring to move until she was certain. It seemed he had truly left, and her breath whistled out.

"Is he gone?" Belle whispered.

"Yes." Thankfully. She was grateful for his help. Truly she was. But she didn't plan to accept more than she was forced to.

"Are you glad?" Belle asked, easing away from the dark corner as if still uncertain it was safe to do so.

"We're finally on our own. Just you and me." Apart from Linette and Eddie up the hill, a cookhouse and cowboys across the road and Ward, no doubt, flitting back and forth. She would have much preferred Ward's isolated cabin, but this would do for now.

"I'm glad, too." Belle turned to study the room. "We gonna sleep here?"

"Yup. Just the two of us. Let's have a look around." The room held a small stove that would serve as a kitchen range as well as a welcome source of heat on cold nights. There was a tiny table, two chairs, a shelf with a few supplies and a bookcase with a few odds and ends. There was another doorway and they went to the small bedroom.

Belle edged over to the bed and touched it. "How long we staying here?"

Red crossed to Belle's side, perched on the bed and caught her sister's chin. "Honey, we need some place until I can come up with a plan. But as soon as I do, we'll leave. We'll find a place on our own where we'll always be safe and always together."

Belle's gaze clung to Red's. She could see her little sister wanted to believe in a future that held promise and possibility. Understood her hesitation to do so. Her faith in good things had been shattered in the past few months.

Red pulled Belle to her lap and held her tight. "We got away from Thorton and Old Mike. They're both in jail and will never hurt us again."

"They'll stay in jail forever?"

"I hope so. But long enough they won't bother us again."

"Red, he prayed. He said we could trust God."

She heard the wistful note in her sister's voice and understood Belle referred to Ward.

How was she to deal with this? She had no trust left. Not for God and certainly not for any man. But how could she admit she felt God had abandoned them and rob Belle of any hope? On the other hand, she didn't want her to trust anyone but themselves for their future. She closed her eyes and tried to marshal her thoughts together. It took too much effort, made her head ache. She'd deal with the matter later.

Belle looked intently into Red's face. "You don't like him, do you?"

The question startled Red. There was something about Ward that got under her skin like a red, itchy rash. His insistence on helping even though it was evident he didn't care a whole lot about her. The way he took objection to her comments. Yes, they might have been a little barbed, but she couldn't help it. It had become part of her armor. Yet, despite his contrary ways, he exuded strength beyond the power in his arms. It came from deep inside him. Born, perhaps, out of his own pain and experience. She had to respect that. Might even find it slightly appealing.

But she could not let herself like him. To like a man, she would have to trust him, and she could not, would not, ever again trust a man.

Belle waited patiently for her answer.

"Honey, we don't know him well enough to have much of an opinion about him."

Taking her cues from Red, Belle sighed. "Too bad he's a man. Otherwise I might like him."

Laughing at her little sister's wisdom, Red hugged her tight. "Let's check out the bed." She pulled Belle down beside her and they flopped backward on the furs. "I think we'll be very comfortable." Sharing a narrow bed with her sister was not going to be difficult. Having her so close, she could feel her breathing would comfort her.

They returned to the other room and examined the items on the shelf. Containers of flour, cornmeal and sugar. "Guess we won't starve to death."

"Can I help you cook things?"

"Of course you can. We will have so much fun. Just the two of us." She glanced at the darkened window. Would they see the mountains through that window? She touched the log where he had threatened to carve words. Her chest seemed wooden as a strange wistfulness filled her. She'd once known a secure home. So had Belle, but she wasn't sure her sister could remember happy family times.

Red didn't know what the future held nor where they would go from here, but perhaps in this little cabin she could give Belle some enjoyable times. Teach her to be happy and trusting again, though not too trusting. Look at the predicament they'd landed in because Red trusted people too much.

Belle stood in the center of the room and spun around. "I love it here." She jerked to a stop so quickly she almost tumbled over. "No one will bother us, will they?"

A storm of emotions raced through Red. Anger that Belle should know such uncertainty, hatred toward the man who'd stolen the innocence of them both, despair at how little she could offer her sister. Then determination, solid as a rock, pressed down all other feelings. She would do anything, everything, she could to protect her sister from any more hurt.

"If anyone bothers us, I'll take a shovel to the side of his head."

Belle's eyes widened. "You'd hurt him?"

Belle meant Ward. Red meant anyone who threatened them. "If he tried to bother us, I would."

Rocking back and forth, Belle considered Red silently. Then she came to a decision. "Maybe you shouldn't hurt him."

Red's head snapped back. This from a little girl who had as much reason to hate men as anyone. "Why do you say that?"

"Well, if you hurt him he might not want to help us. It's scary and dark out there." She tilted her head toward the door and Red knew she referred to the half hour or so she'd hidden in the bushes. "Besides, I like this." She went to the table, climbed up on a chair and pressed her hand to a picture mounted on the wall.

Red hadn't paid any attention to it, but now she moved closer. A sampler done in various stitches, pretty flowers and designs around words. The words, done in black cross-stitch, *"Whither shall I flee from Thy presence? The darkness and light are both alike to Thee."* The words brushed a dark spot deep within. "It's very nice. I wonder who made it," Red said.

"I think someone's mother."

Red sat down on the bed and Belle sat beside her. "Why do you think so?"

"Because Mama made one like this for me, didn't she? Remember? She hung it over my bed and said I should never forget the words."

The memory rushed toward Red. She tried to dam it back. She could not let her thoughts hearken back to those happy, innocent days. Everything about her past filled her with crippling regret.

"I 'member her making it."

So did Red. The dam broke and she was back at her childhood home. She was warm, happy, secure in her parents' love and protection. Seems the house glowed with treasures, each representing love. Mama sat in a rocking chair that had been Grandma's and told stories of sitting on her own mother's lap ensconced in the same chair where Red remembered sitting on Mama's knees and later, where she and Mama took turns rocking Belle. What a sweet baby she'd been. "A gift from heaven for us all," Mama had said time and again. "After losing so many babies, God has granted us Belle to fill our hearts with joy." Indeed the happiness in the house had reached new heights with the safe arrival of Belle. Mama had once said she might not live to see Belle marry and asked Red to promise she'd see Belle was properly cared for. Red had readily agreed, never suspecting an accident would thrust the role upon her so unexpectedly.

"Mama hung it over my bed on my fourth birthday."

"I'm surprised you remember."

"I didn't till I saw this one. Then I 'membered."

"I remember, too." Mama had stitched a cradle with a baby in it, a window behind the cradle with light pouring in. She'd carefully selected the scripture. "I want something that will encourage Belle her entire life. No matter what may happen," their mother had said.

Oh, how disappointed her parents would be that Red hadn't protected Belle as she'd promised. She would live with that regret to her dying day and the moment she stepped into heaven, she would beg their forgiveness.

Not that she was sure God would let her into heaven after the events of the past year and her vow to never forgive Thorton.

"I remember the words, too," Belle said.

Red did, too, though she no longer believed them with childlike innocence and wondered if Belle did.

"'I will never leave thee, nor forsake thee.' Red, do you think Mama would be angry that I did forget them for a little while?"

"I don't think so."

"Red, do you still pray?"

She wished she could avoid the question. She had no desire to rob Belle of whatever faith and trust she still had. But she couldn't lie. "Not much."

"Me, either, but when I was locked in Old Mike's cabin I remembered a prayer Mama said and I said it out loud. That's what I was doing when you came for me."

Her curiosity overcame her doubt. "What prayer was that?"

"'God, You are a very present help to me, and I am receiving Your help even now as I pray. Thank You, Father. You are my refuge and strength, and because this is true, I will not fear anything or anyone.'"

Red pressed her tongue to the top of her mouth. Her nose stung. She could not breathe for dread of unleashing so many frightening emotions she feared she would drown.

Why had God forsaken her? Where was He when they needed help?

"God heard me. He hasn't forgotten me."

Oh, if only she could have the faith of her little sister. But never again could she be innocent and trusting. Nevertheless, she was glad Belle had found comfort in her prayers. She jumped to her feet, ignoring the protest from her injured leg. "Let's make the bed."

Together they folded the fur back. It would be much too warm this time of year. They punched the mattress into better shape and smoothed the blankets. She had no way of knowing the time, but it was dark and she was tired. Enough reason to go to bed. They had no other clothes but what they wore, so preparing for bed simply meant washing their faces and removing their shoes.

They lay curled together, Red's arms around her sister.

"Red?"

"What?"

"We gonna wear these clothes day and night forever?"

Red giggled. "I don't expect they'll last forever."

"Seems I've been wearing the same thing for almost that long."

"I wish I could offer you more, but this is what we have for now." There was a time when loving parents had generously provided all they needed. They would never again know that sufficiency. Truth was, Red had no idea how she would provide even basic necessities for them. Only that she would find a way that did not require depending on a man.

Even if for now, she had accepted help from two men, if she counted Eddie. Knowing it was Linette's will that she and Belle stay in the cabin marginally eased her concern at taking charity from a man. Taking it from a woman was an easier pill to swallow.

A fresh thought entered her mind. Perhaps Ward had come in answer to Belle's prayers. God, no doubt, still heard her words.

She fell asleep, soothed by the gentle snores of her little sister.

The next morning she woke to Belle tickling her nose. "Wake up. It's morning and I'm hungry."

Red groaned. Her body hurt from so many hours on horseback and her leg reminded her of her injury. "You sure it's morning? I don't see any daylight."

"'Cause you got your eyes closed." Belle peeled one eyelid up.

Red brushed her hand aside. "It's cold in here."

"You could start a fire in the stove."

"I could, could I? Or we could wait for the sun to warm the place."

Belle crawled over Red and pushed into her shoes. "I'll help you."

Red rolled over to study her eager sister. "First thing I'm going to teach you is how to build a fire so I can get up to a warm room."

"Okay." Belle rushed out of the room. The stove lid rattled. "Show me now," she called.

With a long-suffering sigh, Red climbed out of bed. Her hair must be a rat's nest, but they lacked comb or brush. She settled for running her hands over her hair to tame it out of her eyes.

"Hurry up." Belle waited in the doorway, her hands on her hips in a pose that reminded Red of their mother.

Pain sucked at her insides. She closed her eyes and

waited for the hurting to disappear. "Let me get my shoes."

Belle tipped her head to one side and sighed as if the request was unreasonable.

Red chuckled. "I'm hurrying." She fastened her shoes, then went to the stove. "First, you need some kindling." She showed Belle how to build a fire and they watched with undue fascination as the flames took hold.

Soon the heat warmed Red and her brain began to function. For a minute she allowed herself a moment of joy that they were alone and safe. Thank God Thorton was behind bars. God had answered Belle's prayers and she was grateful for that.

"What are we going to eat?" Belle asked, eyeing the cupboard of supplies.

"What would you like?"

Belle considered her as if wondering what she could ask for.

"Ask and if it's possible with what's on hand, we'll have it."

Belle held Red's gaze in a hungry look. "You remember how Mama made teddy bear griddle cakes?"

Another memory flooded Red's thoughts. Belle was little, still in her high chair. Mama had stood at the stove, wiping her brow in a weary gesture. Mama seemed to be tired a lot and Red had done all she could to help. But Belle fussed.

"She's got a touch of tummy upset," Mama had said. "I wish I could have kept nursing her. The cow's milk doesn't agree with her."

"But we were so grateful for fresh milk."

"Yes, I still am. God provided generously. Now I'm

praying Belle will adjust to it soon." She had set a place of griddle cakes before Belle.

"I'll feed her."

Mama had nodded. But Belle had refused to eat. In the end Mama had made a thin porridge and persuaded Belle to take a few spoonfuls.

Over the ensuing weeks, Belle had remained fretful, refused to eat more than a few mouthfuls at a time. She started to lose weight, grew peaked. They were all concerned. Mama had spent a lot of time on her knees beseeching God to make Belle strong.

One day Mama got up and fried pancakes in the shape of a teddy bear, round belly, round head and round ears. She had dropped raisins in for eyes. Belle was charmed. From that day forward food took on interest.

How times had changed. Since they'd fallen in with Thorton, she'd had to endure Belle begging for food on many occasions.

Red wanted to forget those worrisome months. Almost as much as she wished she could forget how Mama had prayed. How she constantly gave God praise for Belle's health.

"I don't know if there are any raisins, but we can surely make pancakes."

"Can I help?"

"Certainly. Who knows? One of these days I might be sick and you'll be in charge." She'd been teasing, but at the sudden quivering of Belle's lips she wished she'd considered her words more carefully. She hugged her sister. "I don't plan to get sick anytime in the foreseeable future. Now you get a mixing bowl and the flour and we'll get started."

As they mixed up the batter, the room grew overly warm. "Belle, open the door and let in some air."

Belle paused at the window next to the door. "Everyone will see us."

She understood how Belle felt. The isolated cabin would have been a better choice for them. Maybe she'd convince Ward to take them there. "We don't have to open it all the way." Seeing Belle couldn't bring herself to face what lay outside the four walls, Red crossed to her side. She planted a log on the ground, holding the door open enough to let in the air but not enough for them to see across the road.

As she straightened, sunlight smacked into the mountains. She stared. Dark folds contrasted with shadowy blue. A thousand unfettered thoughts swirled inside her head. Verses her mama had quoted often. *We will not fear though the mountains shake.* Emotions she didn't want to own bubbled to the surface. Hope, joy, longing for things she would not acknowledge.

She was Red. She had danced half-naked before men. She'd been touched in ways that made her cringe. Guilt and loathing quenched all other feelings.

"I like the mountains," Belle said with utmost conviction. "What did he say they made him think about? God is like the mountains?"

"Something like that." She would not repeat the exact phrase: *As the mountains are round about Jerusalem, so the Lord is round about His people.*

"I thought you were hungry."

"I am."

"Then let's get the griddle cakes made."

An hour later they had washed up the dishes and

cleaned the little cabin. Belle avoided the window, but sat cross-legged on the floor where she could see out the ajar door.

Red glanced out the window once, saw cowboys streaming from the cookhouse and jerked out of sight. But the open air beckoned. "Let's go out back." No one could see them behind the cabin.

Belle jerked to her feet and hurried to the table. "There's too many people out there."

Too many men, she likely meant. "I'll make sure it's safe." She edged toward the window and studied the surroundings. Not a man in sight. "Nobody out there. Let's go."

They dashed outside and around the cabin. The shovel stood against the corner and Red took it with them. She hadn't forgotten her promise to use it on any man who threatened them.

They sat on the benches around the cold fire pit, listening to the sound of birds and squirrels noisily going about their morning activities. Red lifted her face to the sun. "It's very peaceful."

Suddenly birds erupted from the trees in a great burst of noise. Sounds of horse hooves thundered through the air.

Belle bolted for the cabin. "Men coming," she wailed.

Red's initial alarm gave way to reason. "Belle, it's only the cowboys riding out to work." This was a ranch, after all. She followed on Belle's heels into the cabin. "They aren't interested in us." But she spoke to an empty room. "Belle?"

He slowed his horse and waved goodbye to Roper and the others. He'd already spoken to Eddie. "I'm asking for light duties around the ranch for a few days until they're settled."

Eddie had readily agreed.

Ward saw Red and Belle race to the cabin. What had frightened them? The door slammed behind Red. Ward studied the area around the cabin. Tipped his head and listened intently. He heard nothing to alarm him. Saw no wild animals prowling nearby. Yet something had sent them fleeing for safety.

Then it hit him. They'd heard him approach and run from him. "Horse, I'm not the enemy here." Yet over and over, he felt like it. If he had a lick of sense he would turn around and head out to the hills with the rest of the cowboys.

But he flicked the reins and continued toward the big house.

He asked Linette for some things the pair could wear.

"Goodness, what an ordeal they've endured. They must be frightened." She waved him inside and instructed him to wait while she found suitable clothing. "I have the things the Arnesons can no longer use." A couple had come to the ranch in the spring, ill and too weak to care for themselves. Linette had nursed them as they grew steadily weaker. When they passed away, Eddie had buried them in a nearby plot. They had earlier lost a child and still had her clothes. She quickly found items for both Red and Belle. And agreed to Ward's request to give Red a day or two to settle before visiting them.

He rode to the cabin, dismounted and paused. "Hello, it's me."

Silence.

"Red. Belle. It's me. Ward. I've brought some things." He stepped forward.

Red emerged from the narrow door, her fingers curled around the handle of a shovel. Her fire-bright hair sprang out in disarray. Her eyes flashed defiance.

He roared with laughter.

She glowered, indicating she didn't find it amusing.

"You gonna brain me with that?"

"If I have to."

"Guess you should have done it yesterday before you decided to come along with me."

"Being here don't mean you can come and go as you please."

His amusement ended abruptly. "Red, I promise I will not come and go without regard to the fact you and Belle reside here. No one will." Eddie had warned the others to give them plenty of space until they were ready to socialize.

"Do you mind putting that aside? I don't care to have my skull split wide open when I turn my back."

She hesitated, then propped it next to the door.

He would have felt a lot better if she'd put it against the outer wall where he'd left it. "No one will bother you here. And the woods belong to God. He won't mind if you enjoy them."

She nodded. "Only until I get on my feet."

"I brought some things for you." He untied the sacks hanging from the saddle.

She said nothing as he carried the supplies to the door.

"You're welcome." He was beginning to think she would rather chew her tongue to shreds than express gratitude to him for anything. "Where's Belle? Some of it's for her."

Belle peeked through the crack of the bedroom door. "What you bring?"

"Well, this bag—" he lifted it "—is heavy with food stuff. Cookie makes about the best cinnamon rolls ever. She has some for you at the cookhouse." He paused long enough for the idea to settle in. Then he lifted the other bag. "This is full of clothes you might be able to use. Linette sent them."

"Belle, you gonna come see?"

Belle opened the door wider but kept it between them. That was okay. He understood her caution.

He tossed the lighter bag on the table and set the heavier one beside it. "Who wants to see inside?"

Belle got as far as the edge of the door and hovered there like a dragonfly.

Red finally left her post outside the door and stepped inside. "Who is Cookie?"

"She's the cook. Big, boisterous woman. Her husband, Bertie, helps her. He's more gentle. But Cookie is a fine cook and a good woman. Every Sunday they hold church services in the cookhouse and Bertie preaches us a sermon. Only it ain't as much a sermon as a friendly talk." He had no idea if they cared about any of this, but he figured if he kept talking about ordinary things the pair might relax. "Linette and Eddie want to get a church built in Edendale—that's the little town close by. Not hardly even a town, but it's growing. I sometimes wonder if Sundays will be any better with a real church and a real preacher. I like Bertie's talks." He ran out of steam. Could think of nothing more that might interest them. Still neither of them moved.

Perhaps the food would hold more sway. He dug into the sack and pulled out the brown-paper-wrapped bundle, set it on the table and folded back the edges. "Cookie thought you might be a bit shy about visiting her this morning, so she sent fresh rolls." The aroma from them was about more than a man could resist. "Cookie says it's best to eat them while they're warm. But I can tell you they're pretty good stone-cold and two days old, too." He reached into the sack again. "Didn't know if you liked tea or coffee so brought them both. Cinnamon rolls with a hot drink is about as good as it gets."

Belle rocked back and forth. He could hear her swallow from where he stood. "What can I drink?"

"Cookie thought of that, too, so she put in canned milk. Says it's real good for making cocoa. You ever had hot cocoa?"

Belle edged closer. "Mama used to make it. Red knows how to make it, don't you?" She appealed to her sister.

"Certainly."

"That's good." Ward waited, wondering if Red would offer to make tea or coffee or hot cocoa. Or would she stand there, guarded and ill at ease until he left?

He shifted his gaze out the window. Up until a few days ago, he'd been content to go about his merry way, writing letters back home, not getting a reply but planning, building and hoping for the time the others would join him. He'd given little thought to how he lived each day. Just did what was next. What Eddie sent him to do or what appeared before him. Choices weren't difficult.

Now he seemed unable to make an ordinary decision as to whether he should invite himself for tea or leave.

All because of one hotheaded, red-haired woman who got under his skin in a way that he didn't mind.

He'd been in such a rush to get things together for Red and Belle, he hadn't even taken time to eat one of Cookie's rolls.

The least they could do was invite him to share the goodies. Ignoring the way Belle drew back when he moved, he reached for the kettle, shook it and discovered it heavy with water. He lifted the stove lid, stuck in a couple of sticks of wood, then set the kettle to boil. "We're going to have hot cocoa and cinnamon rolls, and while the kettle heats we're going to put the supplies on the shelf."

Neither female moved.

He didn't care. He pulled out a jar, held it out to Red. "Where do you want it?" Not that there was much of a decision to be made. The kitchen consisted of two narrow shelves and a larder box.

She scowled at him. Then, her lips in a tight line, she grabbed the jar and stuck it on the shelf.

He took out the items one by one and handed them to her.

Belle slipped forward, one cautious step at a time. She hovered two feet away, swaying back and forth. "Who made that?" She pointed to the picture over the table.

He stopped removing items and looked at it for a moment. His mother had sent it in a package that contained the only letter he'd received from her. Afraid the picture would get damaged kicking about the bunkhouse, he'd asked permission to hang it in the cabin after Linette and Eddie had married and moved into the big house. No one lived in the cabin then, and he thought it would be a safe place for the picture.

At Belle's question, he was awash in memories of his mother making the picture during long winter evenings with Pa at the table reading while she worked. Pa had developed a keen interest in the free land to the west. He slid his gaze to Belle. "My mother did. A very long time ago when my father was still alive."

"Did she try running away?"

"Not that I know of. Why?"

"Doesn't *flee* mean to run away?"

That was exactly what he wanted her to do. Run from that horrible man she'd married after Ward's father had died, and come West where he could look after her.

"Did you?" Belle asked.

"What?"

"Run away?"

Red touched Belle's shoulder. "Don't ask so many questions."

"It's okay. I didn't run away. I left. Like I said, I thought things would be better if I wasn't there. Sometimes to flee means to run toward something, too." He hoped that's what he'd done—run to freedom for both himself and the rest of his family.

"Are you scared of the dark?"

Strange questions, but he could see Belle had a real need for answers so he considered his reply. "No. But it is harder to know what's ahead or what to expect. So I suppose I'm more wary in the dark."

"It was scary dark in Old Mike's cabin."

Red grabbed Belle by both shoulders and leaned over to stare into her eyes. "Honey, no bad man is ever going to hurt you again. You hear?"

Belle nodded.

Red straightened and faced Ward with a fierce look, wordlessly warning him she would not allow him to hurt Belle.

Her continued distrust started to fester. "Not all men are bad. My father wasn't. I'm guessing yours wasn't." He gave them a moment to acknowledge it. "And I'm not."

He and Red dueled silently as she considered his words.

"I'll prove it if you give me a chance." He kept his words low, inviting. Though for the life of him he couldn't explain why it mattered so much.

He only knew it did. He would somehow, he promised himself, win the trust of this pair.

As he waited for some sign of agreement or disagreement from Red, he understood winning her trust might prove a whole lot more challenging than winning that of her little sister.

Chapter Five

The kettle steamed but no one moved. Red felt Ward's relentless challenge. Let him prove they could trust him? How was she to do that without putting both herself and Belle in jeopardy? No. "A person has to earn trust before it is given."

His gaze did not falter, forcing her to shift away to avoid his intense insistence. "True. On the other hand, it's impossible to convince someone against their will. All I'm asking is you stop judging me as being like Thorton Winch."

Belle nudged Red.

Red jerked her attention to her sister. "What?"

"He's not like Thorton."

Red squatted down to Belle's eye level. "Honey, you can never be too cautious."

Belle's eyes brimmed with a combination of assurance and hope. "He prayed. And he has that." She shrugged one shoulder in the direction of the sampler.

"If you're so sure, why are you still afraid of him?"

Belle hung her head for a moment. She shuddered,

then met Red's eyes again. "There's a lot of scary feelings inside me."

Red hugged her sister and looked at Ward, surprised to see a reflection of her own dismay.

"No child should live in fear." His words were solid, full of unspoken promises, as if he vowed Belle would never have a reason to be afraid of him. Their gazes melded. She understood he meant so much more than Belle's situation. Likely his own little brothers. Something inside her wrenched as she felt a sense of connection at shared pain, uncertainty and regret over the past. She recognized in his blazing look a silent vow to make up for what he'd lost, his regret over his decision to leave his family. And more. A deep conviction about what was right and wrong and determination to stand up for the right.

In that moment she allowed herself to think of him as a man who could be trusted. She retracted the thought as quickly as it came. She'd trusted too readily and too often and knew the dangers of doing so. Her willingness to believe Thorton was an honest preacher man had brought disaster.

From now on she would guard her thoughts. And heart. She yanked away from his gaze. Flung about for something to do so she could ignore him. Saw the steaming kettle and snatched it from the stove. He'd set out three heavy china mugs alongside the cocoa tin and a container of sugar. "Why don't you stay for cocoa?" Her words were not overly warm, but it was the best she could manage at this point.

"Thanks." He opened the can of evaporated milk. "Left before I could enjoy Cookie's cinnamon rolls.

Intend to do so now." His tone informed Red he wasn't waiting for an invite from her.

"Well then, by all means."

Belle rocked back and forth, her face wreathed in tension.

Red immediately regretted her reluctance. For Belle's sake, she had to try to be civil when he was around. She pressed back annoyance. Wondered at the skitter of fear that tailed after it. Then smiled—it was forced and false, but it was all she could manage. "Here, I'll measure the cocoa and sugar. You pour in the hot water." She set the kettle on the table between them.

Ward looked at Belle and then back at Red. He smiled, too, though his seemed almost genuine, as if amused at the predicament his presence created for her.

She kept a smile on her lips while signaling a warning from her eyes, informing him she would do her best to ease Belle's anxiety but it didn't change anything inside her. From the way his eyebrows lifted and his smile deepened, she guessed he'd read her silent message. She did not care for the amusement flashing from his eyes.

She grabbed a spoon and dumped a measure of cocoa and sugar in each cup and gave the mixture a quick stir.

Ward moved to her side and tilted the kettle to partially fill each cup.

Belle edged closer. "That how Mama made cocoa?"

Red forced cheeriness into her voice. "That's right. We used to have it every bedtime during the winter. Do you remember?"

Belle nodded.

"Mama did it for me as long as I can remember and then for you as soon as you were old enough. Remember how we would sit close to the stove and Mama or Papa read to us?" Red's voice caught and she pretended to be preoccupied with stirring the hot mixture.

"Did Papa used to read poems?"

Ah. The ache of loss scalded her insides as if she'd downed the kettle of boiling water. How she'd loved listening to Papa's slow, deep voice read poems, filling Red's mind with word pictures and dreams.

"I 'member something about daffodils."

Gentle, sweet memories of a different time and different place flooded Red's thoughts. "William Wordsworth. 'And then my heart with pleasure fills, and dances with the daffodils.'"

Belle clapped her hands. "I remember."

"My pa liked poetry, too." Ward's voice sounded thick.

She was reluctantly pulled into another shared regret. Thankfully he was at her side and her attention on preparing cocoa, so she could avoid looking at him. She failed, however, to avoid a tug of sadness as his loss found an echo in her heart.

She poured a dash of milk into each cup. "I guess it's ready."

Belle hesitated a moment, then slipped to one chair.

Only one remained.

"I'll get a stool." Ward ducked out of the cabin so suddenly that Red and Belle looked at each other and giggled.

Belle leaned over her cup of cocoa. "Smells good. Can I start?"

"I suppose we should wait for him."

Belle looked at the door. "What if he's gone a long time?" Her voice thinned with worry.

A slow anger simmered through Red. Belle was only asking for more pain if she started thinking she could count on a man for anything. "Belle, we have each other. We'll be fine even if he doesn't come back."

Belle's eyes shadowed with doubt, but she nodded agreement just as Ward stepped back inside, carrying a thick log squared on both ends.

Red didn't miss the way Belle visibly relaxed at his return and it served to increase her uneasiness.

He plunked the log by the table, sat on it and pointed toward the second chair. "It's yours."

Still full of caution, Red sat down and pulled a mug toward her.

Ward grabbed the other mug and grinned around the table. "I always pictured sitting around a little table like this with my mother and brothers." His smile faltered a bit. "But it's nice to share it with you." He must have seen the protest on Red's lips and corrected himself, saying, "Nice of you to share it with me." He passed the cinnamon rolls.

Belle took a bite and closed her eyes, sighing with delight. "These are so good."

Ward grinned. "That's what I said."

Red hesitated. She knew it was childish but she didn't want to agree with him, and wished Belle hadn't done so. But she couldn't deny herself a bite of the delicious-smelling treat. As soon as she tasted it, all resistance fled. Pleasantly sweet with just the right amount of cinnamon, the syrup soft and the bread as light as cake dough. It would have been criminal to refuse such delight. But now there was no way she could pretend to disagree with Ward. She would simply keep her opinion to herself, but despite her intentions she sighed with pleasure.

Ward chuckled. "I've never known anyone to voice a contrary notion about Cookie's rolls."

There was nothing for it but to enjoy the roll and take a second one. And allow a certain amount of serenity to surround the trio at the table. It was hard, she discovered, to keep up any level of resistance and annoyance when lost in the pleasures of good food.

Belle must have felt something similar, for she seemed to relax and even took another roll when Ward offered it, and didn't show a bit of fear. Red knew she should be glad, but she couldn't help but worry Belle would only end up getting hurt again.

Finally Ward drained his cup, eyed the bottom as if wanting a refill of hot cocoa. Instead he planted his hands on his thighs. "Were you comfortable last night?"

"We were fine."

"Is there anything you need?" He glanced at Red. She shook her head.

"We're fine."

He turned his gaze toward Belle. She studied him, measuring him. He let her. She ducked her head, but Red could tell there was something on her mind. Hopefully Ward would not be aware of it.

"What do you need, Belle?" he asked.

Ward's voice was soft and inviting. Far too inviting. He shouldn't be allowed to speak so alluringly.

Belle lifted her face to Ward, her eyes wide with hope and longing. It was enough to fill Red's heart with pain that her little sister should have unsatisfied needs. She'd done her best to take care of Belle but knew she'd failed miserably.

"I'm listening," Ward urged.

"A doll." The words seemed to struggle from Belle's throat, yet rang so full of childish dreams that Red closed her eyes to control a rush of hot tears. She sucked in air until she had her emotions under control.

She opened her eyes to see Ward watching her. Tried to hide any remnant of feeling. But it was impossible when his eyes reflected pain and a desire to help this child.

"Red, can I talk to you outside?" He rose and waited for her to follow, taking her compliance for granted.

Belle stiffened. "I'm sorry. I didn't mean to say that."

"Belle, honey, it's okay." Red squeezed Belle's shoulder.

Ward stopped, turned to face Belle. "You have no reason to regret asking. I only want to talk to Red about how we might get you a doll."

Red followed Ward outside into the warm autumn sun. "She didn't expect you to do anything. She was only voicing her longing. After all, she's just a little girl."

"Exactly. And she's been through more than a child should have to endure. So asking for a doll seems to me to indicate she still knows how to be a child. I think we should do all we can to encourage that."

"We?" She tried to sound as if he'd overstepped a line, but to know he felt some call to help a hurting child did something funny to her insides, as if warm, melted butter had been dripped to parched areas.

He narrowed his eyes, maybe expecting her to refuse. She wanted to, but honestly could not think of how she could without making Belle pay for her decision.

Taking her silence for agreement, he said, "I'm pretty good at carving. I think I could carve a simple little doll for her. Nothing fancy. If I ask Linette for some scraps of material, you might be able to make some clothes. What do you think?"

A man who would carve a doll for a little girl? She tried not to think what kind of person would do that— a kind, generous one who cared about the feelings of a child—but the thought burrowed past her barriers and landed behind her heart in a spot full of memories of a different life. She held her breath and forced the truth of who she was to the forefront, blocking out every other possibility.

She was Red. A woman ruined by her life in a saloon. Ruined for a decent man.

Ward watched her. No doubt thought she struggled to deal with his suggestion. Let him think so. It was a much nicer quandary than the real one.

"I won't do it if you have an objection," he said.

Oh, she had objections, but not to getting Belle a doll. In fact, she couldn't even say what they were. Only that they had a Ward-shape to them. Something about him proved a threat to her need to stand on her own. Alone against the world. Her sister's sole protector. A lonely job but a welcome one.

"Go ahead. Carve a doll and I'll make clothes for it. Belle deserves a little pleasure in life."

Ward stepped closer, forcing her to raise her eyes and

challenge him or back away. She would not show weakness, and met his gaze with fierce directness.

"I think we all deserve to enjoy life."

"Yeah? I noticed how some people intend to enjoy themselves no matter what the cost to another." She knew he understood her meaning as his eyes narrowed and turned as icy as a winter river.

"I don't mean that kind of thing, and I'm almost certain you know that."

She wouldn't let so much as a flicker of her eyelids indicate he was right. "Really? So what kind of thing do you mean?"

He held her gaze for a heartbeat and another until she feared she would have to blink first. Then he smiled.

The sudden change made her dizzy. The bang on her head still hurt. No doubt the cause of her slight loss of focus.

"I mean the kind of things God gives us freely to enjoy—the sun." He raised his face skyward and closed his eyes.

She tried not to stare at the look of bliss on his face. Concentrated on studying his rugged jawline, noting his clean-shaven cheeks, his bronzed skin from hours outdoors. But taking stock of that sort of thing proved as unsettling as the longing his words drew from her heart.

"Then there's the mountains." He pointed to the west. "Tell me you can look at that view and not feel blessed."

Thankfully he didn't seem to require a reply because she would have found it impossible to say she wasn't moved. Though perhaps as much by his freedom in expressing his feelings as in the view.

"And need I point out the wildflowers? Have you seen the abundance in the spring?"

"Didn't see much from the inside of a saloon." She hoped her hard words would make him stop. Remind him of who she was.

"You are no longer a prisoner inside a saloon. So stop thinking like one." He studied her, waiting for her reaction.

She vowed she would not give him the pleasure of seeing how his words knifed through her arguments and attacked her resistance. It was true she must now learn to live like she was free. Yet some aspects of her past must never be forgotten. And if she ever thought they could be, then she knew full well someone would remind her.

Ward nodded. "I see you understand my meaning. Are you going to tell Belle we're going to make her a doll, or do you want to keep it a secret?"

Red pulled her thoughts back to what mattered—her sister. "Belle is used to not getting what she wants. So I think knowing she's going to get a doll will give her about as much joy as getting it."

"'Spect you have a point. So let's go tell her."

Red had half a mind to tell him she could give Belle the news without his help, but realized it would be churlish. So she led the way back inside.

Belle sat hunched forward at the table, already accepting disappointment. Her posture and attitude tore at Red's heart and for the first time, she allowed herself to acknowledge the gratitude she felt toward Ward's generosity—not only in offering to carve a doll but also for his hand in rescuing them.

She knelt by Belle. "Ward has offered to carve a little wooden doll for you, and I'll make some clothes for it. Isn't that nice?"

Belle lifted her head and stared openmouthed at Red, then at Ward, who stood so close behind Red she could feel him in her pores. An unsettling feeling.

"Really? Truly?"

Red nodded. "It will take a little time, but you will get your doll."

"And I won't have to wait until Christmas or something special?"

"Nope. 'Cause you're special every day of the year and you deserve a special treat."

Belle threw herself into Red's arms, tumbling her off balance. She fell against Ward's legs. He grunted at the impact, then reached down and planted his hands on her shoulders to steady her.

A thousand sensations raced through Red. Joy at her sister's happiness. And a great longing to know protection such as Ward's hands provided day after day.

How foolish to dream of impossible things.

She knew her life would never include anything but standing firmly on her own. She eased Belle back and scrambled to her feet. Could not look at Ward for fear he would see the longing she must deny.

She could not face denial and rejection in his eyes. Nor the truth about who and what she was.

Ward struggled with a string of warring emotions. Knowing Belle feared to ask for something most children took for granted seared his thoughts. Children should not suffer at the hands of adults.

His anger was laced through and through with regret and doubt. How had Hank and Travers fared after he left? And Mother? Had his stepfather ever used his fists on her? To Ward's knowledge, he hadn't while Ward was still there. The man's anger seemed directed entirely at Ward, which is why he left. Only he could never be sure his leaving solved the problem and he wondered if it had been transferred to the others. Would he ever know?

So when Red had gone all prickly at his suggestion to carve a doll for Belle, Ward couldn't help but point out the truth to her. She was free. But when Belle squealed with joy, and bowled Red off her feet right into Ward's shins...well, he experienced a sensation he could not put words to. He wanted to do more than save them from Thorton. Wanted more than to keep them safe from despicable men. He stared at the tabletop, saw the remnants of their snack. Lifted his eyes to the wall. Beyond it lay the mountains. They represented what he wanted—only he couldn't say what it was. Just knew he'd had it when his pa was alive and they were a happy family.

Perhaps that's what he wanted—his family happy and secure again. Unable to give them what he longed for them to have, he settled on giving it to Red and Belle on a temporary basis. Seemed temporary was all that life offered—temporary happiness, temporary... His jaw tightened as words failed. Seemed love was fleeting at best and a deception at its worst. His insides hardened at the knowledge, and he shifted his attention back to Red and Belle.

Keeping them safe and making them happy would

ease his conscience until such time as they found a more suitable arrangement. He vowed to redouble his efforts to contact his family and persuade them to join him.

"Have you had a look around outside?" he asked.

"Only got as far as the fire pit." Red wouldn't meet his eyes, which suited him fine. He had no wish for her to see his confusion and he already knew her green-eyed direct stare unsettled his rational thoughts. What was there about her that made him turn into an over-anxious schoolboy?

"Come along, then, and I'll show you around."

Ward saw stark terror in Belle's eyes at his suggestion, but before he could assure them he respected their caution, Red spoke.

"No need. We saw the ranch as we rode up yesterday."

"I wasn't thinking of showing you the ranch buildings. But beyond the fire pit is lots and lots of room to roam. You can be as alone as you choose."

He waited as Red and Belle studied each other and knew the moment Belle decided she might like to see the outdoors. Her eyes flared with anticipation.

No doubt Red saw it, too, and sighed.

"Red, I might get a little tired of being shut indoors all the time." Belle did her best to sound reasonable.

"We aren't locked up. We can go out back anytime we want."

"I might like to run." Belle rounded her eyes in appeal.

Ward watched Red fight an internal battle, then she faced him. "Guess we might like to see what's out there."

He chuckled at her begrudging tone. "Then come along." He stepped outside.

Red and Belle paused at the doorway and peered one way and then the other.

Knowing how cautious they were about confronting others, he assured them everyone was busy elsewhere. A quick glance up the hill showed Linette at the window, but he didn't say anything. Linette would give the pair space as long as she thought they needed.

Belle clung to Red's hand, though he suspected it was also the other way around. But they'd soon learn they were safe here.

They skirted the fire pit and he led them to an almost invisible trail through the trees to the edge of the river.

"The water level is low this time of year, but it's deep and fast in the spring." To their left were the empty wintering corrals and the noisy pigpen. "We'll go this way," he said, turning to the right and following the river. The big house stood on the hill, but they veered away from it and continued to climb. He slowed his steps, allowing Red, still clinging to Belle's hand, to fall in at his side.

At the top of the hill he stopped. "Have you ever seen a prettier scene?" The ranch buildings were hidden from view. Before them lay rippling hills that crept up the side of the mountain. The mountains filled the horizon, still wearing tiny snowcaps and shining in the sun. Dark pines filled every crevasse.

Belle broke from Red's grasp and stepped forward. "I guess you can see heaven from here. Maybe Mama and Papa can see us." Her expression rapt, she lifted her face toward the sky.

Beside him, Red jolted. He guessed she objected to

Belle's observation but knew she wouldn't say anything to dispel the child's awe even if they both knew heaven wasn't in the mountains. He reached out, intending to touch Red's arm and signal her to let the child enjoy the moment, but when his fingers brushed her arm she gave a startled cry and jerked about to face him, wariness and defiance warring for supremacy in her eyes. She hastily backed away and her heel caught on a rock.

He lurched forward to catch her but it was too late. She went down with a jarring thud and her head whammed to the ground hard enough to do damage.

Chapter Six

Red lay flat on her back, struggling to get her lungs to work.

Ward knelt at her side. "Red, are you okay?"

His words were but a distraction as she fought to draw in air. He slipped an arm under her shoulders and eased her to a sitting position. "Take a breath."

She spared enough energy to send him a look full of annoyance. Did he think she purposely refused to breathe? And then a gasp shuddered in.

"Thank goodness. You had me worried there."

She leaned forward over her knees, fighting to get enough oxygen into her body.

"Are you okay? You hit your head pretty good."

"Fine," she gasped. "Help me up." She knew she crossed a dangerous line by asking for his aid, but she lacked the strength to pull her body upright unassisted.

He grasped her hand, caught her shoulder and lent his body for support as she struggled to her feet. Swaying with dizziness, she clung to him. He was solid, his touch gentle. She closed her eyes. This might be the closest she'd ever get to heaven.

Heaven. Belle had said something about it. Right. That she wondered if she could see it beyond the mountains. Mama and Papa might be watching. *Oh, dear parents, forgive me for my failure in caring for Belle. For my failure to uphold the standards you set out so clearly for me.* She'd had few options once she'd fallen into Thorton's clutches.

She tried and failed to keep back a groan.

Ward took it for pain and held her steady. "Maybe you should sit down again."

But her pain was not physical. It came from deep inside, beyond human touch. Except, against her inner warning, she found something satisfying in leaning on Ward.

It was only her foolish weakness. She eased away and stood on her own. "I'm fine."

"So you've said a number of times."

"You don't have to sound so doubtful."

He favored her with a lopsided smile. "Are you going to expect me to believe you're fine just because you say so?"

"What a silly question. Of course it's true."

His smile grew more crooked. "See, that's just it. I don't believe it just 'cause you say so. I see the way both of you get all tense when I step into the room. That's not okay in my book. You fall and bang your head for the second time in a matter of days and can hardly breathe. That's not fine so far as I'm concerned." He shifted his gaze toward the mountains. "You are afraid and hurting. Denying it don't change it."

A thousand wishes and regrets roared into her like a storm off the towering mountains, tearing her pretense of being fine up by the roots and leaving her grasping for something to cling to. She fought panic. She frantically sought for some idea to steady her. For a moment she thought she would drown in hopelessness and despair. Then she found the only thing that mattered and her world steadied. Belle. Nothing else had any importance. Only her little sister and doing what was best for her. If not for Belle…

She let her gaze drift as far as the mountains allowed. "How deep into the mountains have you gone?" she asked Ward.

He jerked about as if her sudden change of topic confused him. She felt his steady consideration, allowed herself the briefest glimpse of his blue eyes, then quite determinedly turned back to the mountains.

Slowly he turned and looked the same direction. "I've been several days' horseback ride west. There are some beautiful valleys. But also some treacherous cliffs."

"Streams of fish? Green pastures?"

"Some." Curiosity and a degree of caution filled his voice. "It's wild country. Many a man has gotten lost or been attacked by wild animals." No doubting the warning in his words.

"Are there really caves?" She saw his expression harden, fill with suspicion. "I heard there were."

"I expect there are. Why do you ask?"

"No reason."

"Red, promise me you won't head back into the high country and hole up in some cave. You'd never survive."

It irked that he continued to think she was so helpless and needy. "You might be surprised. Besides, what makes you think I'd consider such a thing?" Did he have to look so doubtful? "After all, I have Belle to consider." She tore from Ward's fearsome glare to watch Belle running about the area, searching for treasures. No doubt she could gather up rocks and sticks to take back. A poor substitute for real toys. It was the reason she'd agreed to let Ward make a doll. She'd make hundreds of outfits for it.

Her gaze drifted to the vast landscape before them. However, if not for Belle…

"No need to go into the mountains. There's lots of beautiful spots in the foothills. My ranch isn't anything like Eden Valley Ranch. It's small. There's a natural clearing big enough for a good-sized farmyard. I thought of building the cabin on the top of the hill but figured it might be buffeted by winter winds, so I chose a spot a little ways down."

As Ward talked about how many cows his ranch could carry because of the grassy hills, Red's eyes sought the distance, drawn by some force she couldn't explain. Perhaps it was the thought of disappearing. Or finding solitude. Solace. Peace. *Whither shall I flee from your presence. I will never leave thee nor forsake thee.*

.They were scripture verses but she had learned to push thoughts of God and any memory of Bible verses from her mind. So why now all of a sudden should those words flood her mind? It was the samplers. The one over the bed made by Ward's mother and the one Belle remembered their own mother making. But where was God when they so desperately needed Him? Where was He when she'd fallen into Thorton's clutches and called out for aid? Now it was too late. Her disgrace separated her from God more effectively than the vast valleys and mighty mountains hemmed her in.

Belle was several yards away, running from one thing to another. "Come along," Red called. "We need to get back. I'm sure Ward has to return to the ranch."

He sighed. "Why is it I get the feeling you are always trying to rush me away?"

"I can't imagine why you'd think such a thing." The man would have to be dull as dirt to not hear her impatience.

He managed a halfhearted chuckle. "Only the fact that you are rather less than hospitable."

"I guess I don't need to point out that I have no right to extend or refuse hospitality." Yes, she and Belle might be safe from the likes of Thorton and his friends, but they still did not have their freedom.

"I don't mean to run roughshod over your need for privacy, as you well know. Only you're afraid to admit it."

"I'm not afraid." Of anything. Except what he could do to her and Belle if he chose. That and facing people with guilt branded on her life.

Belle joined them, making Ward keep any more of his opinions to himself. Only a lift of his eyebrows communicated how much he didn't believe her protests.

"Can we come here whenever we want?" Belle asked.

"Anytime at all," Ward answered.

"Even if you're not with us?"

Ward sent Red a questioning look as if wondering where this line of questioning was going. Red shrugged slightly, indicating she didn't know.

"You can certainly explore without me."

Belle grew motionless. "What if we get lost?"

"I'll make sure you're safe." Red looked about, fixing landmarks in her mind.

"If you always keep in mind the mountains are to the west, you can't get lost," Ward said.

Belle rocked back and forth, her worry unabated.

Ward squatted at her side and turned her toward the Rockies. "See that big round nose of a mountain? It's a landmark. And if you can see it, you know the ranch is straight east of that point."

Red burned the information into her brain.

Not that she'd really rush into the mountains and hide forever, but it was tempting. No men. No probing stares. No whispers behind white-gloved hands of women who would never consider the circumstances that put Red in the saloon. Or if they knew them, would not accept them as adequate excuse.

A cave in the mountains sounded mighty appealing.

But Belle seemed satisfied with Ward's answer and turned her attention to the collection she'd gathered up. Just as Red expected—pretty rocks, bits of wood.

"This one looks like it has a face on it." She showed a rock to Red, then, fighting her fear, she showed it to Ward.

It was true that a child should learn not to fear everyone, but in Belle's case, a little fear and caution was wise lest people think they could take advantage of her. Red caught Belle's hand. "Let's take your things to the cabin."

The look Ward gave her left no doubt that he recognized her not too subtle attempt to keep Belle a safe distance from him.

She blithely ignored him.

They reached the cabin. Just before she ducked inside, she turned to Ward. "Goodbye and thanks for bringing the things." She would wait until he left to look at the items Linette had sent, but curiosity made her wish he'd hurry and leave.

He tipped his head back and laughed. "Red, you are something else. Your hints about me leaving are less than subtle." He held out a hand in protest when she drew herself up to demand an explanation. "Promise you won't hit me with the shovel."

Belle poked her head around Red. "She was going to when you first came."

"I was not."

Ward chuckled. "I wouldn't be surprised." He turned toward the back of the cabin.

"What are you doing?"

He grinned over his shoulder. "Going to chop some firewood."

"I can do it."

"I'm sure you can, but you won't have to." He paused and slowly turned to face her full-on. "Red, it's about time you accept that I aim to make sure you're safe and well taken care of."

"I'm not your mother or brothers, you know."

He considered her steadily, his expression going through a range of emotions. His smile flattened from amusement to sadness.

She shouldn't have mentioned his family, although he made no secret that his guilt over them was the reason he helped her and Belle. And then she detected a flash of anger and she pushed Belle behind her into the cabin and pulled the door closed. She confronted Ward, prepared to deal with whatever avenue his ire took.

But the anger disappeared as quickly as it came, replaced by strong-jawed determination.

"No matter what you say or do, I will not walk away from you and Belle." He ground about and disappeared around the corner. In a second or two she heard the sound of an ax delivering blows to logs.

A thousand regrets and wishes battered the inside of her head. If only she could be Grace again. But it would never be. No point in wishing for the stars when your feet were mired in pig slop.

Tucking away her sadness, she pasted on a smile and stepped into the cabin. At least she had Belle.

Ward swung the ax over and over, neatly splitting log after log. Sure, he laughed at Red's attempts to hurry him on his way, but his amusement was short-lived. Would she ever stop treating him like public enemy number one? After all, he'd gone to a great deal of trouble to help her. Yes, he had ulterior motives and she knew it. She understood he was doing for them what he wished he'd done for his family. Still hoped to do.

He paused and wiped his brow on his sleeve. Would he ever hear from his mother and brothers? He suspected his stepfather waylaid his correspondence, but surely one of them could get the postmaster to slip him a letter or find some way of contacting Ward. He tried to believe there was a good reason for not hearing from them, but deep inside he suspected they'd decided to put him out of their minds. Blaming him for leaving them to manage on their own.

He swung his ax. Again and again. If he could go back in time he would do things differently. Or not. How could anyone be certain of what they would do given another chance?

He had plenty of wood split and stacked most of it in a neat pile inside the shed Eddie had built against the cabin wall. Then he set to work shaving off kindling. Satisfied with the amount he'd created, he filled his arms with wood and headed for the cabin.

The closer he drew to the door, the more he grinned, imagining Red's protest. What would she say this time to encourage him to hurry up and leave?

He paused before the cabin and knocked, then listened to hurried steps cross the floor. The door rattled and Red pulled it open.

"I thought you'd be gone."

"Yeah, you hoped so." But she knew it was him or she wouldn't have opened the door quite so readily. In fact, she might have greeted a caller with the shovel still resting nearby.

She followed his gaze to her weapon of choice. "Never know when you might need a shovel." Her voice carried a shrug.

He laughed. "That's true. I brought wood."

"Who'd have guessed?"

"Woman, you do have a way with words. A person could practically cut your sarcasm with a knife." Yet it somehow tickled him to try and guess what would come out of her mouth. "Too bad it doesn't fill the stomach. Then you and Belle would never go hungry."

"Who says we ever have?"

Ward dumped the wood in the box beside the stove and turned to Belle. "You ever been hungry, child?"

She looked up from her play at the table, her eyes wide as full moons and nodded.

At the stark look in her eyes, he regretted involving her in this exchange. "Belle, I promise you that as long as I'm taking care of you you'll never go hungry."

Her glance slid toward the shelves as if mentally counting the number of meals stored there.

"The shelves will never be bare."

He turned and encountered Red's hard stare. But beneath the surface he thought he saw something else. At a loss to think what it might be and feeling very close to the edge of a precipice, he prepared to leave. "I'll be back later."

Belle glanced up from her play. "Bye."

Red sat across from Belle, studying him.

He waited for her to say not to hurry back or something similar.

Her gaze held steady, driving deep into his thoughts, searching for... He didn't know. Nor if he could provide it. He could provide meat, firewood, even a doll for Belle, but how could he give Red what she needed when he didn't know what it was? So he returned her look for look, silently promising his best.

Then she smiled, a trembling, uncertain flash that disappeared so quickly he almost wondered if he'd imagined it. But he knew he hadn't.

"Thank you for everything." She ducked her head and developed a great interest in one of Belle's rocks.

He couldn't move. He'd come to expect sharpness, sarcasm. Come to half enjoy it. But gratitude? It slipped past his reason for helping them and started a fresh journey in his thoughts. One that had nothing to do with trying to make up for leaving his family behind.

And everything to do with starting over.

He spun on his heel, too confused by this sudden shift in his thinking to know what to say.

He strode away from the cabin with no destination in mind. Then his thoughts cleared. He'd promised Belle a doll and he meant to get started on it. He veered toward the cookhouse, hoping to catch Eddie there.

Cookie greeted him at the door with a welcoming whack between his shoulders. "How'd they like the cinnamon rolls?"

He sucked in air to refill his lungs before he could answer. "They thought they'd died and gone to heaven."

"Good. Good. You think they like them enough to trot themselves over here and enjoy them with me?"

"They're both a little fearful yet." Ward glanced past Cookie. Only Bertie sat at the table, peeling potatoes.

"We'll give them time, won't we, love?" Bertie asked his wife.

Cookie snorted and returned to the stove. "Best thing for them would be to meet us and learn they needn't be afraid of us."

Ward half agreed. "The boss around?"

"Up at the house."

"I need to talk to him." Leaving Cookie muttering about how no one had any reason to be afraid around her, Ward left and jogged up the trail to the big house.

Eddie opened the door. "Come on in. Linette's waiting for a report."

As Ward crossed to the sitting room, he tried to think what he would tell them.

"Are they getting settled?" Linette asked. "I'd feel so much better if they were here where I could care for them."

Eddie took her hand. "You must allow people to deal with things in their own way."

"I know you're right, but they must be lonely and afraid. Ward, how are they? How is her wound?"

"She said her leg is fine." Though he'd noticed her favoring it a time or two. As soon as she realized she did, she stopped. "They're very wary about people. Red hesitates to accept help. I wouldn't be surprised if she suggests a way she can repay you."

Linette smiled gently. "If she mentions it to me—or to you—" she nodded toward Ward "—you say the only thing I want in exchange for what little we can share with her is for her to become secure and confident."

Red's goal was to get on her feet and become independent. "Belle seems to relax when she knows no one will suddenly show up. I took them up the far hill." He told how Belle had played but kept Red's behavior to himself. And his own. The way his heart had thudded when she tripped and fell. Then raced like a runaway horse when she'd taken his hand and accepted his help in getting to her feet. Behind that emotion lay concern about her questions about caves in the mountains. He'd be keeping a close eye on them to make sure they didn't decide to go in search of one and disappear. "Belle said she'd like a doll. I promised to make her one if you don't mind me using some scraps of lumber." He directed the latter to Eddie.

"Help yourself."

He turned back to Linette. "I wondered if you had some scraps of fabric you might give Red to make clothes for the doll."

"I'll do better than that. I'll make them myself."

Ward didn't want to argue with the boss's wife, but he had to give his opinion. "I think it might be good for her to make them."

Linette chuckled. "I expect you're right, and how keen of you to realize it. How did the clothes I sent fit?"

"I left before they looked at them. I'll ask when I see them again."

"And when will that be?" Linette watched him carefully.

"I haven't given it much thought." He kind of thought he'd spend most of the day there, but maybe that wasn't what they needed. "I'm not sure how much to leave them alone. What's best?" Surely Linette would know. She had a knack for helping others.

Linette looked out the window toward the cabin. "Do you know how they got into the situation where you found them?"

"No. Except I know it was not Red's choice."

"You said we all needed to give her time and space to learn to trust us. Perhaps your own words are the best advice for all of us. So long as she has what she needs."

Ward nodded. No doubt wise words from a wise woman, and he would heed them even though he wanted to do otherwise. At least Red was close enough she could call for help if she needed it, and he could see them flit out to the fire pit as he worked in the barn.

* * *

The next morning the sensation of starting a new journey returned. Yes, he might salve his conscience over leaving his family by helping Red and Belle, but it was far more than that.

He'd spent the previous afternoon selecting a piece of pine to carve into a doll. Linette had sent a package of fabric along with thread and needles. Thinking of how Red thought Belle might enjoy the prospect of a doll as much as getting it, Ward decided he would do as much work as possible on it where she could watch.

He hurried through the chores Eddie assigned him so he could start work on the project, but it was Red he was anxious to see. Would she be all prickly today or welcoming? Either way he looked forward to showing her the piece of wood he'd selected and handing her the material for doll clothes.

He found them sitting on the logs beside the fire pit. This time they didn't skitter away at his approach. In fact, Belle waved as he rounded the corner of the cabin. Red never left off watching him.

He greeted Belle, then returned his gaze to Red, aware something had shifted between them, uncertain how to describe it even to himself. He managed a suggestion of a smile before he revealed the length of wood, his knife and the package Linette had given him.

"What's that?" Belle eyed the wood.

"It's going to be your doll."

"It is?" Her doubt was evident.

"You wait and see." He moseyed over to sit on a log a healthy distance from the pair and held the wood for them to see. He'd rough-cut the basic shape and figured they could likely see the shape of a body and head. "This is going to be the face. I'll carve the body here. I figure to attach arms with screws so they move."

Belle edged closer as he flicked open his knife and started carving off curl after curl of wood. She hung back at a safe distance but too far to see how each cut brought out the developing outline of a head.

He held it up. "Can you see the beginning of her head?"

She nodded.

Ward spared a glance toward Red. It was meant to be fleeting but her gaze caught and held his, delving deep, as if searching for answers or something more. He had no idea what she sought or if he could provide it, but he let her look as long and hard as she wanted. She blinked, sucked in air and shifted her attention to her fingers.

His thoughts circled for a way to interpret the moment. He found none and returned to carving the doll, hoping it would tempt Red to move closer, but she seemed lost in contemplation of her hands. Perhaps if he talked about something else, something that might be of some interest to them.

"When Grady came to the ranch, he was awfully scared. Cried if anyone looked at him. Seems no one but Linette could get near him." He concentrated on his handwork for a moment but managed to sneak a glance at his audience. Belle watched every move of his fingers. Red didn't give any indication she heard him except for the way she cocked her head toward him as if anxious to catch every word.

Satisfied he had her attention but wishing for more,

he continued to talk about Grady. "For Christmas last year I carved some animals for him."

"How come he's at the ranch?" Belle asked.

Ward studied his answer. Seems life should be sweeter for children. "His mama died and he had nowhere to go, so Linette brought him with her."

"His papa died, too?"

Ward wondered how much to tell her. "No, his pa is alive but he can't take care of Grady." Or didn't care for the responsibility. Eddie had told him how Linette had challenged the man to take Grady and raise him and how she continued to send letters hoping to persuade him.

"How old is he?" Belle asked.

"He's five."

"He's happy?"

"Linette and Eddie care about him very much." But he knew, as did everyone on the ranch, that Grady would have times of sadness wondering why his father didn't want him.

His answer seemed to satisfy Belle. "How long does it take to carve a doll?" she asked.

"Well, this particular doll is extra special because it's for you. So I might take a little longer in order to make it real nice."

Her eyes sparkled with joy at being made to feel special.

Ward turned toward Red, expecting appreciation in her expression, but instead her eyes were wide and filled with fear. "Red, what's the matter?"

She blinked back her feelings and gave a smile that

went no further than the corners of her mouth. "Nothing. I'm—"

"I know. You're fine." If he heard it one more time… "Only you're not and you might as well stop pretending you are. Your life has not been pleasant. Your future is uncertain. Likely your head hurts and who knows what else is not sitting well with you—"

"Now that you mention it, I am wearing borrowed clothes."

"I noticed. Nice dress." The dark blue fabric made her eyes look more blue than green.

"I got a different dress, too," Belle said.

"I noticed." A faded red dress fit well. "You look very nice, too."

Belle smiled but the tension in the air did not dissipate. It lay so thick between Red and Ward that he was tempted to cut it away with his knife.

"I have something for you, Red." He picked up the package from Linette. However, she refused to move closer so he shuffled over and held the parcel toward her.

She stared. "What is it?"

He jiggled it teasingly. "Only one way to find out."

Still she did not reach for it.

Belle stood inches away, bouncing on the balls of her feet. "Red, hurry up and open it."

Red slowly, reluctantly, took the sack from Ward's hands and opened the drawstring. She pulled out fabric, a pair of scissors, needle, pins and thread.

"For doll clothes," Ward explained.

Belle reverently touched several pieces. "All satiny.

And this one so cuddly. Maybe my dolly can have a blanket, too?" She fingered a soft piece of wool.

"You will have the best-dressed doll ever," Red said. She turned to Ward. "Let me see the size." She measured a bit of fabric against the length of the wood.

Ward held very still as she bent over the beginnings of the doll in his hands. She was so intent on her task that she seemed unmindful of how close they were. He studied her hair. She'd brushed it and tamed it into a thick braid, but already bits of curls escaped and crowned her head.

She marked a couple of places in the fabric with pins, and then sat up straight.

There were but six inches between them, but the distance seemèd vast. He felt alone in a totally foreign way. In an attempt to corral the sensation, he returned to carving the doll.

They worked side by side, she often leaning over to measure this or that, he holding up his work frequently to let them see his progress. Belle sat on the ground in front of them, watching progress on both fronts and playing with her collection of rocks and twigs. At times they seemed to be animals she herded around. Other times she talked to them as if they were family members.

At first Red and Belle said little or limited their conversation to how long would the arms be? How big the head? Did Red think he should carve curls into the head? She did.

"At least they will be blond," she murmured.

Ward studied Red. Shifted his gaze to Belle. Her hair wasn't as curly as her sister's and was more brown than red, though it had mahogany glimmers. He turned back to Red. "You don't like your hair?"

She puffed out her lips in a rumble. "Hate it."

"It's kind of pretty."

The look she favored him with dripped with a load of denial. "It makes everyone stare."

"Yeah, well, only because it's eye-catching."

"I could do with plain."

He thought of her statement. "Don't most women prefer beautiful to plain? Don't they like to be noticed?"

"Can't say being noticed has been such a treat."

Aah. Now it made sense. He tried to think of a way to tell her that people would no longer view her as Thorton had. Nothing came to mind. "What's your real name?" Perhaps if she stopped using Red she might start to think of herself as someone besides that woman.

She didn't even glance up from stitching together a seam.

Belle did, though. "It's—"

"Belle." One word with a heap of warning attached. She flashed a defensive glance at Ward. "Red is the only name you need to know."

He regarded her, waiting for her to meet his look, and when she finally did he saw defiance and perhaps, if he let himself imagine it, a longing that dug deep into his heart. "Someday you will tell me your real name." It was part promise, part prayer.

"Dream on, cowboy." She jabbed the needle into the fabric so viciously he half expected to see her draw blood from her finger. But she deftly guided the sharp point away from her flesh.

Perhaps if he talked about his family it would make

her realize she no longer had to be Red. She could be free of that part of her life and again become the woman she was born to be. "My ma used to say she wished she had a daughter so she could make doll clothes. She told us that when she was a little girl she'd fashioned all sorts of costumes for her doll and dreamed of doing the same for a daughter. She had a collection of paper dolls in families and hundreds of outfits she'd collected over the years. She would let us look at it only under super- vision. She figured—and rightly so—that as boys we might not treat it as reverently as she wanted. If she ever had a granddaughter, she planned to pass the collection on to her." He stopped, unable to go on as a lump of de- spair swelled in his throat. Travers was twenty now. For all Ward knew, he was married and had provided Ma with a granddaughter. Or Ma might have had a child or two in her new marriage. Maybe Ward had another brother or sister.

He stared unseeingly into the distance. An idea— not new to him—plagued his mind. Perhaps he should forget his ranch and go back and see if he could find his ma and family. They might be in the same town, though he no longer thought so. His letters had been returned marked *No Longer Living Here. No Forward- ing Address.*

However, returning was not an option at the moment. Not with Red and Belle to care for.

But would he ever see his family again?

Chapter Seven

Red watched Ward struggle with his memories and emotions. It was bad enough to lose one's family because of death, but to not know where they were or if they were okay… Well, she couldn't imagine how she'd feel if Belle disappeared.

She owed him something even if most of the time his attention was an annoyance. Perhaps she could repay him by helping him now. But how? She couldn't assure him that his family was safe. Nor could she minimize his sense of loss. To do so would be insulting.

Seemed he liked talking about his mother. Perhaps if she talked about hers, he would feel better. Though she shrank back from letting herself remember those sweet, innocent times. But Belle ought to be allowed to remember how precious and loved she was.

So she began a story. "Ma taught me to knit when I was four. I remember so clearly the moment that I finally realized the loop on one needle had to go through the loop on the other. Once I did, I was unstoppable. I knitted a long scraggly-looking scarf that Pa wore everywhere. Said it was his favorite. It finally fell apart when I was about ten." She laughed. "I don't know who was more relieved to see it gone—Mama, Papa or me." She let the memory glide over her regrets and guilt and give her a moment of sweet love. "From scarves, I graduated to doll sweaters and hats. I don't remember using any sort of pattern. I expect Mama told me how to make the sleeves and shape the item. I thought my work was beautiful. It wasn't until after Belle was born and I pulled out my doll stuff to give her that I realized just how crude it looked. So I spent many a happy evening knitting new sweaters and bonnets and leggings for Belle's dolls."

"Red, what happened to my dolls? And all Mama and Papa's things?"

"An uncle inherited everything." The pleasantness of her memory was dashed away at the cruelty of an uncle she'd never met, didn't know existed. Apparently Papa had borrowed heavily from him and part of the agreement required Papa naming this uncle as beneficiary in his will. But the man had no regard for the needs of two girls. And everything that was near and dear to them was junk in his eyes. "He disposed of all the earthly goods as he saw fit." Most of it went to a man who owned a store that handled a variety of goods. Red would never forget the way he'd gloated over some of their treasures. *People love this kind of stuff.* He'd measured the family Bible with dollar signs in his eyes. He did the same for the wall hangings Mama had made and all Belle's pretty little dresses and her cradle.

Slowly, in measured tones, she continued the story, as much to remind herself of how far she'd fallen as for any other reason. To his credit, the uncle secured them a place in the home of a fine family. In return for Belle's keep, Red did housework. She didn't mind. They had their own room and were together. But it proved temporary and they moved. Then moved again.

At that point she stopped talking. She could not bear to recall how Thorton had "taken them on," as he so generously said, promising to take them to his sister where they would "do well."

If only she had known the truth. But by the time she did, she had no option. Thorton kept Belle under lock and key in order to obtain Red's cooperation. He beat Red if she proved the least bit rebellious.

"Then what happened?" Belle's eyes were wide.

Red fought a storm of conflicting emotions—regret at the way she'd failed in her duty toward Belle, guilt at the life she'd been forced to live warred with the joyful, peaceful memories of family life as she'd known it. She tried to control the raging conflagration inside. Struggled to find an answer for Belle.

"We went from one place to another." She tried to keep the bitter note out of her voice.

Belle's expression was wreathed with fear. She shifted back until she rested against the far log bench. She ducked her head and pulled her playthings close.

Red swallowed back regret. She should have stopped talking before she stirred up Belle's memories of the past few months. She turned to Ward, her eyes burning with a warning not to ask for more details.

He smiled narrowly and resumed carving the doll.

She fought to retain her resentment. Instead she found a yearning she would never admit. What sort of man carved a doll for a little girl who wasn't his?

Wasn't even related to him? Or carved little animals for a waif of a boy? Or rescued people who weren't sure they wanted to be rescued? She examined the last question. All that mattered was Belle was safe. But what did her future hold?

Ward looked up from his carving.

She turned away from him but not before he had caught her watching him. She couldn't face him, suspecting her confusion revealed itself in her expression, and she put aside the little dress she was sewing and sprang to her feet, not caring that he might wonder what drove her so urgently.

She stepped away from the logs and the cozy little scene that had drawn her into sweet memories of the past and fears of the future. Two steps in one direction and she stopped. Where was she going? Where could she go to escape both the memories and the uncertainties? Shifting direction, she made several more steps and stopped. If she didn't express some purpose, Ward would think she wandered aimlessly. Or like the daffodil poem Belle recalled... "I wandered lonely as a cloud that floats on high o'er vales and hills." Oh, if only she could float above everything as free as a cloud.

And as lonely.

Despair threatened to choke her. She must not think such thoughts. Her life was worth living for Belle's sake. Curbing her emotions, she stretched her arms overhead. "Got a little cramped sitting for so long," she murmured, hoping she sounded convincing. She picked her way back to the log bench and gathered up her sewing, aware that Ward watched her the whole while.

Even after she resumed stitching together the dress,

his gaze remained on her. She could feel it. Even as she felt his nosy concern. Determinedly she kept her head bent over her task. Let him think what he wanted. Wonder at her strange behavior. He would never understand. Nor would she attempt to explain how precarious was her position in life. She would not fit in any respectable society and had no intention of returning to the other side.

He shifted closer.

She glanced out the corner of her eye, wondering if he would take the hint to keep his distance. Yet, even though there was a yard of log to her right, she did not move. For the life of her, she could not make herself even when his elbow brushed her. She caught her breath, waiting, wondering, then with a heart-wrenching jolt, recalled invasive, cruel touches. She forced herself not to reveal any of what she felt. But her arm stiffened as his brushed hers.

He didn't jerk away, only let their elbows touch. Nothing more. Her heart ticked beneath her ribs, slowly resuming a steady beat. Warmth spread from her elbow to her lungs, freeing her to take a deep breath and filling her with a sweet reminder of being touched out of love. She closed her eyes and forced her lungs to inhale and exhale in a slow rhythm. But trying as hard as she could, she was unable to pretend she didn't feel something that frightened her while at the same time, promised to fill her yearning emptiness.

He leaned closer to whisper, "You will never again have to worry about Thorton or men like him. Not while I'm here to take care of you."

She jerked about to meet his gaze, his face barely six

inches from her own. So close she felt as if she might drown in the blueness of his eyes. And the sincerity of his promise.

What about when he wasn't there? What would people say about her past? It wouldn't be nice; she could guarantee that. And men who would recognize her and think—? She shuddered. Her soul was dirty.

He nudged her elbow. "You're fine. Remember?"

Only she wasn't and she couldn't fake it at the moment, knew her eyes likely revealed her failure to do so.

"Red, you're safe here."

He'd misinterpreted her worry. His dullness edged every thought with annoyance. "I might be safe but I'll never be free of my past." She knew the moment he understood her meaning.

His eyes went from sky-blue to stormy navy. He shook his head. "No one need know about your past."

"There will be those who recognize me." She resisted an urge to cover herself with her hands and protect herself. She tugged at her braid to remind him that her hair was unmistakable. "And even if they don't, I know who I am and I will never forget." Her words came in a hot rush.

She was not surprised when he jerked away to face straight ahead. His elbow lost contact with hers. She knew enough to expect that sort of reaction from decent people. Slowly, every movement a pain, she folded away the fabric, returned all the supplies to the sack and rose to her feet. "Belle, I think it's time to do something else."

Belle scrambled up. "What?"

Red had no idea what they needed to do and grabbed

the first idea that surfaced. "I'll show you how to make biscuits."

She felt Ward's surprise at her sudden decision. She hesitated a heartbeat, wanting somehow to explain. But what could she say? That there was no place in her life for hopes and dreams?

Belle couldn't seem to make up her mind whether she should follow Red or stay with Ward. "Will you come with us so I can see my dolly growing?"

Red kept her groan silent. She didn't want him to follow. "Maybe he has to get back to work." Keeping her back to him ensured she wouldn't know his reaction. But she waited, wondering what he would say.

"Red? Are you trying to get rid of me?" His quiet question opened up a chasm of regret and longing. If only things could be different.

They couldn't, and there was no point in wishing otherwise.

"Red?" He said her name with gentle prodding.

Belle tugged Red's hand. "Can he taste my biscuits when they're done?"

Red stared straight ahead and considered her options. Did she really want him to leave? No. But neither did she want him to stay.

Belle shook her hand as if to remind her of the unanswered question.

Slowly she turned. "Would you like to join us for tea when the biscuits are done?"

He held her gaze in silence as if assessing how much welcome her invitation carried. It carried little. Still he nodded. "It would be my pleasure."

Red nodded and turned her steps toward the cabin. Belle jerked her back. "You gonna leave him there?"

When had her little sister grown so demanding? And so social?

Thankfully Ward answered before Red could dredge an excuse to her brain. "I'll sit out here and work on your doll for a little while longer."

She finally got Belle inside. But the change of scenery did not end Belle's demands.

"How come you don't like him? He's making me a doll."

"That's very nice of him."

Belle crossed her arms, knowing she had not convinced Red of anything. "And he wants to help us."

Red would do anything to take her little sister back to happy, safer times, but with Mama and Papa gone and the two of them at the mercy of those who tried to help, it was time to remind Belle that not all offers of help were sincere. She squatted down to eye level with Belle. If the situation wasn't so serious she might smile at the stubbornness in Belle's blue eyes. Belle was innocently beautiful—subdued, not as eye-catching as Red. Red hoped Belle would never lose her innocence but that didn't mean she could be allowed to be too trusting. "Belle, do you remember the gifts Thorton brought us? The pretty dresses?"

Belle nodded, the stubbornness still evident.

"Do you remember how he promised to take care of us?"

A shadow of doubt surfaced.

"Perhaps you never heard all he said. So I'm telling you now just to make sure you understand what happened. Thorton told Mrs. Stanley, the lady we were working for, that he had a sister back in Baltimore who wanted a young woman for companionship. He assured us all that a younger sister would be an asset and we would be generously provided for. Do you remember that?"

"Some." Belle's expression grew troubled.

"Remember how he carried a Bible under his arm and pretended he was a preacher? You know what happened next."

Belle's bottom lip quivered. "He made me stay in that little room and made you work for him."

"That's right." She tenderly wiped a tear from the corner of Belle's eyes. "I regret reminding you of all this, but you must never forget that not all promises are to be trusted." Her voice hardened until she could barely push the words past her teeth. "Never take anyone at their word."

Belle nodded, her eyes awash with misery. "Does that—" She swallowed hard. "Does it mean I can't have the dolly?"

Red pulled Belle into a tight embrace. "I think it's okay to have a doll. Just don't let it make you forget to be careful."

Belle clung to Red. "I won't."

"Now who wants to learn how to make biscuits?"

Belle pulled away and raised her hand. "Me. Me. I want to."

"Then let's do it." Red promised herself she would live her life for her little sister. Nothing else mattered.

Certainly not the loneliness edging her heart.

Nor the thought of Ward sitting patiently outside, generously carving the figure of a doll for Belle.

Yet awareness of his gentleness to her little sister allowed a tiny bit of regret to sneak past her defenses.

Ward stopped carving to listen shamelessly to the conversation drifting from the cabin. Red had left the door and windows open to let in fresh air but would no doubt shut them if she thought he could hear them.

He'd wondered how they'd fallen into Thorton's clutches. Hearing the trickery of the man made him jab his knife into the log seat beside him. He hoped Thorton suffered greatly in jail.

Of course Red was right to teach Belle to be cautious. And she had every reason to be mistrustful of promises. She had no way of knowing how sincere Ward was.

It was up to him to show her he could be trusted. But how? Every kindness triggered suspicion from her.

The conversation inside the cabin had shifted to "Measure the flour. That's the way."

"Chop until it's all mealy. Good job."

They laughed about something. He imagined the two of them working side by side and smiled. They liked doing things together.

That gave him an idea.

He would work on the doll only when they were with him as they had been this morning. And he'd invent other things to do together.

He studied the toy. The head was taking shape nicely. Soon Belle would have her doll to play with and then he'd start another project. He considered the options.

"Ward," Belle called from the doorway. "I made biscuits. Red says come and taste them."

He closed his knife and stuck it in his pocket. Blew the bits of shavings from the doll and strode toward the house.

Belle waited at the door. "Can I see her?"

He gave her the doll. "You can play with it until I come back tomorrow to work on it some more."

"I can?" Her eyes glistened. She hurried to the corner where her rocks and pieces of wood were arranged, laid her doll down and started whispering to it.

Ward shifted his gaze to Red, saw her struggle with joy for her little sister's pleasure and her ever-constant caution.

He edged closer. "It's a long way from done but she sees the possibilities."

Red's eyes flared like green flames. "A person can be waylaid by the thought of possibilities."

He considered her words. "I get the idea we aren't talking about dolls."

"You sure are astute."

He chuckled.

She scowled.

"I know you're hoping to drive me away with your sarcasm but be warned, it's failing miserably. Red, I like you when you're feisty."

She looked about ready to spontaneously ignite. "You don't know who you're messing with."

That brought a chuckle to his lips. "Or it could be I do."

She jerked her attention from him. Her gaze darted about the room as if not quite knowing how to ignore him. It settled on the plate of biscuits in the middle of the table. "Belle, do you still want to serve tea?"

Ward leaned close to whisper, "Do I hear a broad hint in your voice? Like maybe you'd be relieved if she'd changed her mind so you could suggest I be on my way?"

Her look might have scorched him if he wasn't too busy grinning.

"I haven't changed my mind." Speaking louder, he turned to Belle. "Those are delicious-looking biscuits."

Belle tucked her doll under her arm and trotted to the table. "You like them with syrup?"

"It's all we've got," Red informed them both in her most severe tone.

"I like syrup best of all." He grinned without a trace of repentance, knowing his continued enjoyment of this exchange about drove Red to distraction. He tried to imagine what it would be like if she stopped being all defensive. He got a sudden image of Red smiling and joyful as she served tea to him and Belle. The idea jolted clear through him. It was something he'd like to see in real life. But like Red said, *In your dreams, cowboy.*

He sat on the upright log stool as Belle and Red sat across from each other on the chairs.

It was Belle's tea party and she took charge. "Ward, will you pray over the food?"

Ward didn't dare look at Red, but wondered if she thought the same thing as he.... Did Belle think they might need divine intervention to eat her baking? Most likely she was only playing house. He bowed his head and folded his hands. "Lord, bless this food we are about to receive and bless the hands that prepared it. Amen."

Belle studied him with wide-eyed innocence. "That's me, right?"

He realized she meant his prayer to bless the one who'd prepared the food. "That's right. And Red, too, for helping you." He shifted his gaze to his left. Red stared at the biscuits, her throat working. If he wasn't mistaken, her eyes looked watery. "Red, is something wrong?"

She dashed away any hint of tears. "Something in my eye." Her look dared him to argue otherwise. But they both knew it wasn't true.

He couldn't help wonder what had touched her deeply enough to bring any sign of emotion to the surface. Could he get her to tell him? Smiling at his foolishness—she'd probably tell him anything but the real reason—he split open a biscuit, spooned on syrup and took a bite. "Good. Really good."

Belle beamed with pride. "I like cooking."

He finished the biscuit quickly and scooped up another. "I like eating."

He ate only two biscuits, though he could have downed a half dozen but he didn't want to deprive them of the fruit of their labors and certainly did not want to give Red a chance to accuse him of gluttony. He glanced around the room. He'd been inside a few times when Eddie lived here but having Red and Belle occupy the place gave it a whole new feel. His gaze lighted on the bookshelf. According to Belle, their father had enjoyed reading poetry. Just like his father. It gave him an idea.

"Do you like to read?" He meant the question for both of them but kept his gaze on Red. Saw a sudden, unguarded jolt of pleasure. Knew her answer before she spoke.

Her expression grew disinterested.

How did she do that? Knowing she'd learned to mask her feelings because of her situation with Thorton, he did his best to imitate her skill and hide his anger and regret. "Reading is okay for those with nothing else to do," Red answered.

He chuckled, not surprised that she refused to admit her true feelings. "How busy does this little cabin keep you? Never mind. I only had in mind to suggest a source of books." He let the words sit, waiting for Red to swallow her defensiveness and ask for more details.

Belle, likely knowing her sister would not easily give in, spoke. "I can read a little. Red taught me how."

"You ever had a real reader?"

"No. Red told me she had them when she learned to read. She used newspapers for me to learn." Her eyes sparkled. "One paper had a story in it. You know, a chapter at a time. Red made me skip parts of it." The look of accusation in her eyes brought a chuckle from Ward.

"I can imagine why."

"She said it was too grown-up for me."

"I think there might be a reader or two in the place I mean." He waited, watching Red fight an internal fight.

Finally she gave him a look rife with annoyance. "So where is this secret stash of books?"

"I'll tell you on one condition."

Her eyes narrowed, her lips tightened.

He curled his hands into fists that she still thought he might exact unwanted favors from him.

"Red, just answer one question honestly." He didn't give her a chance to get any more defensive. "Do you enjoy reading?"

Surprise flared through her eyes. She sucked in a gasp as if his question had physically landed a blow to her lungs. For a moment she didn't answer, then she blinked and nodded. "I like reading."

"Wait here." He hurried out the door and jogged across to the bunkhouse, where he snagged up a green canvas knapsack. He hadn't looked at the contents in years but it went everywhere he went. Usually it was tucked under the bed as it had been here.

He loped back to the cabin.

Red and Belle still sat at the table. Belle appeared excited. He'd say Red's expression held more doubt than anything.

Well, he was about to prove to her that her doubts were unnecessary.

"Come and see what I have." He rested the knapsack on the floor and untied the cords holding the top closed. On the top was a worn quilt. His fingers lingered on it. "Ma made me this. Said to always think of her when I saw it. Not that I needed anything to make me remember her." He pushed aside a choking homesickness and set aside the quilt before his feelings grew stronger.

Next were some family pictures. He blinked back the sting in his eyes and instead let pleasant memories crowd his mind. He showed them to Red and Belle. "My parents on their wedding day. And this is me and Travers when we were schoolboys." His voice refused to work and he simply handed Red the picture of Hank at about two.

"Is this your little brother Hank?" Red asked, her voice curiously gentle.

He nodded but kept his attention on the stash of books. "These were my pa's. I took them when I left." Mostly to ensure his stepfather wouldn't destroy them out of spite. He lifted out the first volume. "Pa's favorite book of poetry." The pages were thumbed from much use. "Pa read from that book almost every night, especially during the winter."

To his regret, Ward had often wished Pa wouldn't insist on reading the poems aloud. "Travers and I often got the giggles as we made faces to each other. Pa said nothing but sometimes lowered the book to look at us with a pained expression. If he were alive now I would want to listen to him read each of these poems." He set the book aside and dug through the other until he found the collection of readers. "There you go, Belle."

She took them reverently. "Thank you," she whispered, and shuffled around to sit her back to the wall next to her collection of playthings. No doubt she was as fascinated with the illustrations in the books as Ward and Travers had been at that age.

He turned to Red. "Feel free to enjoy any of these books."

She lifted her face to him. If he wasn't mistaken, tears glistened in her eyes. He tried to think what they meant. Was it something he said? Or sharing memories of his pa? He wished he could retract every word that made her sad. But all he could do was brush a silvery tear from each cheek.

She jolted at his touch.

Had he overstepped the boundaries of what she

would allow? But he did not immediately withdraw his hand as their looks caught and held. Hers full of so many things he couldn't name. How could he make her see he accepted her? No judgment. No expectation of favors.

He waited for her to jerk away. Nail him with a sharp comment, but she only stared at him as if overwhelmed by her feelings.

She looked so sad and lost. If only he could read her thoughts and know where he fit in them. If only he could ease her distress. Without giving himself time to think about his actions, he leaned forward and kissed her.

It could barely be described as a kiss. His lips only touched hers, and then he drew back as startled as she as a hundred surprising thoughts exploded inside his head. He liked kissing her. He would do it again if she allowed.

He knew from the look on her face that she most certainly would not.

Chapter Eight

Red sprang to her feet. How dare he? After all his promises that he expected nothing in return for his help. He wasn't any different than the rest of the men she'd seen while in Thorton's care.

How foolish that she'd allowed herself to think he might be.

All his talk about family had knocked down more than one barrier around her heart and wave after wave of longing had swept over her. She'd once known the kind of life he talked about. Once, even, had dreamed of a time when she would enjoy the same sort of life with a husband and later, with children. Now her past made that impossible. Who would marry her once they learned? Not the sort of man she cared to share the rest of her life with. Most people would assume the worst once they heard she'd worked in a saloon. The cruelty Thorton had subjected her to had never defiled her in the worst way, but it had been malicious. He'd taught her to obey his wishes to avoid his beatings. If that failed, he only had to threaten to give Belle a taste of his meanness.

Ward had stolen a kiss. She scrubbed her hand across her mouth. It wasn't the same as the kisses she'd endured at the saloon, yet it angered her to the depth of her soul…because she'd unlocked gates and allowed him to see far too deeply. And he'd misunderstood it as invitation.

She hurried to the table and gathered up the remains of their little tea party. Even that mocked her. She'd been as guilty as Belle at pretending.

Well, no more. She would accept his help only until she found something else, and she would. She had no idea how, but she would find a way to be on her own. No expectations. No dreams.

He slowly got to his feet. "Feel free to enjoy the books."

"Thank you," she murmured, keeping her back to him.

"I best be leaving." She heard his hesitation, his confusion. His footsteps went toward the door. Stopped.

She held herself so still her muscles vibrated. She would not turn. Did not want to see the look on his face. Didn't matter if it was disgust or something else.

His footsteps resumed. They did not continue to the door but came toward the table.

She forgot how to breathe. Her heart pounded a protest against her chest wall. She stiffened as he stopped so close behind her that she could feel the heat from his body. Now he would no doubt claim what she owed him. The best she could hope for was she'd be able to send Belle outside to play.

"Red?" His voice lacked the harshness she expected. "Red, I apologize. I didn't mean to kiss you. Don't know what came over me. But when I saw you crying, I wanted nothing more than to make you feel better. Somehow I thought to kiss away your troubles. I had no right. I'm sorry. You can be sure it won't happen again."

And then he hurried to the door. She didn't move until his footsteps fade away. Then she crumpled to the log stool, buried her face in her hands and gritted her teeth to keep from crying. Of course he regretted kissing her. He was a decent man. Slowly she brought emotion after emotion back into submission, then pushed to her feet and finished cleaning the kitchen as Belle showed her doll the pictures in the books Ward had lent her. Thankfully her little sister was so engrossed in the books she remained unaware of Red's state of mind.

Red allowed herself a glance at the treasure of books. She loved reading.

Her movements fueled by anger, she grabbed the pictures, intending to stuff them and the books back into the sack.

But her fingers lingered on the wedding picture of his parents. She saw Ward's likeness to his father. Saw a happy couple with dreams of a blissful future. Agony gouged at her innards. Their happy future had been shattered by death.

Seemed even normal people couldn't hope for a pleasant life.

What chance did she have?

None. None at all.

She jammed the pictures into the sack and crammed the books on top, yanked the ties closed and shoved the whole thing into the corner by the door.

Startled, Belle stared at her. "Don't you want to read?"

Her desire to read almost overwhelmed her, but she couldn't pretend she was normal and could pursue normal activities. "Not right now. Do you want to read the story to me?"

"I might not remember."

"You will with practice."

As Belle haltingly read the book, Red pushed her wayward thoughts back into order. She knew who she was…what she was. Her dreams were dead. But she had Belle and would devote her life to raising her sister.

Her emotions settled, she spent a pleasant hour helping Belle read. But despite her best efforts, her mind wandered to events of the day. And Ward's kiss. Meant to comfort, he said. Was it possible he could kiss her and not think of her as Thorton's prize? She shuddered.

Belle looked up at her. "You cold?"

"Let's go out in the sun." They slipped out back, grateful there seemed to be no one about to observe them.

Only she couldn't escape her memories outdoors, either. Seeing the log benches reminded her of sitting beside Ward. She hoped he'd return for Belle's sake to work on the doll. Only it wasn't the doll she thought of. It was the sight of his hands as he worked, the touch of his elbow on hers…

"Belle, let's go for a walk." She didn't give Belle a chance to answer before she headed up the hill. She'd go until the trees hid her.

She didn't follow the river as Ward had shown them, but veered into the woods. The trees thickened about them. Dark shadows covered the forest floor. Birds protested at their intrusion. A raven scolded loudly. But her thoughts did not have the decency to stay behind. No amount of running would outdistance them. In fact, they grew stronger in the shadows. More fearsome until she shivered with tension.

"Let's go home and make supper." Poor Belle had not protested Red's headlong flight. Perhaps she knew something had upset Red. When they started back she took Red's hand.

"We're going to be okay." Her little sister's voice was firm.

"Yes, we are." She would not pay any heed to the frisson of fear shuddering up her spine.

The feeling would not leave her even as she and Belle prepared a simple meal and ate. Thankfully Belle was content playing with her doll and reading the books. Red tried to distract herself from her fearful thoughts by working on doll clothes. But the tingle of worry would not leave her.

She would not give it recognition by trying to decide what caused it.

Later she lay in darkness with Belle asleep beside her and the wooden doll, wrapped in a square of wool, held close.

The sensation of dread, or whatever she chose to call it, hovered on every breath.

It rose with her the next morning. Even the sight of the sun flashing on the mountains did not ease it. She paused in making breakfast to study the sampler on the wall. *Whither shall I flee from Your presence?* Seemed there were two things a person couldn't run from—God and their thoughts. About all she could do was keep so busy neither could bother her. But a little cabin didn't require a lot of work and making doll clothes gave her far too much time to think.

She studied the knapsack. Would reading bring forgetfulness?

But somehow she couldn't bring herself to take out a book. They were Ward's.

"Belle, let's go outside."

They stepped outside. A couple of men rode from the barn and headed west. Red caught her breath and stepped back to the protection of the cabin, but the men didn't even glance her way.

Red swallowed hard. She hadn't bothered to check for the presence of others before they left the cabin. Her confused emotions made her careless. She glanced up the hill to the big house, but the windows were in the shadow of the morning sun and she couldn't tell if anyone watched. The windows of the cookhouse were mirrored by the sunshine and again, she couldn't see if anyone saw her.

Belle had skipped ahead and now returned. "What's wrong?"

"Nothing."

Belle caught her worry and shrank to her side. "Did you see Thorton?" She squeaked the words.

Red forced calm into her heart. "Honey, Thorton is in jail. He'll never bother us again. Now, what would you like to do?" She took Belle's hand and marched around the cabin as if she didn't have a fear or worry in the world.

"Can I play here?" She held her doll. "I think Sally likes this place."

"Certainly."

Red settled on a log bench and watched her sister play. If she had a book to read, she would enjoy the warm sunshine as much as Belle. There were books in the cabin. Ward's books. He'd offered them to her but would he expect anything in return if she selected one to read?

"Sally and I are going for a walk." Belle marched the wooden doll around the clearing. She paused at the corner of the cabin. "Do you think Ward will come back today?"

Red made a noncommittal sound. She wondered the same thing. After her reaction to his kiss yesterday, would he take offense? Decide to let them manage on their own? After all, from the beginning she'd insisted they could. And she meant to prove it.

Belle circled back to the log. "Maybe he'll give Sally arms and legs today."

Red said he might but not to count on it. She would not admit the weight and fear she'd carried since yesterday came from wondering if he would. Insisting that's what she wanted had become hard, heavy work.

It had been a long night for Ward, worrying as he did that Red might not forgive him for stealing a kiss. He'd apologized because he understood it went beyond what Red would accept, but he didn't regret it one bit. He'd fallen asleep with a smile on his lips as he thought of her leaning forward, unconsciously needing, wanting to be kissed.

The early morning hours had dragged. It seemed his chores took longer than usual. One horse needed something for colic. The horses required a ration of oats. One of the cowboys was feverish and Ward had to fetch Linette to check on him.

Linette questioned him as they walked down the hill to the bunkhouse. "Is Red ready for visitors yet?"

"I don't know."

"Warn her I won't be delaying much longer. Besides, Grady is anxious for a playmate."

"I'll mention it." A foolish thought tugged at his brain. He liked having Red and Belle to himself. How selfish of him. And yet it warmed a cold spot behind his heart that had been there since he'd said goodbye to his family.

"If she needs anything, just let me know."

They reached the bunkhouse and Linette examined the cowboy. "He'll be okay. Lots of rest and fluids. I'll get Bertie to tend him."

Finally Ward finished his work and strode toward the cabin. He'd seen Red and Belle sneak around to the privacy at the back.

Not wanting to frighten them, he made enough noise heading after them to give plenty of warning.

Belle ran forward and held the doll toward him. "We've been playing."

He guessed she meant her and the doll. "I hope she's been good company."

Belle giggled. "She's my best friend."

He followed Red's movements as she left the log bench and pressed into the shadows of the cabin. He couldn't see her expression to measure her feelings.

He stepped toward her.

She crossed her arms across her middle as he approached.

His feet were suddenly heavy and awkward. He almost stumbled, though nothing caught his boot. She looked scared and defensive. Had he done that to her? Lord, forgive him if he had. "Hi, Red."

"Good morning."

"Thought I'd do some more work on Belle's doll."

Belle followed behind him. "Here she is. Her name is Sally and she's wondering when she can have arms."

Red's mouth opened and closed. She swallowed loudly enough for him to hear, then stared at the mountains.

Ward took the doll. "She'll have her arms as soon as I'm done giving her a proper head and body."

"Good. She needs her arms to do her school lessons." Belle skipped away and settled on a log bench where she picked up a reader and gave it her full attention.

Red still stared into the distance, her shoulders drawn almost to her ears. Tension seemed to hold her in a vise. "Red, what's wrong? Is it about yesterday?"

She slowly brought her wide-eyed gaze to him. "Sally was my mother's name. I don't know if Belle is aware of that. She was only five when Mama died. How much does she remember?" Her voice was a thin, sharp whisper. She breathed hard and pressed her hands to her stomach as if enduring pain.

He could no more deny her the comfort he ached to give than he could erase her past. He drew her to his chest and eased her around the corner out of Belle's sight, lest the little girl see her sister's distress and be upset.

Red stiffened, refusing comfort in his arms, yet she didn't slip from his grasp as if needing what she would not allow herself. It gave Ward encouragement.

"What happened to your parents?"

She gasped in air.

Perhaps he shouldn't have asked. But he couldn't pull the words back, so he simply held her gently, giving her time to decide if she wanted to answer or not.

"There was an accident."

"They both died at the same time?" He knew what it meant to lose one parent. But two at once? His chest felt like a great weight had been dropped to it.

"Someone from a nearby mine was trucking dynamite through town. Someone explained what happened but I don't remember. I didn't care. Still don't. I went from a happy daughter to a sixteen-year-old orphan with a little sister to care for."

The air shimmered with pain and regret.

"Poor Belle. She was so young. Does she remember any of the good or just the bad?" The agony in her voice shredded Ward's heart. He must reassure her.

"Belle is a happy child and her fears seem to be disappearing rapidly. It appears to me you've protected her from being completely aware of everything going on around her. You should be proud of yourself," he said.

She sucked in air until he thought her lungs would explode. Then let it out in a windy gust, "Proud? How can I be proud? I am ashamed of who I am." She flashed brittle green eyes at him and he knew from the rigid set of her shoulders that she had said more than she intended to.

"You can hardly blame yourself for the fact Thorton tricked you."

Her glower did not weaken. "How do you know about that?"

He smiled uncertainly, wondering how she would react to his admission. "I overheard you telling Belle." She needed to hear the truth plain-spoken. "What happened to you is not who you are."

She blinked. The only sign she gave of hearing him. Then she whispered, "Who am I?"

He silently prayed for wisdom to say the right thing. "You are a good big sister. You are a responsible adult. But above and beyond that, you are loved by God."

The hardness in her eyes grew until he could have been looking at matching emeralds. She shrugged away from the weight of his arm. "I used to believe in God's love."

"He hasn't changed."

"But I have."

"God doesn't." She had to believe it. For her own peace of mind.

"A person can be cast from His presence because of their actions."

He reached for her hand, wanting to pull her back. Not just to himself but to faith in God.

She stepped away.

"Red, remember the verse my mother stitched. 'Whither shall I flee from Your presence? The darkness and light are alike to Thee.'"

"It's easy to believe when you haven't experienced the things I have."

He lifted his hands in defeat. "It's pointless to argue." All he could do was pray for her healing. "I'm going to work on Belle's doll. Why don't you come along and make some clothing?" As he suspected, she put aside her own misery to do something for Belle and retrieved her sewing kit while he settled on the log bench.

After they'd worked in companionable silence for a while, and he reasoned she'd had time for her emotions to settle, he brought up his plan. "I have a surprise." He intentionally spoke to Belle.

Her eyes lit. "What?"

"I brought a picnic lunch. Cookie packed the basket and informed me all little girls enjoy picnics." He hoped big girls did, too.

Belle bounded to her feet and jumped up and down. "I don't think I've ever been on a picnic. Have I, Red?"

Her smile was sad. "Mama and Papa took us on frequent picnics. Do you remember a place by the river where the trees grew together at the top so it was a leafy, green room? That was one of their favorite places."

Belle stared at her sister. "Were there wild roses? With prickles?"

"Lots of them. In June it smelled so good."

Belle looked at a fingertip. "I remember getting a prickle in my finger because I wanted a pretty flower. Papa picked it for me and kissed my finger. He said a kiss was the best medicine."

Moving slowly for fear of startling her, Ward shifted his gaze to Red. She stared at Belle but he saw emotions play across her face. Felt her sadness like someone had lassoed his heart with a tight rope and jerked him facedown in the dirt.

"He used to say that." Her words squeaked from a tight throat. She turned. Her gaze connected with Ward's. Silently daring him to pity them.

He smiled past his pain at what this pair had endured. He wanted her to know he cared how she felt. If a kiss would make it better, he would give her one, or as many as she needed, but somehow he understood—he knew not how—it would take more than a kiss, more than a thousand kisses to fix her pain.

"Then I really, really like picnics," Belle informed them. "Where are we going?"

Ward eased his gaze from Red's. "I think I know a real good spot."

Belle looked skyward. "Is it time for lunch?"

Ward studied the position of the sun. "I think I might have time to carve a leg for Miss Sally first." He could tell Belle struggled with wanting two things at the same time.

"I might be able to finish this dress," Red said, her voice almost normal.

Ward knew she would deny everything he'd just seen—her pain and, beneath it, her hope. He was content to let her take her time in dealing with her past but he prayed God would heal her heart.

They worked steadily for an hour or so but Belle grew more and more restless until finally Ward closed his knife. "I guess poor Sally will have to wait until tomorrow for her other leg." He handed the doll to Belle. "You think it's time to go on our picnic?"

She nodded, mute with excitement.

He turned to Red. "What do you think? Is it time?"

She slowly slid her considering gaze from Ward to Belle and grinned at the little girl's excitement. "I think it must be." She turned back to Ward and her smile faltered only slightly before she ducked her head and gave her full attention to gathering together her sewing materials. She tied off a knot of thread and held up a little yellow-print dress. "It's finished."

Belle squealed. "Oh, thank you, thank you. Sally is going to wear a dress to her first picnic." She hung the dress on her wooden doll. It almost looked like a real doll, though Belle's imagination made it into far more. To her it was real and alive, her best friend. "Aren't you excited, Sally?"

Ward picked up the basket he'd left at the front of the cabin. He led the way, first toward the river. He stopped several times to point out things to them—the tracks of a deer, the tree that had been cut down by a beaver, the sound of water rippling over the rocks.

Red's expression grew more peaceful with every yard they covered. He understood it was difficult to harbor anxiety in the beautiful surroundings. They followed the river around a bend and walked through rustling reeds. He could see his destination and turned aside to an almost invisible pathway. A few more steps led them to a room-sized clearing with fallen trees providing natural seating. The trunks of the trees and the overhead branches formed a secluded room.

He led them to the center. "This is where we are having our picnic. It's like our own outdoor room."

Belle sighed in pleasure. "A picnic room."

Red looked upward to the waving roof of branches,

lowered her gaze to the wild roses. Slowly, she turned full circle. "It's very nice." Her husky voice revealed far more than her words. And the look she favored him with caught him by surprise. "It's a lot like the place Mama and Papa would go. Thank you."

He nodded, his throat too tight to speak. He'd wanted to please her, make her remember better times, but he hadn't expected gratitude. He put the basket down and tried to sort out his thoughts. What else would they do on a picnic? He and Travers had always played tag or hide-and-seek. Was that appropriate for girls? Only one way to find out. "Who wants to play a game?"

"Me. Me." Belle jumped up and down. "What game?"

"You have any favorites?"

She looked confused and he realized she'd been allowed few childhood games the past year or two. "Do I, Red?"

Red's smile faltered only a bit. "You used to like playing chase." The mischievous look she gave Ward tipped his heart sideways. "You would chase Papa round and round until you caught him, and then he had to chase you until he caught you."

Belle eyed Ward with a begging look. "Will you play chase with me?"

"It sounds like a lot of work. And what does Red do?"

She plunked down on a fallen tree. "I watch."

"Uh-huh." How had he gotten roped into this? But he couldn't deny Belle. Any more than he could disappoint Red. Despite her teasing indifference, he knew she ached for Belle to enjoy happy times and happy memories. "Okay. I'll play."

Belle ran away with a scream of delight. "You have to catch me."

How hard could it be for a grown man to catch an eight-year-old girl? He soon found out it was more difficult than he could have imagined. She could slip through tiny openings and duck under overhanging branches that slapped him in the forehead and tossed his hat to the ground. Red chuckled. "Better leave your hat here."

He scrambled over the undergrowth and dropped the hat beside her. She looked up, as innocent as could be except for the flashing amusement in her eyes.

"Why do I get the feeling you are enjoying this more than you should?"

She widened her eyes. "It's good to see Belle having fun."

"Uh-huh." He studied her with narrowed eyes but she kept her expression blank. He turned away. "Funny that it's me chasing through the trees scratching my face." He made a show of rubbing a spot where a branch had attacked him.

Just before he stepped out of the clearing, she giggled. "Yup. It's funny."

He grinned as he trotted after Belle. He didn't mind a bit being laughed at. In fact, it felt downright good. He finally managed to catch Belle and swing her off her feet to a good deal of squealing. Then he had to let her chase him. She seemed tireless but he soon hollered, "Uncle. I give up. Let's eat."

Belle grabbed his hand and marched back to the clearing.

Ward grinned. It felt good to have the little girl's

trust. As soon as Red saw them, her mouth pinched into a frown.

Ward sighed. It was going to be a good sight harder to earn Red's trust.

He could only hope and pray that one day he would. Why did it matter so much? Well, because of his pride. He was a good man, and they ought to know it. But it went deeper. Back to his own family. If he could help this pair find what he'd failed to give his own family, somehow that would help ease his conscience.

If only Red would accept his help as it was given— freely and generously. He wanted nothing more from her. Not favors as she hinted. And not her heart.

Chapter Nine

Red understood Ward was doing his best to bring back good memories for Belle. Just as he made no secret of his desire to help her remember better times. On one hand she appreciated it. On the other, she wondered why it mattered to him. More important, how would Belle feel when they moved on?

If not for disappointing Belle, who could not remember going on a picnic, she would have gathered up her skirt and marched away. Instead, she allowed Ward to pass her a thick sandwich full of savory beef, seasoned with sharp mustard sauce. She tried valiantly to maintain a sense of annoyance but the peace of her surroundings, the enjoyment of good food and her pleasure at watching Belle play defeated her attempt.

Accepting the inevitable, she leaned back and looked up at the bright sky laced with the branches of evergreen trees. There was a time such a sight would have filled her with sweet thoughts of God's love.

She jerked her attention from the sky to the fallen trees. One of them formed a sidewalk for Belle's doll, Sally. Would she ever hear the name, or be able to say it without a thousand regrets and a world of longing catching at her heart?

Ward looked into the picnic basket. "Looks like that cake was the last of it. I hope you both got enough to eat."

Belle glanced up from her play long enough to tell him her opinion. "I did. It sure was good."

"I'll be sure to tell Cookie. She'll be pleased." He turned to Red.

"It was very good," Red allowed. "And I'm plenty full. Give my thanks to Cookie." She wondered at the way his eyes flickered as if remembering something.

"Why don't you tell her yourself?"

She didn't care that her expression likely revealed her surprise and a whole lot more. Did he expect her to walk over and tell Cookie? "You aren't bringing her to visit, are you?"

"Tomorrow is Sunday, and Cookie and Bertie have a little church service in the cookhouse. I thought you might like to go. Then you could thank her yourself."

"It's impossible." How dare he even suggest it?

Belle left her doll stranded on the fallen tree and rushed to Ward's knees. "Would Grady be there?"

Ward's probing gaze left Red just long enough for him to cup Belle's head and smile at her. "He's there every Sunday. He used to be the only child." He made it sound like Red was responsible for the child's loneliness.

She stiffened her spine, preparing to defend herself.

But before she could voice her protests, he turned to her, his gaze intense, demanding, even challenging.

As if he silently dared her to face the crew at the ranch. And maybe even God.

Her own gaze hardened as she pressed her lips into a tight line. Before she could reiterate her refusal, Belle stood before her. "Red, I never had a friend. Not since I was real young. I kind of remember the kids next door. There was a big boy who would give me a push on the swing and another boy about my age. He had a pretend farm under the tree. They had a baby, too. Sometimes I got to hold her. But that was when I was little. Maybe Grady would like to be my friend." She swayed back and forth as she talked.

Red sighed. Belle had already turned Grady into her best friend. And she knew to refuse Ward's invitation would rob her little sister of the chance to meet a child and enjoy a playmate.

From the way Ward grinned, she guessed he knew it, too.

The look she gave him should have erased all amusement, but he only grinned wider.

"Say yes. Please, Red. Pleeeeease." Belle pleaded with her eyes as much as her words.

Red studied her eager sister. She didn't want to face the residents of the ranch. They knew who and what she was. She could well imagine the speculative glances the men would give her. And the censure…

But what about Linette and Cookie? They'd shown friendship.

Their kindness only deepened her guilt and regret. She wasn't sure she could accept any of this.

She especially had no interest in attending a church service.

However, it might afford her a chance to ask Linette if she knew of any jobs a girl like Red could obtain. She clenched down on her back teeth, not wanting to think of the sort of position people might think she was qualified to fill. Finally she nodded. "Fine. We'll go."

Belle squealed and spun in a circle, then raced back to share the news with her doll.

Red would not look at Ward. She couldn't bear to see him gloat.

"I'll take you over in the morning." His voice was gentle, almost soothing. "Red, you won't regret it." He made it sound so simple.

She regretted it already, but having something to gain allowed her to overlook her misgivings. She shivered, but not from cold. "It's time to go back to the cabin."

Ward knew as well as she there was little cause for hurry.

Her promise to go to the service provided her an excuse. "If we're going to church, I need to make sure our outfits are ready. And I'll need to see to baths." She'd already planned the latter even without church attendance. "Come on, Belle."

Her sister walked her doll the length of the log and fell in step behind Ward.

Back at the cabin, he didn't immediately leave despite Red's barely contained hints.

"I'll get a tub for you." He ducked into the wood shed and emerged with a big square washtub. He carried it to the cabin and parked it in front of the stove.

Still he did not leave. Instead, he plunked two big pots on the stove. "I'll carry in some water." He filled both pots and the bucket.

"Thank you." Would he ever leave so she could wallow in her regrets?

He stood at the door, turning his hat round and round as if measuring the brim.

Seems he didn't intend to leave.

"We can manage the rest." She nodded toward the tub.

Dull red colored his cheeks. "That was unnecessary."

She didn't relent.

"Red, stop forming everyone's judgment for them. People aren't nearly as harsh as you make them out to be."

"Is this a warning about tomorrow? You telling me how to conduct myself?"

He sighed. "That is not my intention at all." He crossed the floor to plant his face inches from hers. "What I'm saying is that you should give people a chance rather than slap them alongside the head with comments like the one you just sent my way."

She tried to hold his demanding stare without blinking. But her eyes watered from the strain and she ducked her head. Was she really too defensive?

He made a noise of exasperation and headed for the door. "All I'm saying is let people decide what they want about you. Stop saying things that blatantly tell them they shouldn't like you." He strode from the door.

She waited until the sound of his footsteps faded, then sank into a chair. Did she do what he said? By her comments and attitude inform people how they should view her?

How could she help it? It was how she judged herself.

Determined to ignore her confusion, she searched

through the items of clothing Linette had sent. "I need to thank Mrs. Gardiner for lending us these clothes." Besides the clothing, Linette had sent a brush and comb, hair ribbons and a bar of sweet-smelling soap.

Belle looked up from her play. "Are you going to buy us new things?"

"As soon as I can."

"When will that be?"

Red set aside the soap she'd been sniffing. "I'm going to find a job and we'll have a place of our own."

Belle glanced about. "This is a nice place. Maybe we could stay here."

"No, we can't."

Belle's face wrinkled in confusion and worry.

How could Red make her see the dangers of being so dependent on others? Never again would she allow either of them to be in their situation. Not one minute longer than absolutely necessary. "Belle, I want to take care of us."

"You're afraid everyone is like Thorton." Belle shivered. "Sometimes I think they are and then I look at Sally." She held up her doll. "Ward can't be bad like Thorton."

Red sat back. She couldn't rob Belle of her assurance. "You might be right." She returned to the stack of clothing. For herself, she selected a simple gray dress with white collar and cuffs. With a few tucks here and there, it would fit well enough. For Belle she selected a pretty blue dress. At the rate Belle was growing, these things would soon be too small.

The reality of a child's needs fueled Red's determination. She must find a position soon in order to provide for the both of them.

Later that night, she and Belle were bathed and in clean nightgowns. Belle crawled into bed to play with her doll but Red wasn't a bit tired. She'd already disposed of the water, cleaned the tiny kitchen, swept the floor and even dusted the shelves. She'd worked on outfits for the doll until her neck protested and she'd set the sewing aside. How was she to spend her time? She eyed the knapsack. A book held a lot of appeal.

She knelt before the bag and ran her fingers along the seams. She gingerly loosened the tie and inhaled the scent of mothballs and old wool.

The little quilt lay on top. She lifted it to her face and sniffed. But all she smelled was mothballs. No baby scent. Nothing remotely like the woodsy, leather scent of Ward.

What had she expected?

Her movements jerky, she started to set the quilt to one side, then changed her mind and pulled it to her chest. His mother had made this for him. Ward had experienced a painful family situation and still seemed to know how to be happy.

He'd always been able to choose. He'd been in charge.

She dropped the quilt to the floor. From now on she would be in control of her life.

She turned back to the sack. The first book that came into view was the book of poetry. Her breath stalled halfway up her throat as her mind filled with images of her father reading poetry. It was a regular nighttime habit and had been the background to her evening activities. As she sewed, did schoolwork, knitted doll clothes or played, and later as she entertained Belle, Papa's voice had spoken words of music and imagination. Keats and his "A Thing of Beauty Is a Joy Forever."

Where had the beauty and joy of her life gone?

Probably his favorite was Elizabeth Barrett Browning's poem, "How Do I Love Thee? Let Me Count the Ways." Papa didn't need the book to recite it. He knew it by heart and would say the words to Mama with such feeling she blushed.

Red sat on the floor with her back to the wall, the books forgotten as she wept silently for the parents she'd lost, the life that had been snatched from her and the bleakness of her future. She felt as if she were rudderless, homeless, hopeless. *Oh, God.* But she could not pray, ask relief from a God who'd abandoned her and who would now see her as dirty and shameful.

Her tears dried. She remained on the floor, staring at the darkness beyond the lamplight. Darkness that engulfed her soul. The lamp flickered and she shook her head. She realized that her leg ached where her wound still healed. How long had she sat there? What difference did it make? She turned the lamp down and crawled into bed, trying not to disturb Belle.

The next morning she woke aching from head to toe and regretting her agreement to attend church. With heavy limbs and a heavier heart, she made breakfast and endured Belle's excitement over the outing.

Finally Belle slowed down. "Red, why are you so sad?"

Red tried to dredge up a smile to convince her sister she wasn't. She failed miserably and her lips trembled.

She swallowed hard and widened her eyes, determined she would not cry in front of her little sister.

Belle hurried around the table and threw her arms around Red. "If you don't want to go, it's okay. I don't mind staying home."

Red hugged Belle. She knew how much Belle wanted to go. And she deserved to. It was time life became more ordinary for her little sister. "No, we'll go."

Belle tipped her face upward and studied Red. "Is it because you don't like Ward?"

"I—" She faltered. She liked Ward just fine. But there was no future in it. She closed her eyes and willed in strength. "There are times I miss Mama and Papa so much I can hardly bear it."

Belle crawled into Red's lap and cuddled close. "We have each other."

Red laughed despite her tears. She'd told Belle that was all that mattered so often yet she wondered if either of them believed it. Today it was especially hard to cling to the idea, but she must. It had to be enough. "You're right. Now let's get ready."

A few minutes later they were dressed. She'd pinned her hair back into as tight a bun as she could fashion and hoped it would stay in place. She did not have a bonnet of any sort but, unable to face the shame of appearing bareheaded at a church service, she had fashioned a bit of lace into a covering and hoped it would suffice.

Belle looked sweet and innocent in her dress with her hair curled into ringlets. Thank goodness she had been spared the bright color of Red's hair.

She peeked out the window and watched cowboys file in. Even though no one glanced in her direction, she ducked back out of sight and pressed a palm to her chest as if by doing so she could control the pounding of her heart.

Belle took her place at the window. "I see a little boy up on the hill. It must be Grady."

If not for Belle's eagerness, Red would change her mind about attending.

"Here comes Ward." Belle dashed to the door, pulled it open, and he stepped inside.

"My, don't you two look nice?"

Belle pirouetted. Then grinned at Ward. "So do you."

Indeed he did. Red couldn't help but stare. He wore a crisp white shirt, black jacket and black trousers. His hat was a new brown Stetson. It appeared he had shaved only a few minutes ago. His blue eyes shone like sky reflected in water as he smiled at Red.

If she let it happen, she could momentarily forget her guilt and pain.

She fought a mental battle. If only she could pretend her past hadn't happened but even if she could, others would be eager to remind her.

When Ward offered his arm to guide her across the yard, she hesitated. Touching him only deepened the chasm between who she was and what she wanted. She shifted her gaze past him to the distance between the cabin and the cookhouse. Without something to keep her headed in the right direction, she'd never make it.

She rested her hand on his arm.

And gave him a ferocious warning look.

Ward had prayed long into the night for Red to forget her past and accept the future that lay before her. But from her deep scowl he knew she hadn't yet reached that place. Maybe today would bring a change. He hoped so.

They approached the cookhouse as a Roper, Cassie and their four children stepped inside.

"I don't—" Red started to protest.

Ward pressed his hand to hers, anchoring her to his side. "Settle down. You'll find a warm welcome here. In fact, I better warn you that Cookie has a big embrace."

If he hoped to drive the fear from Red's eyes, he failed. She didn't move. Seemed incapable of it as she stared straight ahead, her expression wooden. "Take a deep breath."

She continued to look toward the cookhouse.

Slim came up behind them. "Morning."

"Morning, Slim," Ward said. Although he sensed Red's anxiety, he couldn't ignore how Slim stood holding his hat and waiting. "Red." He touched her arm to bring her attention back from chasing after her fears. "This is Slim Hawkins. Slim, Red Henderson." He wished he had another name to give, but it was the only one she admitted to.

Red nodded but did not offer her hand. In fact, she shrank back as if afraid Slim might want to touch her.

"Her sister, Belle."

"Nice meeting you, ma'am and Miss Belle." Slim adjusted his hat back on his head. "I'll head inside." He continued to the cookhouse.

While Belle bounced impatiently, Red appeared frozen. Had he made a mistake urging her to attend? But he couldn't believe he had. After all, she couldn't hide forever. Sooner or later, life had to be lived. "Come along." He ushered them toward the door. Getting Belle to move required no effort, but he gently touched Red's elbow to get her attention.

She turned toward him, her eyes stark in a face grown too pale.

"Red, are you okay?"

His words and worry seemed to be just the thing she needed. She blinked. Determination replaced the fear he knew he'd seen.

"I'm fine."

"Not only don't I believe you, I am getting to hate that word. *Fine*. Every time you say it, you mean quite the opposite."

Her look was meant to scald him. "Don't ask if you don't want the answer."

His annoyance fled as quickly as it had come and he chuckled. "I might believe you're fine now because you're feisty."

She adjusted her skirt and murmured, "I am not feisty."

Not freeing her even when she tried to escape his touch, he led her to the door. He paused before he opened the door. "Remember what I said. Cookie is enthusiastic."

Then he stepped inside, Belle at one side, Red at the other. Several of the men sat at the table.

Cassie sat beside Roper, their four children on either side. She saw them and smiled, but waited for Ward to bring Red and Belle forward.

Bertie and Cookie glanced up and noticed he had visitors with him.

"You're Red." Cookie steamed toward them. Belle ducked behind Ward, and Red edged closer to his side.

"And this little one must be Belle. So glad to finally meet you." She reached them and, paying no heed to Ward's presence, grabbed Red in a bear hug.

He'd wondered if Cookie would overwhelm Red, who fought so hard to remain untouchable. He would step in and rescue her if he thought she needed it.

She looked fearful and stiff in Cookie's arms, and then she closed her eyes and he could almost believe she sighed. As if finding something in Cookie's embrace she'd ached after for a long time.

And then Cookie released her. Red stepped back, keeping distance between herself, the bigger woman and Ward. Ward wanted to close the distance, grasp her elbow, but Cookie demanded his attention.

"And where is that little gal? Hiding behind you, I think." Cookie nudged him aside and grinned down at Belle. "I heard you like my cinnamon rolls. Guess what I made for afternoon tea, just for you."

"Cinnamon rolls?" Belle sounded intrigued.

"You guessed it. Now how about a hug?" To Cookie's credit, she let Belle take her time about deciding.

"You won't squeeze me to death?"

Cookie hooted. "Ain't never done so yet. Never hear any complaints, either."

Ward, Slim and Bertie all laughed derisively.

"Pay them no attention." Cookie held out her arms and Belle went into them, getting the gentlest hug Ward had ever seen Cookie give. She released Belle. "Didn't hurt a bit, did it?"

"It was kind of nice."

His nose tingled and Ward didn't dare look at Red for fear of seeing a matching emotion in her eyes that would make him reveal a weakness he didn't care to admit. Men didn't cry over little girls being hugged.

Cookie waved for Bertie to join her. "This here is Bertie, my husband and a fine man, if I do say so myself."

"So pleased to have you join us. Why don't you find a place and make yourself comfortable? As soon as everyone is here, Ward can make the introductions."

Ward headed toward the benches beside the tables. Red caught his sleeve. Surprised at her touch, he turned, saw again the fear that made her eyes too wide. He moved closer to her side and whispered, "What's wrong? And don't even bother with 'I'm fine.'"

She narrowed her gaze. "I just want to ask if we can sit at the back."

He studied her as she allowed him the faintest glimpse of truth in her. She didn't want to sit where she would be more visible than necessary. But she'd trusted him enough to ask. The knowledge dove straight to his heart and made him feel good all over. "Of course." He led them to the back corner and sat between Red and the rest of the room. Belle cuddled close to Red but perhaps as much because she sensed her sister's feelings as anything, as her gaze darted eagerly about the room and she smiled widely at Cookie. Belle appeared to be ready to enjoy the day.

The door opened and Eddie and Linette entered with Grady at their heels.

Belle sat up straight and drew in a quick breath.

Linette and Eddie hurried to them. Linette spoke first. "It's so good to see you again, Red. Are you quite recovered from your wound?"

Ward wanted to smack himself on the forehead. He'd plumb forgot her injury. And she certainly never mentioned it.

"I'm fine. Thank you."

"You're certain? No sign of infection?"

"It's almost better."

"No recurring headaches?"

Red slanted a glance to Ward as if informing him he was her only headache. He almost choked with amusement and knew his eyes brimmed with his silent laugh.

"I'm fine. I never thanked you for caring for me. Thank you. And thank you for the lend of the clothes."

Linette squeezed Red's hands. "Why, it was my pleasure and the clothes are yours to keep."

Red faced Eddie. "I apologize for borrowing your horse without permission."

Ward swallowed hard to contain a burst of laughter. Borrowed without permission, was it? Seemed like another term for stealing.

"In the future, remember you have only to ask if you need something."

"Yes, sir. I appreciate your kindness."

Ward's amusement faded. Why did she sound so sweet and grateful for them, but acted like Ward was an intrusion when all he wanted was to help?

Linette and Eddie greeted Belle, and then introduced Grady.

He hung back.

"He's a little shy but he'll soon get over it," Linette assured Belle when she saw her disappointment at Grady's lack of response.

"Did you see my dolly?" Belle held it out for Grady's

inspection. "It's not finished yet. Ward is carving her another leg and some arms. Did he carve you something?"

Grady nodded.

"Can I see it?"

Linette smiled. "Grady, would you like to show her your animals after church?"

Grady nodded.

"Then it's settled. You'll join us for dinner."

Red opened her mouth. Ward saw a refusal coming and forestalled it by turning to the others. "Everyone, this is Red Henderson and her sister, Belle." He went around the gathering. "Roper, the foreman, and his wife, Cassie. Their children. Daisy, thirteen, Neil, twelve, Billy, who is six, and little Pansy."

"I'se two." The blue-eyed, golden-haired girl held up two fingers.

Roper and Cassie and the three older children all smiled at the little one.

Ward had told Red about how Cassie had come West with Linette and decided to start her own business in Edendale feeding travelers and providing the store with bread and biscuits. Laughing, he'd explained how Roper had found the four orphaned children needing a home and struck a deal with Cassie to help her establish her business in exchange for help caring for the children.

"Now they're married and the children have a permanent home."

Red tried to hide the tears that came to her eyes, but he'd seen.

"Sometimes life has a happy ending." He wanted her to believe in it.

"I've seen the children out playing. I'm glad things worked out for them."

He knew by the hard overtone in her words that she didn't expect the same for herself.

Realizing he'd been sidetracked from his intention to introduce Red to everyone, he turned back to the cowboys and introduced them. There was Slim, Blue and Cal, who were regulars at the ranch, and also a half a dozen other cowboys who would work for the season, then move on. Each one greeted Red and Belle kindly, though he saw a knowing gleam in young Stone. He'd be speaking to the man in private about respecting Red.

Bertie cleared his throat to signal they should all be seated. He waited as they sorted themselves out, then asked them to bow their heads while he prayed. Bertie was simple in his approach to God, but sincere. He'd never come right out and told about his past other than to compare himself to the prodigal son. Following his "amen," Cookie led them in some hymns, her enthusiasm making up for any lack in musical ability.

Ward was used to the plain service but wondered how Red would react.

She sat facing straight ahead, not joining in the singing. Not giving any indication she was even aware of her surroundings. Perhaps she remembered earlier times. Better times. From the things she said, Ward knew she'd been raised in a Christian family.

Which might serve to intensify her guilt over the life she'd been forced to live.

Cookie sat down and Bertie took the floor again. He welcomed Red and Belle and the others. Then he opened his well-worn Bible. It was obvious from the way he handled it that he loved God's word.

"Today, I feel led to talk about the passage in Matthew, chapter eighteen, that tells the story of a man who had a hundred sheep but one was missing. He searched high and low until he found that one sheep and brought it safely back to the fold. He was happier about that one lost sheep than the ninety and nine who were safe and sound. That's how valued each of us is to God."

They were words that reiterated Ward's thoughts. He didn't look at Red, but under the cover of the table he reached over and squeezed her hands, not surprised to discover them clenched tightly in her lap. She didn't give any indication that she was aware of his action, but he reasoned she had to be and chose to allow it. He could only hope and pray she felt the tug of God's love in the search for one lost sheep.

Bertie finished with a reminder that God saw all his little sheep with the same love.

One of the men spoke up. "I heard a song about that. I'd be pleased to sing it, if you'd like."

Bertie waved the man up. "By all means."

The man cleared his throat and began to sing. He had a wonderfully strong voice that carried Ward into the beauty of the song.

"There were ninety and nine that safely lay in the shelter of the fold. But one was out on the hills away…"

By the time the song finished, the room was still and silent except for a sniff from Cookie. Linette dabbed at her eyes with a hanky. Ward didn't dare look about for fear others would see the tears stinging his eyes. Maybe the others felt the same.

Bertie went to the man's side. "That was wonderful. Just wonderful. Thank you so much."

Cookie rose and plowed toward the man and patted his back vigorously enough to cause him to cough. "I'll never forget that song. If you're around for a bit, be sure to favor us with another solo."

The man hurried to his seat.

Finally, Ward allowed himself to look at Red expecting to see a glisten of tears. She faced him, her eyes glittering. But not with tears.

With a fearsome look of disbelief.

He opened his mouth to protest. Had she not heard the words from Bertie's mouth? The song sung by the visitor? The words of God Himself in the scripture?

How could she not believe?

At the look in her eyes he closed his mouth. Now was not the time or place to ask his questions. But he would demand answers at the first opportunity.

Chapter Ten

Only by blocking the words from her mind could Red sit through the service. Yes, the man in the story had gone looking for his one lost sheep. Because it was innocent and pure. Not likely would he have gone looking for a wolf. Or a pig. She knew by Ward's behavior he thought she should see herself as the lost sheep. If it made him feel better to see her as an innocent lamb, well, let him have his pretense.

The man singing the solo had a lovely voice. But she sighed with relief when he finished and sat down.

Now everyone could say goodbye and leave. Except she'd been railroaded into having dinner with Linette and Eddie. Perhaps she could say she had a headache and needed to rest. Linette would doubtless be sympathetic, thinking her recent injury bothered her. It wouldn't be a complete fabrication. She'd clenched her jaw so tight throughout the service that it hurt to the top of her head.

Cookie clapped her hands. "Tea and coffee will be ready in a few minutes. Everyone make yourselves at home." She winked at Belle. "There'll be cinnamon rolls and other goodies, too."

Belle jumped to her feet. "Can I go talk to Grady?"

Red pulled herself away from her thoughts. "Give him time to get used to you." But before Belle got two steps away, Linette and Eddie, with Grady between them, made their way toward Red and sat across the table from them.

Grady shyly went toward Belle and within moments they moved away to play. Leaving Red with no one to cling to. Though she realized the irony of a big sister, who was supposed to be taking care of her younger sister, seeking protection from her.

Her dread knew no bounds. Now Linette and Eddie would quiz her on her family and desire other details about who she was and from whence she'd come. How much had Ward told them? No doubt he'd said he'd rescued her from a saloon. She stiffened her spine and prepared herself for the inquisition.

However, they didn't ask a single question. Instead they talked about the little things Grady had done that pleased them. "He's learning his numbers and letters," Linette said. "I do my best to teach him, but what we really need is a teacher. And a real church." They gave Red the details of their plans for a church in Edendale.

Linette leaned forward. "Forgive us. I'm sure you're not interested in all this talk. Now that you're feeling better—"

It took Red a moment to realize Linette referred to her injured leg and head.

"You can come for tea."

Wonderful how these people were so determined

to take care of her, include her, even though she didn't need it and certainly didn't welcome it.

Linette waved Cassie over. Once the other woman joined them, Linette sighed expansively. "The three of us should get together for a nice visit. The children would enjoy it."

Red watched Belle showing her doll to Daisy and Pansy. Then she turned to Grady and said something that brought a smile to the boy's mouth. Yes, Belle appeared ready to form friendships.

Red wanted only to run back to the cabin and pull the door closed.

Linette continued speaking. "Perhaps we could join forces in teaching the children."

Cassie nodded. "I'd like that."

Red rocked her head back and forth.

"You don't approve of the idea?" Linette said.

Ward had moved away to talk to Eddie. She suddenly wished he was at her side and would intervene. Though what could he say? That a saloon girl shouldn't be allowed to associate with innocent children? Where did that leave Belle? More innocent and undamaged than many people would believe. And not nearly as guarded around others as Red.

But Red was no longer an innocent child. She'd seen the seedy side of life. She'd experienced far too much. Like the day Thorton had convinced everyone he was taking Red and Belle to his sister. Instead he'd taken her to a small house, saying they had to rest for the journey. In the middle of the night, he'd jerked her from her sleep and dragged her from her bed where she'd slept next to

Belle. Her concern for Belle had made her choke back her screams,though she fought like a tiger.

"You're mine," he'd said. "You little redhead."

She'd never hated her red hair more than at that moment, and she'd glowered at him, tried to scratch his face.

"Now it's time you learned to obey me." He'd taken his belt and laid it across her back. Again and again. She tried to fight him off, but he'd grown more violent until she'd finally sunk to the ground in outward defeat, overcome by pain. Inwardly, she'd seethed and vowed she would never be his slave.

Except she was.

Over the months, he'd used the belt time and again if she exhibited any independence. And sometimes out of sheer meanness. She would have fought him tooth and nail, but all he had to do was threaten to do the same to Belle and she would dance, indecently clad, for any man. Anything to protect her little sister.

She pushed the past to the farthest corner of her brain and refused to acknowledge it. But the dirt and degradation would never go away. Even if no one else knew, she could not associate with innocent children.

Thankfully, her troubled thoughts were interrupted as Cookie and Bertie handed out mugs, poured tea and coffee and served a variety of tasty baked goods. Conversation turned to general things such as the beautiful summer weather.

She focused on enjoying tea and cake.

Belle sat beside Grady and kept up a steady one-sided conversation. Even though Grady's shyness kept him quiet, Red suspected he'd have trouble getting in a comment even if he wanted to. His eyes flashed with interest and he seemed enthralled by Belle's attention. Pansy sat on Belle's other side, equally taken with Belle's chatter. Billy tried to pretend disinterest but didn't get far from the conversation, though it would more correctly be called a monologue. Red smiled at Belle's eagerness.

Neil hung about the men, interested in what they had to say.

Daisy, she noticed, never got far from Cassie.

Red rose. "We should be going back."

"Oh, no," Linette said. "Have you forgotten you promised to come for dinner?"

Red hadn't forgotten but hoped Linette had.

Linette continued. "It will allow the children to play together longer." She turned to Cassie. "You and Roper and the children are invited, too, of course."

Cassie shook her head. "Thank you, but I think we better get Pansy home for a nap." She spoke to the other children. "If you want to play with Grady and Belle until mealtime, you may."

But the three elected to leave with Cassie and Roper.

Linette watched them depart. "I don't think the children are ready to be parted from their new parents yet. Ah, well. In time they'll grow secure." She gave her attention back to Red, which made Red want to twitch. "Bring Belle to the house so Grady can show her his things. You're welcome, too, Ward."

Trapped. Unable to say no without appearing rude and denying two children the pleasure of a playmate, Red murmured thanks and followed Linette and Eddie up the hill. Ward tagged along at her side. Her thoughts churned. This would provide an opportunity to speak to Linette. She must ask about a possible position.

A little later as the children played, the four adults sat in the room overlooking the ranch buildings with the mountains rising in the background. On the walls hung spectacular paintings.

"These are beautiful." Red rose and circled the room, admiring the pictures of the mountains, the ranch, bright flowers and serene wooded scenes.

Eddie came to her side. "Linette's handiwork." No doubting his pride at his wife's accomplishments.

Linette joined them.

Red smiled at her. "You're very talented."

Linette thanked her. "Would you like to see the rest of the house?"

"I'd love to. Especially if there is more of your artwork on display." And especially if it would get her away from Ward, hovering at her side as if he feared she couldn't manage without his help.

Linette laughed merrily. "When I look out my window and see such lovely views, it's hard to stop drawing or painting." She led the way through the house. "It is fashioned after Eddie's family estate back in England. Of course he and his father expected it would be used for fancy entertaining, but they didn't take me into account. When Eddie and I fell in love I made it clear I would use the extra rooms to help others."

"Like me?"

"You and others. Whoever the Lord brings to my door, I will welcome. No judgment, no turning my back on people regardless of race or position in society. At first, his father balked at the idea but soon realized things are different in the New World. People are judged differently…by who they are, not where they've come from."

Red didn't say anything, wondering if Linette spoke of her background and if she meant the words for Red or spoke generically.

They stepped into Grady's room. A pencil sketch of him hung over his bed. "Oh, it's sweet." She'd love to have a similar drawing of Belle but didn't dare ask.

"I sent a smaller version to Grady's father in the hopes it would melt his heart toward his son."

"What do you mean?"

Linette told of meeting Grady's mother on a ship crossing the Atlantic and how, when she lay dying, the woman begged her to take Grady to his father in Montreal. Linette readily agreed. "But he took one look at Grady and said he had no use for a little boy. He signed over guardianship to me. But I am determined to see them reunited."

Red had heard a condensed version of the story from Ward but hearing it from Linette gave it power and emotion that seemed to thicken the blood in her veins.

Linette's expression grew fierce. "Every child needs and deserves approval and acceptance from their father."

The words churned through Red like a sudden storm. She'd once known her father's approval. She closed her eyes, not allowing herself to think how disappointed he would be with her now.

"Well, never mind. I know God will answer in His time and His way. In the meantime, Grady is loved here. In fact, I almost fear having my prayers being answered.

I would miss him terribly. It's a good thing there will be another child in the New Year." She fairly glowed as she patted her stomach.

Red had guessed she was in the family way and congratulated her. They moved on to tour the kitchen. Soon they would rejoin the men.

"Linette, maybe you can help me."

"If I can, I most certainly shall."

"I need a position or job of some sort so I can provide for Belle and myself. Would you know of anything? Perhaps you have a friend that needs a maid. Or someone who needs a housekeeper."

Linette brushed her hands along Red's arm. "You're welcome to stay here."

"I need to establish a life for Belle and myself."

Linette considered Red's request a moment, then shook her head. "I wish I knew of something. I'll ask around." She lifted a finger. "But you might send an advertisement to the *Macleod Gazette* offering your services as a maid or housekeeper or whatever you've a mind to do."

"I'll do that. Do you have an address?"

"Better than that. I have some old copies of the paper. You might even find something in one that is what you desire." She gathered a handful of papers from a shelf in Eddie's office. "Here you go."

"You're sure Eddie won't mind?"

"He's done with them. We always pass them on to whoever comes by. This time it's you."

Red took them. "Thank you." She hesitated. Hated to ask for anything more, but she couldn't write a letter without paper. "Would you mind lending me paper and an envelope?" There was pen and ink at the cabin.

Linette pulled open a drawer and removed an envelope, affixed a stamp and handed it over along with several sheets of paper. "Consider it a gift. My contribution to your future. And I will certainly pray for you."

Red nodded. "Thank you." Too bad someone hadn't prayed months ago. Or offered to help. But with the possibility of finding a job filling her mind, she didn't dwell on what might have been.

Later, as Ward escorted them back to the cabin, he commented on the newspapers. "Trying to catch up on the news?"

"It's a start." Not wanting to get into an argument about whether or not he could take care of her, she did not tell him the real reason for wanting the papers.

But that night she pored over the pages, searching the advertisements. She found one that made her laugh.

Wanted: Hardworking young woman who is capable of caring for six motherless children and doing farm chores. Must be pure of heart and sweet of spirit. Willing to marry suitable candidate.

The requirements certainly eliminated her. Not that she had any desire to take over a farm home with six motherless children.

What did she want?

Or more to the point, what job was she suitable for? She doubted anyone would let her be around children or proper ladies once they discovered her past. She could try hiding it. Change her name. But her hair would give away her true identity to anyone who had ever seen her. So that left chambermaid in a hotel, a cook, or perhaps a hired girl on a ranch like Eddie's. She truly didn't care, so long as she was left alone and could care for Belle.

But there were no such ads in the paper. Discouraged, she set them aside.

The next morning, Red's determination returned, renewed and strengthened. She would find a job somehow, and silently worded an advertisement.

A knock sounded on the door.

"Come in." Ward didn't usually come until later, when he'd attended to his chores.

The door opened and Eddie stood in the opening with Grady at his side. Eddie nudged the little boy.

"Can Belle come out to play?" Grady asked.

Belle sprang up from the corner where she sat surrounded by her playthings. "Can I, Red? Please?"

Red wanted to slam the door, keep the world away from them. She knew it was only a matter of time before her past would confront them in a cruel fashion. But she couldn't deny Belle. "I don't want you wandering away."

"We'll stay close to the cabin."

"Very well."

Eddie squeezed Grady's shoulder. "Have fun. I'll return for you later or if you want to go home, you go up the hill." He shifted his attention to Red. "If he chooses to go home, could you watch and make sure he gets back safely?"

"Of course."

With a tip of his hat, Eddie strode toward the barn. Red saw Ward in one of the pens. He seemed to be studying her. No doubt wondering how she would handle this intrusion into her privacy.

She stiffened her spine. She'd handle it just fine. Without anyone interfering, thank you very much.

Belle carried her doll in one hand and picked up as many of her other things as she could. "Did you bring your animals?" she asked.

Grady dug little carved animals from his pockets.

"Good," Belle said. "We'll start our own ranch." She led the way to a tree beside the cabin, its green leaves dancing in the gentle breeze. It stood tall and proud in full view of everyone in the cookhouse, the big house up the hill, the barn, the pens....

Red stared out the door at the pair, already organizing the play ranch. She wanted to keep an eye on them, make sure Belle remembered how to play with other children.

She picked up her sewing, pulled a chair toward the open door and sat so she remained half-hidden from view. From her perch she watched the children, happy for Belle's sake. Her attention wandered. Beyond the children, Ward held a horse by a rope lead and guided it about in a circle. Each movement was sure and gentle. She caught wisps of his voice, steady and assuring. At first the horse pranced and tossed its head, but Ward's manner soon calmed it.

She couldn't take her eyes off the man and animal. Uncertain emotions trembled through her. The horse recognized Ward's gentleness. It soothed its fears. Ward had that way about him.

He led the horse to a post, snubbed it up tight and went inside the barn.

Red sighed and shifted her gaze back to the children. With twigs they had created corrals for Grady's little animals.

Belle looked up. "Red, can we get some pieces of wood from out back?"

"Go ahead."

The pair trotted around. She listened to their murmur as they discussed what they needed.

The horse in the corral snorted. Red looked up. Ward placed a saddle blanket and saddle on the animal. Even from where she sat, she saw the way it trembled, sensed the fear. Her heart kicked against her ribs, then took off in a gallop.

"No," she whispered, seeing Ward prepare to swing to the saddle. Every fear, every worry consolidated into one thought. He would be thrown. Hurt.

She jerked to her feet, moved outside where she could see better.

He settled into the saddle and nodded. She hadn't noticed Eddie. Why didn't he stop Ward? Instead, he loosened the rope and set the horse free. It shook from head to tail, tossed its head, reared once, then bucked in a fury to get Ward off his back.

Red edged closer, unable to breathe, but not wanting to take her eyes off Ward. If he got injured… A vise held her lungs.

The bucking stopped.

"Open the gate," Ward called, and Eddie did so. Ward rode the horse through the opening and headed down the trail away from the ranch.

What if—

She would not let her thoughts go that direction.

"He's a good horseman. He's in control."

She hadn't been aware of Eddie standing at the corner of the corrals, watching her.

"Of course he will." She returned to the cabin, grabbed up her chair and parked it in the sunshine. After all, the day was far too pleasant to spend indoors. What's more, she could see the mountains from where she sat.

Eddie moved away, apparently unconcerned with Ward's well-being.

The children played in the shade of the tree.

Red studied the distant mountains. But not until she saw Ward and the horse trotting back to the barn did she notice how the sky formed a perfect blue background to the jagged ridges of the mountains.

Ward waved.

She nodded. She'd only been apprehensive because she knew he couldn't do his job if he had a broken limb. That was all. Nothing personal about her feelings. She picked up a dress that needed mending and jabbed her needle through the fabric.

Eddie collected Grady at lunchtime.

Belle chattered so much over lunch that Red finished long ahead of her. "Eat up," she said.

"Okay." Belle ate her meal hurriedly. "Can I go out and play again?"

"Let's go out back."

"Can Grady come, too?"

Red couldn't say no to her little sister, though she feared the risks involved in getting too close to anyone. Sooner or later someone would discover the truth about them and point it out. But her argument lay flat and lifeless. Linette and Eddie must surely know where Red had been and what she'd been forced to do. Yet they welcomed her. And what had Ward said? Something about letting people get to know her and decide for themselves what they thought of her? Did he mean to suggest they would accept her?

She didn't see how that was possible. Not when her own heart condemned her.

"Can he?" Belle asked again.

"If he comes, you can play with him."

But it wasn't Grady she listened for that afternoon. When the little boy came midway through the day, Red resumed her place outside the cabin and continued the mending as the children played together. After a bit, she returned inside to start supper preparations, leaving the door open so she could keep a watch on the children. Each time she glanced out the door to where they played, her gaze drifted onward to the corrals, the barn and beyond. Previously she'd known only gratitude when no one hung about, but today the place seemed deserted. Where had Ward disappeared to? No, she corrected herself. Where was everyone?

Eddie took Grady home later. Belle came in to wash for supper. They ate fried steak, boiled potatoes and green beans that Cookie had preserved from the garden. Earlier Red had made bread, and they had thick slices of it with syrup for dessert.

Belle helped clean up and dried dishes as Red washed.

At the sound of footsteps nearby, she forced herself not to turn and see if Ward approached. A quiver in the pit of Red's stomach made her think she had forgotten to eat even though she washed the dishes that proved otherwise.

"Hello." Ward's firm, steady voice greeted them from the open doorway.

Something wrenched inside her. A syrup-sweet sensation of hope and despair.

"Hi, Ward." Belle bounced to his side. "Did you see the farm Grady and I are building?"

He cupped his hand over Belle's head, adding to the sweetness in Red's heart.

"I did. It looks to me like you and Grady had a great deal of fun playing together."

"We did. Grady says he can come every day if it's okay with Red." She flung about to confront her sister. "It's okay, isn't it?"

Red nodded, her tongue strangely wooden.

Ward flashed a smile full of summer sky, then turned to Belle. "Maybe you won't need your doll so much anymore."

"Oh, yes I do." She ran to the corner where Sally sat amidst the playthings. "She really needs all her arms and legs. Are you going to finish them?"

Ward pulled pieces of wood from his pocket. "I thought I would. Are you ladies wanting to sit outside and enjoy the evening?"

"I am." Belle dashed outside and disappeared around the corner.

"I'll be along in a minute." Red wiped the basin clean and hung the towel to dry. She expected Ward to follow Belle, but he waited.

She adjusted the chairs around the table and delayed the moment she would have to go to his side. Her feelings were too fresh, too fragile, too foreign to feel comfortable around him.

Finally she could delay no longer and pasted a brave smile on her face. "Shall we?"

"Yes, ma'am." His grin slipped past her defenses and landed in her syrupy heart. But she wouldn't be controlled by foolish emotions, and lifted her chin, faced straight ahead and marched out the door.

How could she appear calm and collected when her insides bounced about? But she needn't have worried about it. Belle chattered nonstop as Ward carved a leg and arms for the doll.

Belle leaned over his shoulder, watching. "You're almost finished."

"Your Sally will soon be whole."

Belle giggled.

Then he would no longer need to visit every day. About time, Red told herself. But it wasn't relief she felt.

Ward attached the arms and leg and handed the doll to Belle. "There you go."

Belle pressed the doll to her chest. "Oh, thank you. Sally says thank you, too."

Ward pushed to his feet. "It's time to say good-night."

Red stood, too, and they moved to the cabin. As soon as they entered, Belle rushed to the bedroom. "I'm going to get ready for bed. Me and Sally."

Red turned. "Thank you and goodbye."

"Goodbye? I'll be back tomorrow afternoon."

Relief rushed through her. She cut it off. He didn't need to keep checking on them. Sooner or later they would have to manage on their own. Just as soon as she found something. Tonight she would write an advertisement and send it to the paper. "We'll be fine on our own." She said it as much for her sake as his.

"No doubt. But I need to get more wood."

"But—" She hadn't even considered the amount of wood they consumed. From now on, she would ration its use.

He brushed her cheek with warm fingertips. "Red, stop scheming on how not to use wood. There's lots out there for the taking. I don't mind bringing in more."

His touch did things to her insides she didn't want to admit. Filled her with such longing. Had she fallen into a pretend spell, like Belle with her doll, letting herself act as if this could be her life? It could not. Neither she nor Ward truly thought so. He liked to think he could take care of her more as a way to prove to himself he could, rather than because she mattered. What he really wanted was to take care of his mother and brothers. She was only a temporary substitute.

Ward watched her carefully. Did he see a glimpse of her confusion? "Promise me you won't try to get along without using any wood. You need to cook meals and soon you'll need to warm the cabin."

Did he mean in the fall? She wouldn't be here that long. He caught her chin and stared into her eyes. "Red, promise me."

"If we need it, I'll burn wood."

He sighed. "Why is it I don't feel like that's the promise I want?"

She shrugged. "Must be because you have a suspicious nature."

He laughed. "Something you've taught me." His gaze, warm with amusement and welcome, slipped past her defenses. Oh, she wished he wouldn't laugh so easily, smile so broadly. It made it so difficult to keep her guard up around him. Made her wish she could be something else—someone other than who she was. A draft of loneliness blew through her.

He sobered. His gaze intensified, silently laying claim to her emotions. Then slowly, as if anticipating each second, he lowered his head and kissed her.

She had plenty of time to turn away but she didn't. Somehow, despite all her arguments to the contrary, she wanted the assurance and protection his kiss signified. The touch of his lips slipped into her heart and grabbed it like a giant fist squeezing out a drop of longing, threatening to turn it into a rushing stream that would drain her. Leaving her empty and powerless. Still she could not end the kiss.

He lifted his head. His eyes were awash with yearning.

She didn't want to see it. Admit it. Knowing as she did that once the emotion died, reality would set in. And remembering who she was, what she'd done, the look in his eyes would turn to loathing. She stepped back. Crossed her arms over her middle as if she could hide the truth.

"I'll see you tomorrow." He hurried out.

She told herself she didn't notice a husky tone in his voice. She'd heard passion-thickened voices before and dared not believe it wasn't the same thing she heard in Ward's voice.

That night she waited until Belle had fallen asleep to sit at the table. Before she began her letter she had to find the address, and she spread out a paper to search for it.

That's when a headline caught her eye. She bent over the page and read the story carefully. When she was done, she sat back. This was it. Where she would go.

Chapter Eleven

Ward hummed as he strode to the bunkhouse. He'd given Red plenty of time to turn from his kiss. But she'd lifted her face in welcome. Then let the kiss continue. She was changing. Beginning to believe she was a good person. Worthy of love and respect. What happened to her was not of her doing. No one should blame her for it. She shouldn't blame herself.

Perhaps she was beginning to see that.

He realized he hummed a little tune, and stopped before he stepped into the bunkhouse.

Cal looked up and chortled. "Look at the smile on his face. I'd say he's fallen for that redhead across the way."

Ward waved away the comment but he didn't deny it. Yet he couldn't admit it even to himself, knowing Red might let him kiss her but she wasn't ready to open her heart and life to him.

Or anyone.

He climbed into his bunk and stared at the ceiling. Not that he needed to worry. She wasn't looking for love. He thought of his little cabin and the fledgling ranch. His goal had been to provide a home for his mother and sisters. Now Red fit so easily into the picture that he felt guilty. He'd abandoned his family once before and here he was mentally doing the same… putting Red in their place. His heart beat slower, each pulse heavy with determination. He could see how letting himself fall for Red could prove a substitute for missing his family.

He flipped to his side. He couldn't let that happen. His family must come first. He wasn't so foolish as to think love would satisfy the deep longings in his heart.

But just before sleep came, he smiled and thought of Red's kiss.

The next day Eddie kept Ward busy. Not until after supper did he have time to hitch a horse to the stoneboat and head over to the cabin, intending to bring in more firewood for Red.

First, he stopped to speak to her. "I would have been here sooner—" he started to explain.

"I expect Eddie thinks you should do some work once in a while. Besides, when will you learn I don't need you taking care of me?"

He ignored her gibe. "I see Grady was here again. That's nice. Everyone needs a friend. Friends make each other happy." He wanted her to accept him as a friend. To allow him to make her happy. To help her. Take care of her. Knowing she would object to the latter statements, he added, "Seems to me friends help each other."

Neither of them broke from staring at the other. Neither of them relented from their position.

"You got an objection to being friends with me?"

She sniffed. "Seems to me friends don't push at each other, making impossible demands."

"Push? Impossible demands? Red, I have no idea what you are talking about. All I've done is rescue you and Belle from Thorton, bring you to a safe place and make sure you're taken care of. How is that pushing and making demands?"

She sniffed again and gave him a look dripping with disdain. "I guess it meant nothing to you, but I recall a kiss or two."

He took off his hat and scrubbed at his hair, not caring that he likely turned it into a rat's nest. Then he gave her a look rife with disbelief. "Didn't see you resisting."

"Maybe," she said with annoyance in every syllable, "I was just being polite."

"Polite?"

"Stop sputtering. Yes, polite. Or maybe I thought you would tell Eddie to toss us out to fend for ourselves if I didn't let you."

He would not sputter but he sure felt like it. "You know that's not true. I can't make it any plainer that I'm happy enough to make sure you're safe."

"You make it equally plain that it's only because you haven't been able to contact your mother and brothers."

He slammed his hat on his head. This was not going at all the way he had planned. She was supposed to welcome his offer of friendship, admit that a kiss or two was appropriate, see that his desire to help was genuinely generous. Maybe even confess to liking, to even a small degree, having him around. "It's not just because I haven't been able to contact my family."

"So you're doing it to give you the right to steal a few kisses?"

"Woman, you don't know what you want, do you?"

He turned to leave, then remembered he meant to chop wood. He confronted her. "I did not steal any kisses. You gave them. Freely, and I'm pretty sure you liked them. You don't fool me one bit."

She threw a towel at him. It fluttered ineffectively to the ground.

He laughed and continued on his way. Recognized another hole in her argument and called, "Besides, if you're so all fired set on leaving, why do you care if refusing a kiss might make me tell Eddie to throw you out?" As if Eddie would contemplate such a thing. But why should he encourage her to trust Eddie when she wouldn't trust him? "You aren't making any sense."

She slammed the door.

He headed for the woods, muttering under his breath about how difficult it was to figure out a woman like Red. But before he had placed three logs on the stoneboat, he started laughing. One thing about Red, she had a way of keeping him guessing and right now he was guessing she didn't like him pointing out she hadn't resisted his kiss. He could hardly wait to see what she would do next.

As Ward returned with wood, Red did her best to avoid him. She washed the windows and scrubbed the log walls. Both activities enabled her to keep an eye on him. To make sure he didn't sneak up unexpectedly, she told herself as she secretly watched him sweat over his labors.

"Sure putting a lot of elbow grease into this place," he commented as he passed with a load of wood. "Especially for a woman who says she doesn't care."

"Who said I don't care?" Oh, she should not have said that. It sounded as if she wanted to stay. "I'm only making sure no one will regret offering me a temporary home." Her heavy emphasis on the *temporary* was unmistakable. As was the flash of impatience in his eyes.

He gave her a long-studied look that threatened to pry open secret places in her thoughts. She did not want them exposed. Wouldn't allow anyone access. Not even herself. There were simply things that no longer existed for Red. Like home, acceptance, love.

She puffed out her lips. She didn't need love. Didn't want it. Knew she would never receive it. Not with her past.

Ward continued to watch her and she realized she'd let her emotions play across her face. "Better get at your work," she said. She made little shooing motions with her hand.

He dropped the reins and stalked toward her, a dark, unreadable look on his face.

Alarm skittered up her nerves. Had she angered him? Would he exact payment in one of the ways Thorton had used? She glanced about. Could she hope to outrun him?

But he was already at her side and caught her by the arms, his touch surprisingly gentle. She kept her head down-turned, afraid of what she might see.

"Red, you are so prickly. Sometimes it wearies me. Yet there are other times when it catches at my heart and makes me want to hold you and kiss you until your fears subside. This is one of those times."

Before she could think what to do, he caught her chin, tipped her face upward and kissed her thoroughly. He ended the kiss and pulled her against his chest. "One day you'll admit you are safe with me. You'll realize just how nice it is." He released her and strode away, picked up the reins and drove to the woods without a backward look while she struggled to maintain her balance.

Why had he kissed her again?

And why, oh, why did she like it so much?

She rushed into the cabin. Belle played outdoors so Red sat alone at the table. She planted her face in her hands and moaned. She must get out of here as soon as possible.

She picked up the letter awaiting dispatch. Tomorrow was Sunday and she'd take it to church service and ask Linette to see it got to town. She could only hope the response would be swift and agreeable.

The next day she managed civil conversation with Ward as he escorted her across the road to the cookhouse. She'd planned to leave early and avoid his company, but he must have guessed her intent. When she opened the door, he leaned against the outer wall, all fresh and relaxed, his chin so clean-shaven she wanted to touch it. His white shirt provided a contrast to his bronzed skin that let the word *handsome* spring to her mind before she could stop it. And why did he rest one boot on its toe so he created the perfect picture of masculinity?

He grinned at her.

It was as though the sun touched her with unseasonable warmth and she jerked away. She had tried all night to forget the feel of his kiss, to forget his assertion that she might like it.

She pressed her hand to the letter in her pocket.

This position would provide the perfect opportunity for Red and Belle. She couldn't have asked for more if she'd prayed for a miracle. Yet excitement did not race through her veins. Or even satisfaction or gratitude or any number of things she should be feeling. What she felt was a long ache for what she could not have.

Remembering Ward's kisses, she brushed her fingertips over her lips. Then, lest he read something into the gesture she didn't care for him to, she jerked her hand to her waist and pretended to adjust the fabric.

A woman like her could never entertain the sort of dreams that haunted her restless sleep. The warmth of his arm brushing hers tempted her to ignore the truth. Knowing she could never afford to forget the facts of her life, she pretended a great interest in something to her right and used it for an excuse to put a healthy six inches between them.

She felt his considering stare and knew he was aware of what she'd done, but she would not risk a look at him, having discovered that her resolve weakened when he smiled at her. Besides, he seemed to have developed the unwelcome ability to read her thoughts.

"I wonder how long this warm weather will last," she commented. Weather was always a safe topic to discuss.

"Not long enough." He sounded amused, as if recognizing her intent to divert him from—what? Only it wasn't him she meant to sidetrack, she wanted to stop her thoughts from admiring him, wondering if he wanted to kiss her again.

They reached the cookhouse and were greeted with the welcoming scent of cinnamon and Cookie's exuberant hug. Red successfully dismissed her wayward thoughts.

Belle waved at Grady. "Can I sit with him?"

She'd noticed the children sat with their parents throughout the service and then were free to go to the others. "I prefer you to sit with me. You can talk to him afterward."

They sat on the back bench. Ward quirked an eyebrow at her when she made certain Belle was between them.

Let him think what he wanted.

Again, Cookie led them in singing a few hymns. Not wanting to attract unwanted inquiries about not joining in, Red moved her lips silently. Then Bertie got up to speak. She closed her mind to his words, though once or twice his sincere tones drew her reluctant attention. She heard enough to know he talked about the lost being found. Maybe it was his favorite topic.

The service ended and Linette and Cassie moved over to sit across from Red.

"Grady is certainly enjoying playtime with Belle," Linette said. She turned to Cassie. "Why don't you send the children to join them?"

She took Red's agreement for granted but then it was Linette's house, her yard. Why shouldn't she?

"I might send Daisy down with the two little ones. Neil prefers to be with Roper. If you don't mind?" She addressed Red.

Red nodded. "That would be fine. I'm sure Belle would enjoy it." At this rate, her little sister would soon be a social butterfly.

Cookie again served goodies. Red guessed they were

delicious, but for her they had a cardboard flavor. She excused her tension as trepidation over the response to her letter, uncertainty about the future or even reluctance to venture into the unknown. Certainly not as already missing Ward when she left. That made no sense. She would not even entertain the idea.

She hoped to have a quick private word with Linette but no opportunity presented itself.

"You'll come up to the house?" Linette asked.

Red nodded. How else was she to deliver the letter to Linette without everyone knowing?

"You, too, Ward."

The man grinned from ear to ear and fell in at her side following Eddie and Linette. The two children scampered ahead.

"Red," Ward murmured. "You're awfully quiet. Is something wrong?" His gentle, caring words scrubbed every reasonable explanation for her behavior from her mind. Ward-shaped longing and missing rushed through her like a flash flood leaving the bare rocks of truth exposed. She wished with all her heart she could dream of being more than someone for him to care for…a way to ease his concerns about his family.

She couldn't be.

Why, she'd never even seen his little ranch, though he talked of it often enough. She recognized how far that thought had veered from insisting she couldn't be more—didn't want to be.

"Only thing wrong with me is I didn't sleep well last night."

"You're not sick are you? Your leg is healing okay?"

She let out a gusty breath. "Ward, I am fine. Just fine."

He snorted. "Huh. Seems to me people who are just fine sleep peacefully."

"And who appointed you the expert on sleeplessness?"

He chuckled. "Nice to see you back in form—all feisty."

"I am not being feisty." She emphasized each syllable to make sure he understood. "I'm just pointing out that you have no way of knowing why I didn't sleep well."

He stopped directly in front of her, forcing her to halt.

She kept her attention on the tips of his boots. A little dusty now after walking along the trail, but he'd obviously polished them in honor of Sunday. Something about that fact twisted through her brain…a cruel corkscrew.

"Red Henderson, or whatever your name is, I'm guessing your sleep was disturbed with thoughts of a kiss you pretend you didn't want but enjoyed despite yourself."

"How dare you?" She shot him a look of denial. At the warmth in his eyes and the way his gaze darted to her mouth, she wished she'd continued to stare at his boots. "I do not… Did not… Am not…" Oh, she had no idea what she meant, and closed her mouth lest she say something she'd regret.

"Ah, but I think you are." He cupped her elbow and proceeded up the hill as satisfied as a well-fed cat.

"You might not be as smart as you think you are." She knew she sounded petulant. The letter that had weighed on her mind all day now promised relief and freedom. She couldn't wait to give it to Linette.

A little later when Ward and Eddie excused themselves to look at one of the horses, she got her chance. "Linette, I'd like to request another favor."

Linette nodded. "All you have to do is ask."

She extracted the letter from her deep pocket. "Will you post this for me?"

"That is too easy to be a favor."

Red's smile felt a little crooked. "There's more. When I get a reply, will you make sure to give it directly to me?"

Linette didn't answer for a moment. "You're saying you don't want me to give it to Ward to deliver? Why?"

She waggled her hands. "I don't want to argue with him about me leaving." It didn't begin to explain her reasons, which were less about what Ward might do and a whole lot more about fearing her own weakness. It wouldn't take a lot of arguing for her to agree to stay.

However, that was not possible.

Linette laughed. "You know there's only one reason he'd argue with you. He cares about you."

"I don't fancy having to defend my decisions. Promise me you won't give the letter to Ward. Please."

"Very well, if that's how you want it. But why are you running from him?"

"I believe it's for the best that I move on."

Linette considered her so long and hard that Red pretended a great deal of interest in the painting beyond Linette's shoulder.

"Red." Linette's soft voice drew Red's eyes to her.

"There's no need to run and hide. You are a beautiful, competent woman any man would be honored to love."

Red ached to tell Linette exactly what she'd endured for Thorton's amusement and then ask if she still felt a man would be honored to love her. But she knew the answer and didn't need it spelled out for her. She took the letter from her pocket and handed it to Linette. "Thank you."

Now all she had to do was wait for a response.

She could only hope it would not be long in coming.

"We'll be gone ten days to two weeks," Ward said to Red. "The heavy rains to the west are threatening to flood the lower pasture. We need to move the herd to higher ground." Eddie and the other cowboys were mounted and ready to go. A chuckwagon had already departed.

"I can manage quite fine on my own."

He laughed. "Try not to miss me too much." And with a saucy salute and a flashing grin, he rode away with the others.

Now, only three days later, she stared down the trail as dusk settled into the hollows and wondered if he'd come to his senses while he was gone. Would he think about the sort of woman Red was? What would his mother think if he ever located her?

She turned back to the interior of the cabin, determined to ignore such foolish contemplations. If she received the response she hoped for from her letter, she would soon move on. And if the reply was not what she wanted, she would continue to look for something else.

Several times, Daisy had brought Pansy and Billy to play. Belle enjoyed it thoroughly.

"I like having friends to play with," Belle said, pulling Red from her musing. "Billy knows lots of games."

"You'll have to do your lessons in the morning before you can go out and play." Her little sister could read fairly well and had improved in her sums. But it would be wonderful if she could go to a real school.

As soon as dishes were done, they sat at the table. Belle played while Red read the papers, though she'd read every word twice already. If she had yarn she could knit, but she lacked the materials and would not ask Linette for any. She owed her far too much already.

The hours trudged along until Belle's bedtime. And then hollow silence filled the room. Red wandered from one side of the cabin to the other, touching objects now grown familiar—the red checked curtains at the windows, the handle of the shovel she kept close to the door, the smooth wood of the shelves, the stack of wood that reminded her of Ward's care.

She shook her head to clear her thoughts. Ward could not figure so hugely into her life.

Her eyes lighted on the picture over the table. It lay in shadows so she couldn't read the words. Not that she needed to see them to know what they said. *Whither shall I flee from Your presence?* Crossing her arms across her stomach, she stared at the picture. If only she could hide from God. The best she could hope for was to block thoughts of Him from her mind. Which was increasingly hard to do, thanks to the constant reminder of the wall hanging, the Sunday services at the ranch and in no small part, Ward's gentle words. He'd often said God forgives, doesn't see our past.

Easy for him to say. What had he ever done wrong?

Her steps long and hurried, she crossed the cabin, spun around and made a return trip. Back and forth, chased by churning thoughts, driven by a relentless restlessness.

"Enough," she murmured, and sat down on a chair. Her gaze slid to the knapsack. She drummed her fingers on the table. A book would relieve her boredom. But she did not move. She'd long ago stuck the one book she'd glanced at back in the bag, finding the poems triggered a flood of memories she didn't care to deal with. Besides, the books were Ward's. Just holding them would make her miss him.

But surely she could read one without her emotions raging wildly. She stared at the bag, her heart pressing to her ribs as she tried to convince herself she didn't want to read. She failed that argument. They were only books, she reasoned, nothing more.

She edged toward the bag. It meant nothing that she accepted his invitation to enjoy his books. He need not know. She lifted the flap, hurriedly shoved aside the quilt, not allowing thoughts of his mother to enter her mind.

She grabbed the first book her fingers touched, making certain it wasn't the poetry book.

"Thank goodness it's a novel." She returned to the table, pulled the lamp close and opened the pages. Two hours later, she reluctantly closed the book and made her way to bed.

The next day she hurried through her chores and

read as Belle worked on her sums. In the afternoon, Grady, Pansy and Billy came to play with Belle. They ventured outdoors and Red sat at the open door, enjoying the story.

A cold wind came up. Daisy came to get Pansy and Billy and Eddie took Grady home. Belle and Red retreated indoors and closed the door. She was grateful for the warmth from the stove and wood to burn. Thanks to Ward.

She made soup and biscuits for supper, read to Belle and tucked her into bed.

This time, Red didn't mind when darkness descended. She sat and enjoyed reading. She felt an unreasonable gratitude toward Ward for providing her this pleasure. Not that she would tell him.

He'd been gone a week. Not since she was a child anticipating Christmas had Red counted the days and seen them pass on such reluctant feet.

It didn't help that Belle asked several times a day when he was coming back.

"He said they'd be gone up to fourteen days."

Belle's dramatic sigh echoed the emptiness in Red's heart.

How could she have allowed herself to grow so fond of the man? Did she secretly want to be hurt?

Of course she didn't. But at some time in the past weeks she'd allowed a crack in her armor without realizing it.

Belle stared out the window. "Grady's coming," she shrieked.

It had been cold and rainy for the better part of two days, preventing the children from playing outside.

Red joined her sister at the window. "Linette's bringing him." This was the first time Linette had visited the cabin and would no doubt expect to be invited in. Red hustled to fill the kettle and put it on the stove, then rushed to open the door.

"Please come in, though it feels strange to invite you into your own house."

Grady darted over to join Belle at her toys.

Linette chuckled. "My house is up on the hill."

"I know. But you spent the winter here."

Linette grew wistful. "I did and it was a lot of fun." She accepted Red's invitation to sit at the table. "Did anyone ever tell you about it?"

Red poured water over the tea leaves and put out a plate of cookies. "A bit."

Linette chuckled. "I came out expecting a marriage of convenience. My father had arranged for me to marry a much older man back in England." She grimaced. "I couldn't bear the idea and I was so sick of the restrictions of my life. I was friends with Eddie's fiancée, and she showed me the letter she wrote telling him that she'd changed her mind and couldn't marry him. It was her suggestion to tell Eddie I'd be willing to take her place. So when two tickets arrived, I thought they were meant for me. But Eddie hadn't received his fiancée's letter and meant the tickets for her." She grinned. "He wasn't pleased when I showed up instead."

Red gaped. "What did he do?"

"Because of the weather he said I could stay until spring. By then we'd fallen in love."

"That's amazing." Red tried to sound enthusiastic but the ache in her heart made it difficult. She could never hope for such a sweet happily ever after. She poured the tea and offered cookies, taking some to the children.

"Oh, I forgot the reason I came, though it is only an excuse. I've been dying to visit." Linette glanced about. "I know you think you have to run and hide. But I hope and pray you find love and happiness here as I did." She dug into her pocket. "I have a letter for you."

Red took the envelope and studied the return address. This was the letter she'd hoped for. "Thank you." It felt heavy in her palms, though it weighed no more than a sheet of paper should.

When Linette saw that Red didn't intend to open the envelope while she was there, she turned to other things. "Do you need anything? Firewood? Food?"

"I'm fine. Thanks. Ward made sure we had a good stock of supplies before he left."

Linette grinned. "I guessed as much. Ward's the sort you can always count on."

"Yes." She wouldn't let her thoughts pursue that idea. It was his family that he wanted to be taking care of, not Red and Belle. She understood it. Didn't feel any resentment.

A little later, Linette announced she had to leave.

Red escorted Linette and Grady to the door. "It was nice of you to visit."

"I'll come again, if you don't mind."

"I'd like that." It surprised her how much the idea appealed.

The pair departed.

Red stared at the letter, afraid to open it for fear it would not be what she hoped for.

"Aren't you getting cold?" Belle called from the cabin.

Realizing she stood in the open door letting out the warm air, Red returned inside and put the letter on the table to consider it.

"We have a letter?" Belle managed to sound curious and worried at the same time.

Her words spurred Red into action and she slit the envelope open, unfolded a sheet of paper and read it through twice. Her eyes hot with tears, she finally turned toward the anxious Belle. "It's a place for us to go."

Belle's expression turned stormy. "We have a place right here. I like it. I like Grady and Cookie and Pansy and Ward. I don't want to go someplace else." Her bottom lip jutted out.

"Honey, this was never meant to be for long. This is Eddie and Linette's cabin. We can't continue to use it. It's time for us to move on and become independent."

Belle backed away, fire burning from her eyes. "You just don't want anyone to help us. You don't want people to like us."

"Belle, that is not true." Except a shiver of truth traveled through her brain. If she didn't let people like her, then she wouldn't have to endure their shock and horror when they discovered the truth. She grabbed the paper and showed Belle the picture of three women and two men standing before a square, two-story building. "Here, look at this. This is a new mission in Medicine Hat where they want to teach school, and help people who are abandoned or homeless. You know where that is. South of here, close to the American border. Just think, you could go to a real school."

Belle examined the picture, then handed the paper back. "I don't want to go. My friends are here." She silently challenged Red to dispute the fact.

She couldn't.

"Ward is my friend even if you won't let him be your friend."

Red ignored the accusing words. Friends? That's what Ward had asked for. And she'd basically refused his offer. Why? What harm would there be in friendship?

The answer ached through her. She didn't belong in decent society. At the mission she would be accepted as a needy, damaged person. "Belle, they said we were welcome and they could find work for me, so we're going and that's all there is to it."

Belle grabbed her doll and retreated to the far corner of the room, her back to Red. The words she mumbled to her doll informed Red that her sister considered her unfair and mean.

Belle would adjust to the new situation.

Red would, too. She wouldn't let regrets and longings and dreams of things that couldn't be stop her from moving forward.

Something argumentative bounced around in her brain. She kept saying people wouldn't accept her. Yet Ward knew of her past and wanted to be friends. Linette knew and had been kind and accepting. No doubt Eddie knew and he allowed her to live in his cabin. Cookie included them. Cassie and Roper allowed their children to play with Belle.

Was Ward right? Did she need to forgive herself and accept that God forgave and loved her?

She might have believed it based on how those at the ranch had welcomed her.

Except for one thing.

They didn't know the whole truth. They only knew she'd been forced to dance in a saloon to protect Belle. None of them knew how Thorton had humiliated her until she hated not only her red hair, but her entire body, both inviting men to leer and touch her without her permission. And certainly without her wanting them to. She shuddered. A mission for outcasts was the best place in the world for her. And it would suit Belle fine, too, once she got used to it.

Despite her positive considerations, a sorrow as deep as eternity filled her soul.

She turned her back to Belle and buried her hands in her face, lest her little sister see the tears flowing down her cheeks. The way Thorton had treated her had left her hating herself.

Chapter Twelve

Ward rode after a wayward cow. He always enjoyed being out in nature, riding behind the cattle. He drank in the pine scent, the air so fresh it likely came off a glacier higher in the mountains. Here and there, wildflowers of pink, yellow, orange and red dotted the alpine meadows. The sky was as blue as deep water with only a scattering of fluffy clouds.

He was anxious for the day when he'd have his own herd to move. In fact, he might buy some cows this fall and take them to his ranch. What would Red think of his little cabin? Not that it mattered. He'd written a number of letters to his mother, his brothers, every neighbor he could remember, the postmaster, the schoolteacher, the church, even addressed a letter simply to "The Lawyer" in the town where he'd last seen his family. Surely someone would know where they were and be able to get a message to them.

If only they'd come west and join him. His usual enjoyment of nature dimmed this year. A week of trailing after a herd of cattle seemed like eternity. He wanted to spend the time with Red. And Belle, of course. The little girl was a joy to play with.

Red remained a mixed joy as she continued to present him with nothing but her feisty side. Not that he hadn't seen more. So much more. He'd seen tenderness and longing in those unguarded moments, especially after he'd kissed her. She would vehemently deny it if he was foolish enough to point it out.

Mostly she seemed intent on proving she didn't need or want anyone. In the depths of his heart he understood why. She couldn't believe anyone would let her forget her past or be prepared to overlook it. No words would convince her so he quit trying. But as far as he was concerned, she wasn't responsible for what happened to her. She'd been tricked and forced to endure unspeakable things in order to protect Belle. In his eyes that made her noble and strong.

And if anyone dared to condemn her in his hearing, they would regret their words. *Lord, help her realize she doesn't need to dwell on the past.*

A cow veered away from the herd and Ward rode after it. A few more days and they'd be back at the ranch. Maybe his absence would make Red miss him. He grinned at the idea. What would it take to make her confess such a longing?

Perhaps given enough time…

If she stayed for the winter, he could make sure she had plenty of food to eat and wood to keep warm. He could help her pass the long winter afternoons. They'd talk about their hopes and dreams, play games with Belle. He might even pull out his father's poetry book and read a poem or two to her. Would she think it too romantic?

He figured time would heal her wounds and wanted to be there the day she realized she was free of her past. They could celebrate with a kiss or two.

Realizing his grin seemed permanently fixed to his lips, he glanced around to make sure none of the cowboys observed him. He'd take a razzing if they did. Thankfully they were occupied far enough away they couldn't see him.

Three days later they drove the last of the cows to the lower pastures and headed for the bunkhouse.

"I'm going to have a nice long soak," Ward announced, which brought a burst of snickers from the others.

"Got courting on yer mind?" Slim asked, his innocent voice not fooling Ward or any of the others.

"Could be," Ward allowed.

The others jeered, though he knew they would all head out for town or to the nearby ranch where a couple of single gals lived.

"Just so long as you remember I get first dibs on the tub." He kicked his horse into high gear and headed for the bunkhouse accompanied by yells from the others as they raced after him.

A few hours later, he strode across to the cabin, certain he smelled much better than when he rode into the yard. He'd donned a clean pair of denim jeans, his favorite blue shirt and polished his boots. He couldn't wait to see Red.

Belle raced from the cabin. "Ward. Ward. You're back."

It was a greeting to warm a man's heart. He waved and called a hello to her, then his gaze riveted to the doorway. Would Red come out or would she make him go in search of her?

Then she stepped into the sunshine. Her red hair glistened like a welcoming fire. Her eyes remained guarded but pink stained her cheeks. She would no doubt deny it, but he figured it meant she was happy to see him.

He was so glad to see them, his heart squeezed like an overactive fist. He jogged the last few steps, caught Belle and tossed her in the air.

She squealed in delight.

The child still in his arms, he moved to within a few inches of Red, brushed her cheek with his fingertips. "Glad to see me?"

She shook her head no, but her eyes said yes.

He put Belle down and moved closer to Red, drawn by the secrets in her gaze, hoping those secrets included feelings for him she wasn't ready to admit.

"She's gonna make us leave," Belle said.

Ward's heart spasmed like someone had stomped on it. He'd misread her expression. The secret she held was continued resistance. All joy fell out the bottom of his heart, leaving him empty and hollow.

Red hurried inside, Ward on her heels and Belle right behind.

They faced each other like wary boxers waiting to see who would make the first move.

Belle spoke before Ward could bring his thoughts into rational order. "You tell her she's wrong."

Ward pulled a small carved dog from his pocket.

"Belle, take this outside and play. Stay out of the wind."
Rain had been threatening all day.

With a disdainful sniff, Belle grabbed her sweater and left.

Red didn't give him a chance to say a thing. "I'm not wrong."

"You don't have to leave."

"I can't be a substitute for your family." Her eyes had developed blinkers so he couldn't gauge her feeling.

"You aren't a substitute. Stop saying it. You are safe here. Don't you like it?"

Something flickered through her eyes but disappeared before he could do more than guess she liked it but would never admit so. He changed tactics. "Belle is happy and safe," he said.

"There's a school where we're going. She can have proper instruction." She grabbed a newspaper from the table. "Here. Read it. I've already written and received a warm invitation."

He barely glanced over the news article. "You don't have to go. I don't want you to."

She rocked her head back and forth.

He took it for an internal struggle. Suddenly he understood what bothered her. She figured sooner or later someone would point out her background and the gossip would force her to leave. Probably thought it better to go now than later when Belle—and perhaps Red—got too fond of the people and the place.

All he had to do was make it permanent. "Red, marry me. I will take care of you." That didn't seem to convince her. "Just think how good it would be for Belle. For both of you."

* * *

It took Red two full minutes to catch her breath and answer. "Marry you? That's insane." She must have misunderstood him. "You can't mean it."

"It's the perfect solution."

People didn't marry because it provided a solution to where they would live. Or perhaps they did. But he didn't love her. Not that she expected him to.

"I—" She meant to say she couldn't, but failed to force the words to her mouth. Yet she could not deny the appeal of his offer. Would marriage give her what she longed for? Would she be allowed to forget her past? Or would it haunt her? Most important, would others let it go?

"Think about it."

He had no reason to sound disappointed, as if she should jump at the offer.

"Tomorrow is Sunday," he said. "Is that long enough to consider my offer?"

She laughed—a sound as much mockery as amusement, though she couldn't deny a jolt of pleasure at his eagerness. "Give me until Monday." Why was she even letting him think she'd consider it?

"Agreed."

They nodded. She wondered if he would offer to shake hands on the agreement or— She couldn't resist a glancing look at his mouth.

He chuckled as he pulled her into his arms. "Red, do you have any notion of how transparent you are at times? I only wish you would be so all the time." He stroked her head, smoothing her tangled curls. "You have the prettiest hair."

She jolted back. "It's not pretty."

Looking deep into her eyes, he spoke volumes without uttering a word. She let herself drink copiously of his assurance that he liked her hair, maybe even liked her a tiny bit.

Liking, caring…were they enough reason to marry?

He dipped his head and caught her mouth with his own—a gentle kiss.

Belle banged on the window. "Does that mean we're going to stay?"

Red sprang away from Ward.

He roared with laughter as he went to the door and threw it back. "You might as well come inside."

Belle shut the door behind her. "Well, does it?"

Ward repeated his offer of marriage.

Red sent him a cross look. "You said you'd give me until Monday."

"You better make the right choice." Belle's warning look reminded Red of their mama. It stole away her breath.

Ward noticed her quick intake of air. His eyes narrowed with concern.

She turned away. Thinking of Mama and Papa only confused her more. What would they advise? She dare not think of the looks they would give her because of the way she had lived not so many weeks ago.

Ward plunked down on the log stool he had claimed for his own. "Who wants to hear about the cattle drive?"

"Me. Me." Belle climbed to her chair and planted her elbows on the table, her expression adoring.

"I'll make tea." Red couldn't stand to watch them. Belle would be happy to become a permanent part of this place and have Red marry Ward. Was it reason enough to risk marriage?

She wished she could say it was. In the depths of her being she wanted to marry Ward and spend the rest of her life with him, but how could she? She was dirty, soiled, spoiled. He would soon come to despise her. Even as she despised herself.

If only there was some way to erase the time she'd belonged to Thorton, go back to the innocence of her early years.

However her past could not be washed away, forgotten or ignored.

Ward recounted many amusing tales of his adventures, but Red barely heard as her inner war continued. He drank tea and ate cookies, all the while talking to Belle, yet his gaze followed Red as if waiting for some sign of what she felt. But how could she reveal anything when she didn't even know what to think?

By the time Ward returned the next morning to escort them to church service, Red had convinced herself of one thing—her brain had ceased working. She had no idea what she wanted or what was best or what she should do.

It would require little effort for her to beg off attending church service, but Ward would no doubt badger her for an explanation, so she allowed him to tuck her hand over his arm and didn't make a fuss when he pressed it close. His warm presence partially calmed her inner turmoil, though she would never confess it to herself or anyone else.

She knew what to expect at the service and prepared

to close her mind to whatever Bertie had to say. Except today her brain had not only stopped functioning, it had holes in it that allowed Bertie's words to sneak in. Within seconds she was caught up in his tale of a wild youth.

"I'd been raised in a godly home. My father was a preacher of sorts. Yet I turned my back on it and did all manner of despicable things. I hated what I had become, feared what the future held. Likely prison or worse if I didn't stop. But I thought God would never forgive me for the horrible things I'd done. Nothing anyone said or did convinced me otherwise. Until the day I fell on my face in self-loathing."

Red sat straight and unmoving, her fingers twisted together in a white knot. She knew exactly how he felt.

"It was there in the dirt that I found what I needed. Forgiveness."

She sat back. That was too simple an answer.

Bertie wasn't done. "I deserved punishment and somehow I suppose I thought if I received it in my flesh it would erase what I'd done. But God reminded me of a verse my father had us children memorize at an early age. John 1:9, 'If we confess our sins, He is faithful and just to forgive us our sins, and to cleanse us from all unrighteousness.' I'd never before noticed that tiny little word *all.* That's when I realized the cleansing was all from Him. There was nothing I could do to add to God's generous forgiveness. I rose from the dirt and went forward a new man."

Red found it difficult to swallow. He made it sound so easy to start over. But how could one forget the sin of their past? Even if it were possible, would others let her forget?

She pushed her questions into a dark corner of her heart and turned her attention to the snacks Cookie handed out. Somehow she made it through the afternoon, answering Linette's questions, saying the right things at the right time. Or so she thought until she noticed Linette's curious study and forced herself to participate more. But she was grateful beyond measure when Eddie ended the afternoon early.

"I hope you all don't mind if I take Linette and Grady away. We have a lot of catching up to do."

Linette sent Red an apologetic look. "We'll get together another time."

Red nodded, relieved she wouldn't have to spend any more time under Linette's watchfulness.

Ward rose, too. "I want to get these ladies home before the rain begins in earnest." He walked them back to the cabin.

"Thank you," Red said at the door, hoping he would take the hint and leave her alone so she could sort out her thoughts. Instead, he opened the door wider and urged her inside, then followed. Belle moved away to play and Ward pulled two chairs close to the warm stove.

"Red, I couldn't help notice Bertie's sermon upset you. Want to talk about it?"

"You're mistaken." But her voice caught, betraying her lie.

He covered her hand with his.

She jerked away.

Ward studied her silently but she kept her attention on the front of the stove.

He sighed and shifted his attention away, allowing her to draw in a strengthening breath.

"I'm not mistaken and you know I'm not. Red, I understand your past is painful, but don't you think you should stop blaming yourself for something you couldn't help?"

She shivered. "Sin is sin."

"And God is God. Like Bertie says, He forgives."

"It's too simple."

He rested his hand on her shoulder, filling her lungs with immovable steel.

"It's too simple, for sure. But still, it's God's way. He offers us complete forgiveness. What do you think we can add to what He's done?" If his voice had been impatient or argumentative she might have objected, might have found an answering argument. But his gentle, caring words erased everything but a long, heavy guilt. There was nothing she could say to explain the weight of it.

When she didn't answer he squeezed her shoulder tight. "I'll pray for you."

The wind shuddered around the cabin.

He pushed slowly to his feet as if reluctant to leave her. Listening to the wind increase in strength, she wished he didn't have to go out. If they married—

She jumped to her feet and walked him to the door.

Marry simply to keep a person from going into the weather? Now that was the stupidest reason ever. She watched his departure from the window. Almost as stupid as wishing she could be worthy of his love.

* * *

The next morning dawned still and bright. She stepped outside to a much more pleasant day and lifted her arms to the sky.

"We're staying, aren't we?" Belle demanded for the seven hundredth time since Ward left last night.

"Belle, I told you I'll let you know when I make up my mind."

Her little sister jammed her fists on her child-sized hips and looked impatient. "You're just being prideful and stubborn."

Red couldn't help but laugh at the grown-up words from Belle. "Where'd you hear that?"

"Grady says that's what Mrs. Gardiner said to Mr. Gardiner when he refused to let her go to town. He said it was too muddy. But she said he was prideful and stubborn."

Red nodded, her grin still in place. "Maybe a person has to be sometimes."

"I don't think so." She marched away without a backward look.

Chuckling as she worked, Red hauled in several buckets of water and filled the tub to heat for laundry. She should have filled the tub last night but the rain made her choose to stay inside. Today was a nice day. She could hang the clothes outside to dry.

She'd said she'd give her word today. If he hadn't changed his mind, she would agree. He could take care of them and it would make him feel better. It would give Belle all the things Red wanted her to have—home, security, acceptance, maybe even love. He would never love Red. She didn't expect him to. It wasn't necessary.

She would require only one thing from him—his promise to never hate her for her past.

As she tidied the cabin and sorted the items for washing, she continually glanced out the window, wondering when Ward would appear to demand his answer. She glanced up at the sound of hoofbeats and saw Ward and Slim ride away from the ranch, Slim going south, Ward north. She pressed closer to the glass to keep them in view.

Just before Ward rode out of sight, he turned and waved his hat in her direction.

She half lifted her hand to wave back, then dropped it at her side. If he still wanted to marry her it would be a businesslike arrangement. No need for her to get all eager and adoring.

She scrubbed the clothes, rinsed them and twisted the water out of each garment. She hung the items to dry, all the while her ear tuned to the sound of a returning horse.

Hours later, the laundry had dried enough and she removed each piece carefully, folding it into the laundry basket in preparation for ironing.

The sound of hoofbeats thudded in her ears and she spun around. But only one rider returned—Slim. Red sucked in air and turned back to her chore. Ward would return later.

In the meantime she had work to do and hoped it would keep her thoughts from rushing ahead to his visit.

She carried the laundry inside, heated the sad irons and began the job of ironing each item. It consumed her minutes but not her thoughts. Perhaps he purposely stayed away because he'd changed his mind about the marriage proposition.

Thankfully Grady came to play with Belle so Red could glance out the window every few minutes without alerting her sister to her anxiety.

But after Grady left, Belle confronted her. "What did you say to Ward?"

"What do you mean?"

Belle's look was rife with accusation. "You chased him away."

"Why do you say that?"

"Today you were supposed to say you'd marry him. But he hasn't come. You said something."

"No, I didn't." Though Belle's suspicions closely echoed her own. He'd changed his mind but not because of anything Red had said. "He hasn't come because Eddie sent him to do something. Didn't you see him ride away this morning?" Was it only today? Less than twelve hours ago?

"So you're going to tell him you'll marry him?" Belle chortled, then threw her arms about Red's waist. "I knew you'd come to your senses."

Red patted Belle's back. "I haven't said anything yet. You'll have to wait until Ward comes so I can tell him my decision first."

"You like him. You'll do the right thing and marry him." Belle was so convinced that she knew what was best that Red laughed.

"We'll see."

Later, they made supper, cleaned up, then sat and stared at the door. Darkness fell. Still no sign of Ward. Had he returned and she missed it? Was he over in the bunkhouse trying to decide how to retract his marriage offer?

"It's time to get ready for bed," she told Belle.

"No."

She might have scolded her sister except for the fact her lips quivered and her eyes shone with tears. "Belle, you can't stay up all night."

"But you said he'd be back. I want to hear you tell him you'll marry him."

"Belle—" How could she tell her that Ward might not want to hear the words? But she couldn't destroy Belle's dreams until she had to. "He said he'd come so he will. But not tonight. It's too late."

Belle nodded and sadly prepared for bed. When Red went to tuck her in, Belle threw herself into Red's arms and sobbed quietly.

"Honey, don't cry. No matter what happens, we have each other and we'll be fine. We can still go to the mission in Medicine Hat."

Belle sobbed harder. "I don't want to go anywhere," she hiccupped.

"I know. But we're strong. We'll do whatever needs to be done."

Belle flung herself back on the pillow and glowered at Red. "You're talking like we're going to leave. You promised we could stay."

She only wanted to prepare Belle for bad news but what was the use? If bad news came they would deal with it. Nothing would ever be as bad as what they'd already endured, but Belle didn't need to think along those lines.

"Honey, I'm sure he'll come in the morning."

"I know. He said he'd be back." Belle seemed satisfied, and Red kissed her good-night and left the room. If only she could find the same solace.

Chapter Thirteen

Next morning Belle rushed from bed to the window. "I don't see him."

Red laughed, though it sounded tinny even to herself. "Maybe because it's not light yet."

"Almost. I see Slim and Cal going to the cookhouse." One by one she called out the names of the cowboys as they entered the house across the road. "Where's Ward?" Belle flung about and gave Red a demanding look.

Red shrugged and kept her attention on breakfast preparations. "I'm sure I don't know."

Belle stomped over and sat at the table, her elbows practically digging holes in the wooden top. "I still think you said something to him Sunday. You looked mad when he left."

Red sighed. Nothing she said would convince Belle otherwise. She served breakfast but Belle spent more of her time glowering at Red than eating.

"Are you done?" Red asked after she'd given Belle more than enough time to finish.

"Not hungry." She pushed the plate of food away.

"It's a long time until lunch."

"Who cares?"

"You might not have enough energy to play with the other children."

"Don't feel like playing."

"Fine." Red gathered up the dishes and scraped the wasted food to the slop bucket. "Good thing the pigs will enjoy your breakfast."

Belle's only reply was a long sigh.

"I'll wash and you dry."

"Don't I always?"

Red almost bit her tongue to keep from scolding Belle for her rudeness. She wouldn't normally tolerate it but this time she let it go because it reflected her own feelings. If Ward had changed his mind he could at least have the decency to tell her instead of putting her through this torture.

The dishes were almost finished when a knock sounded on the door.

"It's him. About time." Belle was at the door before Red could take a step. She paused and gave Red a squinty-eyed look. "Now, you be nice to him, hear?"

Red laughed. "Yes, boss."

Belle yanked the door open. And her shoulders sank like the air had been sucked out of her insides. "Hi, Mr. Gardiner."

Red composed her face. She would not reveal the same disappointment Belle did.

Eddie stepped into the room, twisting the brim of his hand. "I thought you might be worried about Ward."

She nodded, not about to share her silly thoughts with him.

"He should have returned last night."

The meaning of his words made their way slowly to the center of Red's brain, and then exploded. She grabbed a chair and sat down before her legs gave out. "I thought—" Her worries seemed so selfish.

Belle's eyes were far too wide. "He's gone?"

Eddie glanced from one to the other. "No need to worry."

A little late to tell them that. "But you're worried?"

"I'm sure he's fine, but I'm going out to check on him."

Belle's breath released in a moan.

Red pulled Belle to her. She meant to soothe the younger girl but clung to her, finding comfort and strength in her warm little body. She burst with questions she dare not voice. Where was Ward? Was he hurt?

Eddie jammed his hat on his head. "I best be on my way." But he didn't immediately turn. Instead, he tipped his head and signaled he wanted to speak to Red.

She stood and eased Belle to the chair. "I'm going to say goodbye to Eddie. You wait here."

Eddie held the door for her and she stepped outside. He closed it firmly behind him. Her nerves jarred with the sound.

He rubbed at his forehead. "There's more." He leaned closer, his expression filled with urgency. "Ward told us about Thorton Winch. Constable Allen rode up to the ranch with news that he's escaped. He feared the man was headed this way."

Red collapsed against the wall. Thorton! If he found her... Then a second, more dreadful thought burned through her mind. "Do you think he ran into Ward?"

"I don't know what to think. But I want you and Belle to stay up at the big house until we can be sure you're safe. Go pack up whatever you need."

She heard his words, understood what he wanted, but she couldn't move.

"Red." Eddie shook her gently. "You need to hurry."

She nodded once but couldn't think what he meant her to do.

"Red, I can't go after Ward until I know you're safely in the house with Linette."

She nodded. Over and over.

He opened the door and gave her a little shove through it.

Her legs like log posts, she stepped inside, looked around and then reality hit her. Thorton had escaped. Ward was missing. And she delayed Eddie in searching for him.

She forced her trembling limbs to pull out the sack Linette had sent items in and tossed in the clean clothes stacked in neat piles.

Belle pushed her chair back with a clatter that shrieked along Red's nerves and she rushed to Red's side. "What are you doing?"

"We have to leave here immediately."

Belle pushed Red away from her task. "We can't leave. I want to stay forever and ever. If you're going to run away from Ward, then I'm not going with you."

"Belle, we're only going to the big house. Now gather your things together as quickly as you can." She couldn't get there soon enough. The idea of being caught by a vengeful Thorton brought bile to her throat.

"I'm not going." Belle plunked down on the floor.

Ignoring her, Red continued to stuff in items, urgency making her movements jerky. She saw the book she was reading and added it. "I'm ready. Belle, come on." She tossed a sweater at her sister.

Belle crossed her arms and refused to move.

Eddie knelt before Belle. "You can't stay here. It isn't safe."

"Why not?" Her stubborn tone informed them she thought Eddie only said it in the hopes of making her move.

"It just isn't. Red isn't running away. But we need to get you to the house where you'll be safe."

"Ward said we're safe here."

Red sighed. "Belle, we aren't right now."

"You're just saying that."

Red considered her options. Belle left her little choice. "Thorton has escaped from jail. We'll only be safe with Linette and Grady."

"There's a man watching the house at all times," Eddie assured them.

Belle bolted to her feet and grabbed the sweater. Finished, she looked at Red, her eyes wide with fear and disappointment. "You said he would never bother us again."

Eddie took the sack Red had packed, gave a quick glance around the place, paused to push the wood away from the fire. Then he eased Belle toward the door.

They hurried up the hill. Every step drove shards of fear into Red's heart. Where was Ward? Was he injured? Or had Thorton captured him? She could well imagine him taking delight in torturing Ward.

Red closed her eyes in a vain attempt to stop the

horrible pictures flooding her mind. She stumbled and Eddie caught her by the elbow.

"You need to stay strong," he murmured.

She nodded. She must not let Belle guess at her fears. By the time they reached the house she ached all over from tension.

Eddie turned them over to Linette, then hurried away.

"Grady," Linette said. "Why don't you show Belle the new toys Papa gave you?" Linette had explained how Grady wanted to call Eddie "Papa."

Belle's eyes were still much too large and she grabbed Red's hand. "I'm scared."

Red managed a smile and took Belle to the windows. "See Slim out there? He'll make sure no one gets into the house."

"We're safe? Thorton can't lock us up?"

"Thorton will never lock us up again. I promise."

Satisfied, Belle went to play with Grady.

As soon as she was out of sight, Red groaned.

Linette hugged her. "I've been praying ever since we heard what happened. We must trust God to protect us."

Red tried to convince herself it was enough.

"Come. I've prepared tea." They sat before the windows overlooking the ranch where they could watch all the comings and goings. Eddie and Constable Allen left the barn, climbed the hill and stepped into the house.

Constable Allen took off his Stetson and tucked it under his arm. "Ma'am, Mrs. Gardiner. I just wanted to update you on what's going on. All the ranchers in the area have been notified about Winch's escape. They'll be on the lookout. I've organized several of the men into a posse to find Thorton and Ward. It's only a matter of time until both are located."

Linette twisted her teaspoon round and round. "Thorton isn't the only danger Ward faces. What if he's injured? Lost? Or something equally as dreadful?"

Eddie answered, "Ward is careful, cautious even. I can't imagine something like that happening to him."

"We'll find them both wherever they are, I assure you," Constable Allen said.

At the way the Mountie kept linking the two names together, the alarm Red had been struggling to keep under control scooped her insides hollow. If she hadn't been seated, she knew she would have fallen to the ground like an old rag. He was suggesting the only thing that would delay Ward would be Thorton.

"How would Thorton know we're here?"

The Mountie answered, "He persuaded a guard it was his right to know who was responsible for having him arrested. The guard foolishly gave Ward's name. Thorton wrote to the land agent asking after Ward Walker, claiming to be a long-lost brother. The agent gave him all the information he had."

"Including where his land is?"

The Mountie nodded, his eyes full of apology.

She shuddered. Thorton knew far too much. "Does he know Ward works here?"

The Mountie gave a tiny shrug. "It would be easy enough information to get."

Ward was in mortal danger. "Find Ward." She squeezed the words from a tight throat.

Constable Allen gave a tense smile. "Trust me. We'll

find him. We'll find both of them. We'll keep you informed as best we can but now my job is to locate them."

Red watched him depart as a thousand fears dragged talons across her heart.

Linette rushed after Eddie. "I expect you home safe and sound."

Eddie kissed her and left.

Red and Linette watched the pair hurry toward the barn.

Roper and Cassie and the children came into sight. Roper paused to speak to Eddie, then continued toward the house. Linette went to let them in.

"I'm going to join in the search but I don't want to leave Cassie and the children unguarded."

"Of course not. They can stay here. Come in. Children, Grady and Belle are in the kitchen."

The children went to play under the watchful eye of Daisy, and then Cassie and Linette returned to the sitting room.

Cassie squeezed Red's arm. "They'll find Ward."

At least she didn't link Ward's name with Thorton's, for which Red was grateful.

A few minutes later the men rode away to the west.

Red jerked forward. "I should have told them to check his ranch. Maybe he stopped there."

Linette gripped Red's elbow. "I'm sure they'll check. Let's pray for safety for all of them." She didn't give Red a chance to either agree or argue but bowed her head and prayed fervently God would protect them all, help them find Ward and help the Mountie capture the fugitive. "Amen."

Cassie had taken her hand during the prayer. "Amen," she said, and released her grip on Red's hand.

"Amen," Red added. She could not pray, though she wished she could. What was the use though when she knew God would not hear her?

The minutes passed, heavy and cold. Finally Linette pushed to her feet. "The children will be hungry. I'll see to lunch."

Red helped with preparations, sat at the table with the others, ate the food set before her but she couldn't even say what it was.

Gloom crept into the corners as they watched out the window. As night fell, the men returned to the barn.

Eddie and Roper staggered into the house and sighed as if weary to the soles of their feet.

The women sprang forward. "Did you find him?"

"Not a sign anywhere," Eddie said. "We went to the cabin. It was empty. There is no trail, no clues indicating either of them. Ward has no reason to hide his trail. But Thorton—" He scrubbed at the back of his neck. "The man is a magician at hiding his tracks." He looked from Linette to Red to Cassie. "We'll be out again at first light."

Red clamped her lips together. She would not let her wail escape. Excusing herself under a mumbled excuse, she hurried from the room and sank down on a chair in the kitchen. Ward was gone. All her fine talk about how she could manage on her own meant nothing as truth after truth bombarded her. He had been nothing but kind. He had the sweetest smile, the nicest eyes. His voice triggered happy feelings inside her. She clamped her hand to her mouth. Her heart squeezed tight. How could she have been so blind?

Because even if he didn't love her, she loved him with an ache the size of this house. She'd treated him unkindly. Would she get an opportunity to make it up to him?

Her insides felt sucked dry as she contemplated her situation.

She wanted to spend the rest of her life with him. Would she ever get the chance?

What had become of him?

But she had no answers by the time Linette showed her and Belle to a guest room. Cassie and the four children had returned to their house with Roper.

She prepared for bed and lay beside Belle until her sister's breathing deepened, then she rose. Unable to even pretend sleep, she circled the room, looking at each object. Some of the paintings she recognized as Linette's work. A bookshelf hung on one wall. She lifted each book and examined it. One was a hymnal. She paged through it, remembered standing between Mama and Papa as they sang the familiar words. A folded piece of paper fell from the pages. She picked it up and opened it. Someone had written a poem, perhaps meant to be set to music for a hymn. Because she didn't want to think beyond the walls of this room, she read the words.

Grace that exceeds our sin and our guilt!
Grace that is greater then all our sin. Dark is
the stain we cannot hide. What can avail to wash
it away?

It was the anguished cry of her heart. Was there forgiveness for what she'd one?

Brighter than snow you may be today.

She fell on her knees. Was it possible God could forgive so great a sin as hers?

Oh God, is Your grace meant for a sinner such as I?
I was once an innocent believer.
Can I be a tarnished, forgiven believer?
My grace is sufficient.

The words were from the Bible but filled in the spaces between each heartbeat.

Sufficient even for someone with Red's past?

Sufficiency from God's almighty, powerful, everlasting hands. From the Creator of heaven and earth. The God that parted the Red Sea and could move mountains.

How much more could she ask?

Lord, forgive my sin, wash me until I am white as snow.
Cleanse me from those awful things I was forced to do.

She pressed her face into her palms and let the words of the poem speak her heart and her pain.

Blessed, joyous release came. She laughed softly so as to not waken Belle. God did forgive sins, even those as loathsome as hers.

Free to now pray, she silently beseeched God to keep Ward safe. Then she fell into bed and slept.

Ward smiled into the empty landscape as he rode away from the ranch.

One of Eddie's prize imported bulls was missing.

He and Slim had been dispatched to locate him. He planned to ride far, wide and hard, find the bull if the animal was in his circuit and get back to the ranch as fast as possible.

His insides sang with anticipation. Would Red agree to marry him? He couldn't imagine anything more pleasant than taking care of her the rest of his life. Just the thought of it oiled his insides with peace. He'd never lost the idea he'd failed his mother and brothers, but if Red gave him a chance, he would never fail her. Not so long as it depended on him. He wasn't foolish enough to think he might not make mistakes, but he would certainly pray for God to help him. He would win her back to her own faith in God. She'd once believed. She would learn that God never changed and she could trust Him as much as she'd done as a child.

Marrying to keep her safe and take care of her made perfect sense. But could he keep her safe? He'd failed to do so with his brothers and mother. Instead, he'd abandoned them. He vowed if Red agreed to marry him, he would never leave her and Belle. He would do his best to protect them. And should he fail, he would simply keep trying.

The bull wasn't in the lower pastures so Ward headed toward higher ground, his mount clattering over a rock-infested ridge. He rode through brush and searched around hills for the missing animal.

"Okay, bull, where are you? I'd like to get back as soon as possible."

His search would take him within a couple of miles of his ranch and he veered in that direction. Could be the bull might take it in his head to pay the empty place a visit.

He reached the crest of a hill that allowed him a view of his ranch. The buildings sat in a natural clearing that was big enough for a good-sized farmyard. Like he'd told Red, he'd thought of building the cabin on the top of the hill but figured it might be buffeted by winter winds, so he chose a spot a little ways down. All he had at this point in time was a small log cabin, a wood shed and some corrals. He'd build a fine barn one of these days. He turned in his saddle. To the west lay rippling hills that crept up the side of the mountain. The mountains filled the horizon, shining in the sun. Dark pines draped from every crevasse.

"It's a beautiful spot," he murmured. "Red and Belle will love it here." Only one dark spot remained in his plans. He had not heard from his mother and brothers. He longed to give them a home as well.

Ruminating would not find the bull and get Ward back to Red to hear her answer. He'd seen the acceptance in her eyes and already knew what she'd say, but he still longed to hear the word *yes*.

They climbed higher. Reached a plateau, and Ward gave his mount a chance to relax a bit as he glanced about for any sign of the missing animal.

"Nothing," he muttered. The sun had already dipped into the west. He'd have to turn back now to reach the ranch before dark.

Something stirred the bushes across the coulee. He urged his horse toward the rim of the plateau to get a better look. The purple shadows deepened so he couldn't make out the dark shape. He needed to get closer, and searched for a way to get down the incline.

Spotting a narrow ledge, he reined the horse toward the path.

The animal sidestepped and tossed his head, indicating he didn't care for the direction Ward indicated. Why had he picked this particular horse to ride? Paddy was known to be a knucklehead who shied at shadows.

"Now, look here, Paddy. The sooner we have a look, the sooner we can head back. You won't be getting any hay or oats until we're done. So best you choose carefully where you put your feet and get us off this plateau."

The horse responded to Ward's firm hand and started down the trail. It was narrowed more than Ward anticipated. In hindsight, he should have ridden several miles to the east where he knew there was a gentler trail. But it was too late to do anything but keep going.

"Steady there, old boy." He murmured encouragement to the frightened horse. "We'll be okay." But the sun had lowered enough to make it difficult to see.

He gently urged Paddy to put one foot in front of the other. "Look, I'm not enjoying this any more than you are. But the sooner we get to the bottom, the better for both of us." Every nerve tensed for the smallest clue to guide them safely.

Without warning the ground gave way beneath them. Ward's heart jolted as they dropped into nothingness. His heart bounced to the roof of his mouth and stayed. He kicked free of the stirrups and threw himself off the saddle. He might fall a hundred feet and land on rocks but he still preferred his chances on his own to being rolled on by a horse.

For an immeasurable moment he hung in the air, and

then landed on one shoulder, his air leaving his body in a whoosh. He rolled several times and came to rest on something solid. Pain crisscrossed his chest.

He blinked to clear his vision but all he saw was shapes. He squinted, saw a dark shape to the side. The cliff. He shifted carefully, uncertain if he had stopped partway down or reached the bottom.

Before him spread a gray blanket. He tried to get to his feet but swayed as pain shot through his head. He sank back to the ground.

"Paddy? Come." Through the deepening darkness he saw the horse trot away and settle down to enjoy the green grass. Stupid animal. He wouldn't even go home and alert Eddie and the other cowboys of Ward's dilemma.

Ward turned and tried to make out the cliff but his eyes refused to focus. He'd never be able to navigate a climb without proper light.

He'd have to spend the night here. He shivered. If only he had the slicker tied to his saddle. "Paddy," he called again, forcing false cheerfulness to his voice. "Oats, boy. How about some oats?" But he couldn't shake a bucket and tease him closer.

With a sigh that tore at his bruised ribs, he shifted about and got as comfortable as possible. He groaned. His situation left something to be desired. Determined to ignore his discomfort, he shifted his thoughts to other things. What would Red think when he didn't show up as he'd promised? Likely that he'd changed his mind. No doubt he'd have his work cut out for him convincing her he hadn't.

The cold stole up his legs. Thoughts of Red warmed his heart.

Why hadn't she jumped at the chance to marry him? It provided the perfect solution to her problems. Safety and the protection of his good name.

He couldn't see anything but the blackness of the night but he squinted as he considered his question. Should he have offered her more? Should he have said he loved her? He rubbed at his cold chin. Love was a highly overrated commodity in his thinking, though the love he'd seen between his ma and pa had been real enough. Yet his stepfather had vowed he loved Ma and her sons. His actions proved otherwise. Ward loved his ma and his brothers. Yet what did it mean? He'd left them. Perhaps with the best of intentions. But still, he'd left and had no way of knowing if they were safe or suffered the daily beatings meant for Ward.

Nope, far as he could see actions meant a whole lot more than words of love. He figured what Red needed he could provide without letting love cloud the issue.

The air grew colder. He was high enough up the mountain that he'd have to endure a long, cold night.

Several hours later his head jerked to his chest and he bolted awake. *You must get back to Red. Take care of her. She needs you even if she won't admit it. You can give her what she needs. Safety. Protection.* It was enough. It had to be. Would she ever tell him her real name? Wouldn't she have to if they married?

Something stung his eyes. He blinked. Sunshine. His limbs ached with polar ice. Cold sunshine. But at least he could find his way out of there. The sun was already high in the sky despite the fact it seemed to lack warmth.

He staggered to his feet, pins and needles of pain informing him of returning circulation. He had to get to Red. Had to tell her something. He shook his head. He couldn't remember what he was supposed to tell her.

He swayed as he fought for balance. "Paddy, come here. That's a good boy." His words were mumbled sounds but the horse understood his meaning. But would he trot to Ward so he could ride out of this predicament? Of course not. He tossed his head and ambled several more yards away to make sure Ward couldn't catch him.

Ward looked about him. A hundred yards to the east he made out what appeared to be a path wide enough to allow a man to the top. Stepping gingerly on tender feet, he climbed to the top and headed across the plateau in a direct line to his ranch. Every bone in his body hurt. Every breath ripped from his lungs. But he pushed aside the pain. He had to get back to the ranch and Red.

The sun shone bright enough to hurt his eyes but failed to warm him. Several times he staggered and righted himself. How long had he been walking? He squinted at the sky. The mountains were at his back. He turned and the sun hit him in the eyes. Already afternoon. He checked the pain in his leg, saw a deep gouge that oozed blood. Wondered about the pain in his arm. Nothing he could do for it. Had to keep going. Get back to Red.

He reached an open area where he'd chopped trees not long ago. He'd soon be at his cabin and he picked up his pace in anticipation.

In his haste, he fell. *Get up. Get up.* His body slowly obeyed. *Red.* He breathed her name in and out on each breath. Each breath hammered against the inside of his skull. *Red.* He focused on her name and found strength to continue.

He staggered and righted himself. Was that the cabin? He squinted. Tried to bring his vision into focus. The walls of the cabin wavered ahead of him. It was only a few yards away. He ran. More precisely, he lurched toward the cabin. Reached the door and leaned on it. The latch released and he tumbled to the floor and lay there, beyond caring.

Inch by inch he pushed his face off the floor, got to his hands and knees and looked around. The bed beckoned and he crawled to it, pulled a blanket over himself and fell asleep.

Chapter Fourteen

Something nudged Ward from his dreams. A blow to his boot. He surfaced slowly, loath to leave the dream he'd been having about Red. They were married and living in this cabin. Only it had many, many rooms. Each room seemed to evolve from the previous one until he was lost and calling for her. *Red. Red.* Her voice answered, telling him he was safe but he couldn't find her.

His first conscious thought was how strange that she was telling him he was safe. Wasn't it the other way around? Wasn't he the one who promised safety?

The blow to his boot came again. Someone was in the cabin and it wasn't Red. It was a man.

Ward was instantly alert but he calmed himself and faked being half-asleep as he studied his guest. Thorton. Holding a gun and wearing a self-satisfied smirk.

A thousand fearful thoughts clogged Ward's brain. How had this man escaped? Had he harmed Red and Belle? Best move slowly. Find out what was going on before he did something he might regret. Like choke the man with his bare hands.

"Well, lookee here. If it ain't the man who stole

my girls from me." Thorton's smile belied the evil in his eyes.

Ward edged his feet over the side of the bed to face Thorton. Sleep had helped to restore his strength. "There's laws against owning people. Or keeping them against their will."

Thorton's laugh rang with embedded evil. "Red could have left anytime she wanted."

"You know she would never leave Belle in your clutches."

"Poor Belle. You taking care of her as well as I did? How about Red?" His eyes glinted with knowing mockery.

Ward curled his fists. He must not fly at this man even though he ached to. He had to outsmart him.

"At least I don't have to force her to stay by locking up her little sister."

Thorton's amusement died. "Thought you'd have them here with you. Where are they?"

Ward allowed his eyes to give away nothing. Thorton didn't know her whereabouts? Or was he only taunting Ward? "How'd you find me?"

"Told the land agent I was your long-lost brother. He readily told me where you had this ranch." He snorted. "Looks like your ranch is only in your imagination. You figure on bringing Red here to live?"

Ward shrugged.

"Well, sonny, you ain't never gonna get the chance. Where's my girls?"

"Can't say."

Thorton's gaze was as cold as the metal gun in his hands and Ward wasn't fooled. He was just as dangerous with or without a gun. "You've got her, and I want her back."

So he didn't know where Red was.

"You're going take me to her or else."

Ward leaned back, guessing his expression was as mocking as his feelings. "And if I don't?"

"I could shoot you on the spot."

"Wouldn't help you find Red though, would it?"

Thorton considered the question for several seconds.

Ward used the time to mull over his options, but trying to figure out several things at the same time with a brain that hadn't had enough sleep and was distracted by having a gun leveled at his heart proved a challenge.

"Where are they?"

What would best serve to get Thorton distracted from searching for Red and Belle? Besides a bullet straight through his heart.

Thorton jammed the gun up Ward's nostrils. "Take me to them."

Ward sucked back caution and a goodly dose of fear that drained his heart of blood and left him as cold as the dead of winter. He tried to gauge the time of day. A slice of a glance toward the window showed the sun gleaming on the Rockies. He must have slept several hours.

"I expect they're with friends."

"And where exactly might that be?" The gun bit into his flesh. Ward knew hatred like he'd never known in his life, not even when his stepfather had beat him. Not even when the man had beaten Travers just to get a reaction from Ward. Thorton wanted Red for all the wrong reasons and Ward would not allow it. He could only pray that Eddie knew of Thorton's escape and had taken Red and Belle into his house for protection. "I might take you where they are." He would never take him to the ranch but perhaps he might get a chance to disarm the man if they rode down the trail.

"You take me there. Then I'll decide what to do with you."

"Fine. I don't have a horse."

"I found one a ways from here. Might be yours or not. Don't matter. It will serve the purpose."

"I need to give him a few oats if he's going to make the trip back to the ranch."

"Forget the oats." Thorton urged him to the door without any kindness in the way he jabbed the gun in Ward's ribs. At least it was out of his nose. He had a rifle on the saddle. Always carried one in case he met a pack of wolves or an injured animal. If he could distract Thorton long enough to get it…

The horse that Thorton had found was knuckle-headed Paddy, all right. Ward approached the horse.

"Hold up there." Thorton's voice rang with warning. "I think I'll relieve you of this." He reached around and removed the rifle from the horse. "Don't guess you're going to be needing it. I got all the firepower we need." He tied a rope around Ward's waist and pushed him to mount.

"You best keep an eye out for wolves, then. I saw a pack several times in the past week. Other cowboys have seen them, too," Ward said.

"You're just saying that to make me nervous. Hoping you might distract me."

"Don't deny that I might not like to see you take that gun off me, but I ain't making it up about the wolves.

Just saying you ought to keep your eyes on more than just me, seeing as you're the only one with a gun. I ain't got no desire to be wolf bait."

Thorton laughed, a sound full of evil mockery. "I wouldn't mind seeing you devoured by a pack of wolves. Seems fitting after you stole my girls away as sneaky as any wolf I ever saw."

"Be that as it is. I 'spect if they get me, they'll get you as well." He enjoyed the way Thorton's eyes darted from one side of the clearing to the other. He didn't mind a bit seeing the man get all nervous and swallow hard at the thought of wolves on his trail. Despite Thorton's pretense at being convinced that Ward joshed him, it was plain he didn't fancy being wolf food, either.

Ward decided to take advantage of Thorton's nerves. "You ever seen a wolf up close? Man, when one of them bares his teeth it's enough to make the bravest man cry for his mother."

"You, maybe," Thorton said. "I ain't never cried for my mama."

Ward bit back the remark burning the tip of his tongue. He doubted the man had a mama. At least one he could remember.

Ward decided he'd pushed hard enough, but he hoped he'd given the man something to fret about. A man tensed up was a dangerous man. But Ward counted on Thorton taking chances that would give him an opening.

"Get in your saddle and show me where Red and Belle are. I intend to get back what is mine."

Ward swung up and headed down the trail. Somehow Thorton's little brain hadn't noticed there was only one trail out. 'Course he might have come that way and discovered the fork in the trail.

He led the way, but Thorton kept a firm hold on the rope around Ward's waist to make sure he couldn't pull any "funny stuff," as Thorton called it.

Ward's mind clattered with all sorts of ways to distract Thorton. If he could get the gun…

But Thorton didn't give him an opening.

Ward prayed. *God, help me stop him. I don't want him to ever find Red and Belle.* In fact he would not let it happen. He would die stopping Thorton if necessary. He hoped it wouldn't be. He wanted to spend years and years with Red. Loving her. The truth caught his breath and stopped it halfway up his throat. He loved her. He didn't care if love was risky or foolish. He didn't care if Red ever loved him back. It was enough to love her and spend the rest of his life showing her. Or die protecting her. He chuckled. How ironic that he'd discovered the truth about love only to face never having the chance to live it.

Thorton jerked on the rope. "What you laughing at?"

"Thinking of Red."

Thorton yanked the rope so hard Ward had to turn the horse to keep from being pulled from the saddle.

"You keep your thoughts off her. She's mine. Why, I bet she never even told you her real name." His voice grew low. "I could tell you." He laughed a sound so harsh and bitter that it sent cold fingers up and down Ward's spine. "But then I'd have to kill you."

Ward reined his horse forward and continued down the trail. He had no mind to discover Red's real name from the poisoned mouth of Thorton. No, sir. He wanted to hear it from Red's lips. He knew the day he did it would signify that she had let her past go. *God, help her find release from her past.* He smiled at the thought of sharing his life with her. Would he fail her as he'd failed his family? *And help me be strong and make the right choices.*

A dark shadow in the trees to the side caught his attention. He stared after it. Saw another. "Thorton, don't look now but there are wolves following us."

"Yeah, like I'd fall for that trick."

Ward kept his eye on the trees. "Give me my rifle." His low, controlled voice must have said something to Thorton.

"Not going to happen." But he turned to follow the direction of Ward's gaze.

Another shadow flitted past.

Thorton let out a cuss. "Sneaky things. Why don't they come out in the open where a man could shoot 'em?"

Ward thought that was reason enough for them to hide, but knew Thorton wasn't looking for an answer. Another shadow slipped by. "That makes four. There's probably more."

Thorton shot into the trees. Aiming at shadows made for poor target practice. Ward knew he missed hitting anything but trees. He shot five more times. Ward counted the shots. When he knew the gun was empty he spurred Paddy toward the other man. Paddy leaped forward in surprise. Before Thorton could realize his danger, Ward grabbed his wrist and whacked it across the saddle horn. The gun went flying.

Ward roared in rage and grabbed Thorton by the

throat. The pair tumbled to the ground. Both horses snorted and backed away. Thorton twisted and punched and cursed. No doubt he feared for his life, and well he should because Ward didn't intend he should continue to threaten Red and Belle. The man fought hard but Ward had far more at stake. Ignoring the pain in his ribs and limbs, he pummeled the man. He intended to live to tell Red he loved her. He planned to marry her and enjoy many, many years with her. She needed to know she was loved as a woman should be. Forever and always.

Riders approached. Were they friends of Thorton's? "Hello, it's Constable Allen. You can let him go now."

But Ward wasn't letting anyone go. Not until he was done with the man.

Hands pulled him off.

Constable Allen slapped cuffs on the struggling Thorton. Ward was pleased to see Thorton's nose bleeding and a lump swelling his eye.

"Good job of stopping him."

Ward shrugged away from the restraining hands. "If you hadn't come along I would have given him what he deserves."

"Don't worry. This man will get what he deserves. He killed a Mountie."

Ward's laugh was short and bitter. "See he doesn't escape again." He leaned as close to Thorton as the men would allow. "You ever show your face around here again and you're a dead man. Stay away from Red and Belle or you'll regret it. For about a minute as you draw your dying breath."

The Mountie dragged Thorton to his horse. "Get him out of here."

Constable Allen gave Ward serious study. "You're looking a little ragged around the edges. Eddie has men searching for you." He nodded toward two men. "See that he gets back to the ranch safely."

"They'll just slow me down." Ward swung into his saddle and kicked Paddy into a gallop. He had to get to Red and Belle.

Vaguely he was aware of the throbbing in his side as he rode for the ranch.

He leaped from his horse as he approached the barn and left the animal to fend for itself. He dashed for the cabin and threw the door open without pausing to knock. "Red!" he bellowed. The word echoed. "Red? Belle?" They must be out back.

He dashed around to the fire pit. Nothing. He kicked the ashes. Cold. They hadn't been there today.

He returned to the cabin and slowly began to notice details. The stove was cold. The corner where Belle played, empty.

The cold gripped his insides as the information seeped into his thoughts. No dolly. No doll clothes. Not giving any thought to intrusion, he strode over to the bedroom door. No clothing items hung on the hooks. The whole place had the air of being uninhabited.

His legs turned to cotton and he fell against the wall. Was she up the hill with Linette? But wouldn't someone have told him? Had she gone to the mission? Was this her answer?

He'd stop her. Tell her he loved her. Persuade her to change her mind. He spun about and raced from the room, not even bothering to close the door behind him. His pace increased as he headed for the barn.

Cal appeared in the doorway.

"Saddle me a horse," Ward called.

Cal jerked back. "Ward? Where did you come from?" Then he laughed. "You look downright awful. Like you've been dragged by a horse."

"Never mind. Get me a horse."

"There ain't much here in the way of mounts. Everyone is out scouring the country for you and that escaped criminal."

"Constable Allen has the man in custody. And I'm okay, as you can see. There has to be something left to ride." He headed around the barn to the pasture where they kept a string of horses. About half of them were gone. "One of those will do."

"I don't know what Eddie will say. They were rode hard all day yesterday."

"One of them is going to ride hard again today." He slipped through the gate, eyed up the horses and chose the sturdiest-looking one of the bunch. He grabbed a halter from the fence where someone had carelessly left it. Roper would have something to say to the culprit. Then he eased about and dropped the halter over the horse and led him into the barn.

Cal followed him. "You mind telling me where you going in such an all-fired hurry?"

"How come you aren't out looking for me and Thorton along with the others?"

"The boss left me and Slim to guard the big house. Make sure the jailbird didn't sneak in."

Ward tossed a saddle blanket onto the horse, then a saddle.

Cal grabbed his arm. "Man, you're bleeding. You ought to let Linette look at that."

Ward glanced at his blood-soaked sleeve. "It'll keep. I got more important things to tend to."

"So it seems. Exactly where are you headed? Just in case Eddie wonders."

Ward slowed down and sucked in air that tortured his ribs. "Guess I should let him know what I got in mind. I aim to go after Red and bring her back."

"Huh. You need a horse to do that?"

Ward shook his head. Cal could be a little thick-headed at times but this was worse than usual. "I'll follow her all the way to Medicine Hat if I have to. I'm not letting her go."

"Guess you've got the love bug, huh?" Cal grinned like a fool.

"I don't have time for your silly games."

"You got more time than you think you do."

Someday, if Ward lived long enough, he might see Cal grow up enough to make sense. "I'll be on my way. Tell Eddie I'll be back with Red and Belle."

A number of horses clattered into the yard. Cal went to the door and stared out. "Guess you can tell him yourself. He's back."

Ward gritted his teeth. Another delay. He'd never catch up to Red at this rate.

Eddie strode in. "Cal, look after the horses." He stared at Ward. "Constable Allen told me what happened. He said you'd be back here. Said you looked pretty beat-up. He didn't exaggerate. Thorton do this to you?"

"Thorton and a fall down a mountain."

"I'm guessing that's why you didn't return when you were expected?"

"Made for a bit of a delay."

Eddie eyed the freshly saddled horse. "You running out?"

"Going after Red. Figure she's halfway to Medicine Hat by now, but I'll catch up to her."

"You're after Red, huh?" Eddie grinned. "Good to hear."

"I'd like to get on my way, if you don't mind."

"I think you better come to the house before you leave."

"Boss? I'm in an awful hurry."

"Nevertheless, if you want to ride my horses until they're wasted and worn, you come to the house before you leave." He turned away, taking Ward's compliance for granted.

Ward didn't move. "I don't need any more delays."

Cal, carrying gear to the tack room, heard him. "He's the boss." Did the boy ever stop grinning?

"Yeah, guess so."

Still he hesitated. He could delay long enough for Eddie to get out of the road, then ride away. Eddie might send someone after him. Might dock his wages when he returned. Might be angry enough to fire him, but at the moment Ward only cared about finding Red.

Red finished helping with lunch dishes and the women returned to the little sitting room with Linette to watch for riders. Red prayed she'd see Ward return. Instead she watched Eddie and half a dozen men ride to the barn and dismount. Eddie ducked into the barn. Cal came out and helped the men tend to the horses.

No Ward. A chill weaved along the length of Red's spine and drove icy spears to her heart. What had happened to him? Was she destined to lose him just when she'd decided she could love him?

She clenched her fists. *Please, God. Bring him back to me. Please.*

Eddie stepped from the barn and headed up the hill.

Linette clutched Red's curled fists. "It must be good news or they wouldn't have come back."

She nodded. Didn't Linette realize Ward wasn't among them? The thought wailed through her head, sucked the blood from her heart.

Eddie stepped inside. "Good news, ladies. Thorton is under guard. He shot a Mountie while escaping so he'll hang for sure."

"Ward?" Red choked the word out.

"He helped capture Thorton. The way Allen tells it, they had to pry him off the man."

"Is he okay?" Linette asked on Red's behalf.

"He's a little worse for wear. Guess he fell down a cliff or something. I didn't get too many details."

"Where is he?" Red wailed.

"He should be here by now." He moved to the window. "I don't believe it."

Red saw Ward leave the barn, leading a horse.

She held her breath, waiting for him to head up the hill.

Instead he turned the other way.

Wasn't he coming to see her? Had he changed his mind? Was it too late for her to tell him who she was and what she wanted? "I must speak to him." She rushed past Eddie, paying no attention to his words. She trotted down the hill, almost losing her balance in her haste. "Ward," she called. "Wait."

But he didn't hear her.

She continued her flight past the cookhouse. Didn't slow until she reached the barn.

Ward argued with Slim at the corral corner. "I don't care what Eddie said. I'm taking a horse. I intend to find Red."

Slim grinned at Red over Ward's shoulder. "I don't think you'll need a horse."

"Get out of my way."

"Turn around."

Ward tried to push past Slim.

He intended to find her. But why did he need a horse? Finally able to speak, she called. "Ward?"

Ward jolted like he'd stepped on something sharp. He lifted his head and stared at Slim then slowly turned. He saw her and blinked. Shook his head. "Red? What are you doing here?"

She smiled. "Waiting for you."

"But how? Why?" He swallowed hard. "I thought you must have gone to the mission."

"And you were planning to ride there? Why?"

Slim disappeared into the barn and shut the door firmly.

Ward closed the three steps separating them and touched her cheek. "You've been here all the time?"

"Eddie said we'd be safer in the big house." She caught his hand. "Come inside, and I'll tell you what happened."

Her touch brought him from his stunned state.

They crossed to the cabin. She wondered when the door had blown open. They sat side by side and she began her story.

"When the Mountie informed Eddie that Thorton had escaped, he insisted we stay with Linette." Still clutching his hand, she turned to study each dear feature. "Where were you? I've been so worried."

He told her of his accident. His gaze grew sorrowful. "When I came here and you were gone…" He shook his head. "I imagined you'd gone to the mission." He clasped her shoulders. "You're okay? You and Belle?"

"We're both very well." She let herself float in the warmth of his look. But there were things she must tend to. "Ward, my name is Grace. Grace Amanda Henderson. And God's grace has shown me that He loves me despite what I've done."

He cupped her cheek and rubbed his thumb along her face. "You did nothing wrong. Grace? I like it. It suits you." He searched her features as if memorizing them. A skitter of fear raced through her. Was he memorizing them because he meant to say goodbye? Had she changed too late?

"Grace, I have been a fool."

She pulled away, her heart threatening to crack with sorrow. He regretted asking her to marry him.

"I wanted to take care of you. Thought it was all you need. You were right. It was my way of making up for not being able to care for my mother and brothers. But I learned something in the last couple of days." He pulled her toward him, tipped her face toward him.

She kept her eyes lowered, unable to endure any more of his regrets.

"What I wouldn't admit to myself and wouldn't share with you is that I love you."

Her gaze flew to his face. Filled with amazement and sincerity. "You love me?"

He chuckled. "I do. In a thousand ways. 'How do I love thee? Let me count the ways. I love thee to the depth and breadth and height my soul can reach.'"

As he quoted the poem her father had so often spoken to her ma, her eyes filled with tears. He brushed each away with his finger.

"Don't cry. Please don't cry."

"These are happy tears." She sucked back an uneven breath.

He kissed her damp cheeks. "And I shall quote it to you every chance I get." He jerked back. "I'm jumping to conclusions here. Grace, will you marry me?"

She saw the need in his eyes. The need for something only she could give him. "Ward Walker, I love you. I have from the time you stood up to Thorton in that saloon. I will be honored to marry you and share my life with you." She had to be certain of one thing. "My life and my little sister."

"That goes without saying." He kissed her cheeks again.

She lifted her face and offered him so much more. Her heart, her life, her future.

He claimed her mouth and gave her a kiss full of promises. Then he pulled her into his arms and told her of his experiences the past two days.

"I am so thankful you are safe and sound. I prayed God would protect you and He has."

"I had to get a chance to tell you I love you." He kissed her again to emphasize it.

Safe in his arms, she told him of the past, not minimizing her fear and loathing at how Thorton had humiliated her.

"Grace, you did nothing wrong, though I understand how you might feel. But God has washed your past away."

She clung to his reassuring gaze. "I know. It's marvelous to feel free." She rubbed her cheek against his shoulder. "And to know the love of a good man."

"I'm blessed to know your love."

Later, having opened their hearts to each other and shared their deepest longings and fears, they walked hand in hand up the hill to the big house.

Linette greeted them at the door. "I wondered how long before you two chose to join us." Her wide smile and flashing eyes informed them that she shared their joy. "Belle's been anxious to see you."

Belle rushed toward them. "Where you been? Red, did you say you'd marry him?" She left no doubt that if Grace did not do so, she would be a sore failure.

Grace and Ward both squatted down to face Belle. Linette slipped away to give them privacy.

"You can call me Grace again. And yes, Ward and I are getting married."

Ward pulled Belle into a three-cornered hug. "Belle, I love your sister and I love you. Will you accept me as your brother?"

Belle pulled away to give him a look rife with disbelief. "I don't want a brother. I want a father."

Grace choked back a sob. If she wasn't mistaken, Ward's eyes showed the glisten of tears.

"I'd be pleased to be your father."

They hugged long and hard.

Then joined Linette in the sitting room. "I don't need to look at you twice to know you have good news."

Grace smiled. "We're going to get married and start a new life." It would truly be a new life. One blessed by God's gracious love and forgiveness.

Linette hugged her tight. "Are you going to wait until we get a church in Edendale?"

Grace looked at Ward for his opinion and laughed out loud at the shock and refusal widening his eyes.

Her eyes twinkling, she turned back to Linette. "We haven't discussed it but I don't think we want to wait that long."

Linette grinned. "I kind of suspected that would be your answer. Now let's have a look at Ward's injuries."

Grace helped cut Ward's sleeve to expose a deep gash. "It's dirty. I hope you don't get infection."

As Linette left to get water to wash his cuts, he leaned over and kissed Grace. "I won't get sick because I have far more important things to do. I want to show you my ranch. I want to get married and start life together there."

She concentrated on his injury.

"Red—Grace, what's bothering you?"

His tender question opened her heart. "What about your family? What if you find them? And they want to join you?"

He took her hands and gently rubbed each knuckle. "It would be an answer to prayer. I can't think of anything I'd sooner have than my old family and my new family on the ranch."

"You'd have room for all of us?" From what he'd said she expected a small cabin much like the one she and Belle presently shared.

Ward chuckled. "Not in the same house. But with two brothers I think we could put up another house in short order." He sobered. "I only wish it was something I needed to do."

"Me, too." Hearing Linette's footsteps, she stole one more kiss and whispered, "I love you."

His eyes shone as bright as a summer sky.

Linette laughed. "I'm happy for you both."

Chapter Fifteen

Ward's injuries weren't serious. Only some cuts and bruises that healed quickly, though his ribs continued to feel like he'd been run over by a herd of stampeding cows. Eddie insisted he take it easy for a few days and he didn't argue.

"I want to take you and Belle to see my ranch," he told Grace, pleased when she seemed eager for the trip.

Early one morning, he pulled the wagon to the cabin and helped Grace and Belle to the seat. "It's going to be a beautiful day." Truth was, even if the sun wasn't shining so bright and the sky wasn't clear from horizon to horizon, even if a cold north wind buffeted them and rain peppered their skin he would think it a beautiful day with Grace pressed to his side.

The air was golden. The trees flicked their dark green leaves.

He glanced about at the spot where he'd seen the wolves. Thankfully, none appeared. Eddie assured him they had been driven from the area, but Ward wouldn't be taking any chances with his precious cargo.

A few minutes later, they turned past a thick stand of

pines and the ranch lay ahead of them. He stopped the wagon. "There it is. My ranch and our future home."

Grace sighed.

"I'm hoping that's a good sound."

"It is." She squeezed his hand. "It's a beautiful spot." Trees dressed in dark green formed a backdrop to the north.

"I hope you'll like the cabin. It's small but I plan to add on."

She laughed, the sound ringing in the rooms of his heart. "I think you'll find I'm not fussy." Turning so she could look deeply into his eyes, her smile filling her face. "I'm happy simply to have a home."

Her words pinched his brain. "And love?" he prompted.

Her smile deepened until it felt warm and rich. "And love," she whispered.

He understood she still struggled with her doubts and vowed to spend the rest of his life erasing them. "I love you, Grace Henderson. Soon to be Grace Walker." He leaned closer and caught her lips in a kiss.

She pressed her hand to his back as if she wanted to assure herself that he wouldn't withdraw...not only from the kiss, but from his promise of love.

"Hello," Belle said. "I'm here."

Grace jerked back, her cheeks pink with embarrassment.

Ward wrapped an arm about her shoulders and pulled her close. He nudged Belle. "Get used to it. I intend to show your sister how much I love her every chance I get."

"At least when I'm not stuck on a wagon I can go somewhere else."

Ward laughed. "Who wants a closer look?" Without waiting for an answer, he flicked the reins and continued. "There's only a small enclosure now." He pointed out the corral pen. "But I'm going to start building a barn right away. Eddie agreed to sell me a few head of cattle so we can start our own place."

He stopped the wagon before the cabin. Belle jumped down before Ward made it around to lift Grace to the ground.

Belle stared at the mountains to the west. "Wow. They're so close."

Ward grinned down at Grace. "The view is the reason I built the house here. Come and see." He led her inside. "It's not much yet." Two rooms. The larger area served as living quarters, the other, a small bedroom. "I'm going to add on right away so Belle can have her own bedroom."

"How long will it take?" Belle wanted to know.

"Not long. The logs are ready and waiting."

"Do we have to wait until it's done?"

He felt the impatience and uncertainty of the pair. "What do you want to do, Grace?" They'd discussed it and she said she didn't see any reason to delay their wedding.

She shifted away, avoiding his eyes.

He caught her chin and brought her gaze back to him, saw the uncertainty in her face. "Grace, I only ask to give you a chance to say what you want." He lowered his voice. "Not because I want to delay. And I certainly am not looking for a way out." His words grew strong as he spoke.

She nodded, her uncertain gaze shifting to blinding joy. "We can live here while the new rooms are built."

"Good. Then we'll proceed with our plans. Now come and sit at the table." He'd designed the kitchen so a window provided a view of the mountains and placed the table before the window.

She sat down, turned, saw the view and gasped. "I could never get tired of seeing the mountains."

He pressed his cheek to the top of her head. "I will never get tired of sharing my life with you."

Belle groaned. "I'm going outside."

Grace and Ward laughed. Grace explored the cupboards, then looked at the wall over the armchair. "We'll hang the sampler there." She meant the one he'd hung in the cabin back at Eden Valley Ranch.

They brought in supplies from the wagon and stocked the cupboards. Grace made lunch and grinned at Belle and Ward at the table. "Our first meal together in our new home."

Ward thought his heart would burst from his chest with a joy he could hardly contain.

They returned to Eden Valley Ranch later in the afternoon. He put the wagon away, then went to the cookhouse for supper.

Cookie jostled him. "My cooking's not good enough for you? You found yourself a new cook."

"Cookie, your cooking is just fine. But there are other considerations."

The men hooted and laughed.

Cookie thumped Ward on the back. "I'm glad for both of you. You deserve to be happy."

"And I will be."

A short while later he took some things to the bunkhouse and saw a letter on his bed. "Who would be writing me?" he wondered, and then his heart broke into a gallop. His mother! He grabbed the letter and read the return address. It was from Travers. From a town miles from where they used to live. He slit the envelope open and read the letter.

He couldn't wait to share the news with Grace and jogged over to the cabin. "A letter from my brother."

She sank into a chair as if the news was too heavy for her. "What does he say?"

"He says our stepfather moved the family several times. He doesn't know how my letter found him. It had been forwarded a number of times. He says the beatings continued after I left, though they weren't as vicious. He and Hank figured out how to avoid them for the most part. Says he followed in my footsteps and left home when he was fifteen. Three years ago our stepfather had a stroke." Ward turned to the letter and read,

He was a crippled old man after that. Ma nursed him. I tried get her to leave but she said it wouldn't be Christian. She stayed with him until he died over a year ago. A few months ago, she sold the house 'cause she couldn't abide the memories. I'm going to visit her as soon as I mail this letter to you. I don't think I'll have any trouble persuading her to accept your invitation to join you. If you don't mind, I'd like to go West, too, and see if I like it better than here.

His grin threatened to split his face in two. "Isn't that good news?"

But Grace looked as if he'd told her he meant to send her back to Thorton.

"Grace, what's wrong?"

She rolled her head back and forth.

If he wasn't mistaken, unshed tears glistened in her eyes. He caught her chin and waited for her to bring her gaze to his. At the murky depths he groaned. "What is it? Tell me."

She swallowed loudly. "Now you can take care of them."

"I can give them a home. And I'm relieved they are okay and free from the tyranny of my stepfather."

She nodded. "It's what you've always wanted."

"Yes, it is."

She lowered her gaze and refused to meet his eyes even when he lifted her chin higher. "You don't need to take care of us now."

The meaning of her words hit him and he sat back. "Grace, do you still think you are only a substitute for my mother and brothers?"

She met his scalding look with quiet stubbornness.

He leaned forward until he saw nothing but her fearful green eyes. "Grace Henderson, I love you. I want to share my life, my heart with you. Taking care of you is only one way of doing that."

She didn't blink. "You're sure you won't want the cabin for your family?"

"Oh, Grace. I'm not going to change my mind about us. The cabin is our home. You and me and Belle. I'll build a new one for my mother just like I said."

Hope flooded her eyes.

He got to his feet and pulled her into his arms, tipping her head back so he could watch her expression. "I mean exactly what I say. I love you with my whole heart and soul and plan to spend the rest of my years enjoying your company. Okay?"

She brushed her fingertips over his cheek as wonder and amazement filled her eyes. "I have trouble believing that I—Red—deserve your love."

"You aren't Red anymore. You are Grace and soon to be my beloved wife."

"Ward, is it any wonder that I love you so much my heart sometimes hurts."

"Let me fix that for you." He claimed her lips in a gentle kiss. He knew exactly when she let go of her doubts, for she wrapped her arms about his neck and returned his kiss with an enthusiasm that made him chuckle.

"Only one thing."

She grew serious, guarded, and he kissed her again. "Stop being so uncertain of my love."

She brushed her hair from her cheek. "I'm learning. You have to give me time. Now what is it you want?"

"Do you mind delaying the wedding until my family arrives?"

"I think that's a wonderful idea if they aren't too long in getting here."

He laughed. "Oh, Grace. You will keep me on my toes, won't you? One minute all uncertain and the next anxious to start our marriage."

She pulled his face toward her and kissed him soundly and sweetly. "I'm learning."

Epilogue

One month later Grace waited in the upstairs of Linette and Eddie's house. She glanced at her silvery-gray dress. The silk fabric was so soft.

Linette turned from fixing Belle's hair to study Grace. It had taken a while but all of them had grown used to using her real name—even herself. She no longer thought of herself as Red.

"The cut of your gown is perfect," Linette said. "You look positively regal, especially with your curls piled on top of your head like that."

Grace had wanted to pull it into a tight bun, but when Ward heard of her plans he'd begged her to show off her curls. "You are the most beautiful woman in the whole West and I like to admire you." So she'd agreed. She turned to the mirror. It did look rather regal.

Belle's reflection joined Grace's. "Am I pretty, too?"

"You're beautiful. But remember, I'm the bride so Ward is supposed to admire me." She tickled her little sister, and they both giggled. Ward made no secret that he loved Belle as much as he would a child of his own.

Eddie came to the door. "Are you ready?"

Grace nodded. Today was the day she'd been waiting for ever since—well, truth be told, she'd waited for this kind of love all her adult life.

Belle went first, descending the stairs to the main room. Cassie and Linette followed, then Grace rested her hand on Eddie's arm. "I can't thank you enough for all you've done."

He'd sold Ward enough stock to start his ranch operations. He'd sent men to help construct a barn and add two rooms to the cabin and put up a second cabin. They'd finished the projects just in time.

Grace and Ward had spent many pleasant hours overseeing the construction and discussing plans.

"Shall we?" Eddie said, and together they went down the stairs.

Ward watched for her from the front of the room, his smile lighting a path to her heart. She saw no one else as Eddie led her to Ward's side. He tucked her hand possessively to his side, then they turned to the visiting preacher to exchange vows.

Several minutes later the preacher said, "I now pronounce you man and wife. You may kiss the bride."

And Ward kissed her for the first time as her husband. A kiss full of sweet promise.

Then they turned toward their guests. Ward's mother and two brothers were the first people she greeted. "I'm so glad you got here in time for the wedding." The trio had arrived a week ago.

Ward's mother looked weary and worn but her eyes had the same bright blueness of Ward's.

Thirteen-year-old Hank was shy and had a woundedness about him that Grace recognized. Time and love would heal those inner bruises. Eddie recognized it, too, and offered the boy a job at the ranch. Twenty-year-old Travers had been angry and standoffish to begin with, but he and Ward had spent time riding together, working together and putting finishing details on the second house. He'd accepted Ward's offer of making him a partner in the ranch. Grace knew it would take time for the hurt to heal but the process had started.

The crowd enjoyed the huge feast that Cookie had prepared.

Finally Grace and Ward could leave the party. He helped her into the wagon and they drove away from Eden Valley Ranch.

He stopped at the door of their new home and swept her off her feet to cross the threshold. "Welcome home, Mrs. Walker." He lowered her to the floor but kept her in his arms as he gave her another kiss.

"Mmm. Seems I've waited a long time for this day."

"I know what you mean. It's only been a month but all my life I've had a hole in my heart that only you can fill."

He spoke so freely of his love that her heart constantly rejoiced.

"No regrets?" He spoke the words into her hair.

She wrapped her arms about his waist and squeezed him tight. "Not for one moment."

Ward eased her back to study her face. She let all her love and joy shine from her eyes. "You don't think Belle minded that we left her with Linette and Eddie, do you?"

Grace giggled. "She doesn't mind. She sounded so

grown-up when she said, 'You two need time alone right after your wedding. A honeymoon.'"

Ward chuckled. "She was very pretty in her new dress." His smile deepened. "But not half as beautiful as her big sister. It was the nicest wedding I've ever been to."

Grace only smiled. She knew he'd been to very few and one was between his mother and stepfather. Not exactly a charming memory. "Linette was disappointed that we didn't wait for the new church to be finished." The foundations had been laid, the lumber brought in.

"It was nice of her to contact a preacher friend who was willing to come and perform the ceremony."

"Now let's enjoy our new home."

Hand in hand, they walked into the new part of the cabin. Three bedrooms.

"Three?" she'd said when he told her his plans.

"One for us. One for Belle. And one for brothers for Belle."

"No sisters?"

"They can share Belle's room until we're so crowded we have to build on again." Across the yard, far enough away to provide privacy, was the cabin he'd built for his mother and brothers.

Inside, Grace glowed with joy and thought likely she glowed outside, too, she was so happy. "I am forever grateful for God's grace that sees beyond my sin and offers forgiveness."

"I have something else to show you." He wrapped his arm around her shoulders and led her to the window over the table.

"I'm so glad you put the table here under the window

so we can see the mountains every day. I will always remember you saying they made you remember how God's love is round about those He loves."

"I will always remember you declaring so fiercely that you were fine. I got a little weary of you insisting you were fine."

She rubbed his cheek. "You threatened to carve the words into the log."

"Look." He drew her attention to a log by the table.

She gasped. "You didn't?"

"Read the words."

"'Because of His grace.'"

"I thought of carving in the words 'we're fine,' but I realize it is only because of God's grace that I have my Grace whole and ready to love. I don't want us to ever forget it."

She pulled his head down and kissed him soundly, then nestled against his chest.

She laughed. He did, too, his voice reverberating in his chest.

Later, they stood before the cabin and watched the sun set over the Rocky Mountains. She stood with her back to his chest with his arms wrapped about her, feeling his warm breath on her cheek.

"I will never forget this, our wedding day," she whispered, her heart too full to say more.

He nuzzled her neck. "You are my Grace, my love and my joy." He turned her so he could kiss her.

Her heart overflowed. Ward was all she'd ever dreamed of…the dream she'd given up while in Thorton's clutches. She would never stop thanking God for

His abundant grace and for the love of a man like Ward.
She thought of her parents and felt their approval.

Life filled with love was so good.

* * * * *

Dear Reader,

Bad things happen in life. It might be an accident that leaves someone with a permanent injury. It might be cruelty and abuse. Or it might be day after day of struggle that leaves us whimpering and defeated. Where is God in all this? And why are people allowed to be so evil? Worse, why are we so bad at times? In this story, I attempt to deal with how such an incident affects people. But this is a work of fiction and the answers are not complete. If you struggle with the feeling of being unworthy of God's grace, I beseech you to find answers in His word and seek help from Godly people.

I'd love to hear how this story impacted your life. You can contact me through my website www.linda-ford.org where you can also catch up on new books and bits and pieces of my life.

Linda Ford

Questions for Discussion

1. Red made a choice that got her into this situation. Do you think she made that choice in good faith? Is there something she might have done differently?

2. What hold does Thorton have over Red? Could you suggest a way she might have escaped him sooner?

3. Do you admire her or criticize her for the life she lived and how she dealt with it?

4. What strengths do Ward and Red each bring to their relationship?

5. How do you feel Belle has been impacted by their time with Thorton? Has Red made it easier for her? How?

6. Eden Valley is a little community of its own. What does it offer to someone like Red?

7. Do you think Red—Grace—will find censure in the future? If so, how do you see her dealing with it?

8. What do you think happened to Ward's family in the past that they didn't contact him? Do you foresee problems with his family in the future? If so, what?

COMING NEXT MONTH
from Love Inspired® Historical
AVAILABLE JUNE 4, 2013

THE BRIDE NEXT DOOR
Texas Grooms
Winnie Griggs

Newspaper reporter Everett Fulton can't wait to leave his small Texas town. But when he's involved in a scandal with bubbly newcomer Daisy Johnson, will their marriage of convenience stop him in his tracks?

THE BABY COMPROMISE
Orphan Train
Linda Ford

Socialite Rebecca Sterling and rugged cowboy Colton Hayes are both determined to find a home for the last child from the orphan train. Despite their differences, can they find a home with each other?

THE EARL'S HONORABLE INTENTIONS
Glass Slipper Brides
Deborah Hale

After years at war, widowed cavalry officer Gavin Romney has a chance to find healing in faith, family and the love of his children's governess. But will his quest for justice leave him with nothing?

THE UNINTENDED GROOM
Debra Ullrick

To realize her dream of establishing her own theater, Abby Bowen must take on a male business partner. She doesn't count on falling for the handsome widower who answers her wanted ad or his twin boys.

Look for these and other Love Inspired books wherever books are sold, including most bookstores, supermarkets, discount stores and drugstores.

LIHCNM0513

REQUEST YOUR FREE BOOKS!

2 FREE INSPIRATIONAL NOVELS
PLUS 2
FREE
MYSTERY GIFTS

Love Inspired

HISTORICAL
INSPIRATIONAL HISTORICAL ROMANCE

YES! Please send me 2 FREE Love Inspired® Historical novels and my 2 FREE mystery gifts (gifts are worth about $10). After receiving them, if I don't wish to receive any more books, I can return the shipping statement marked "cancel." If I don't cancel, I will receive 4 brand-new novels every month and be billed just $4.74 per book in the U.S. or $5.24 per book in Canada. That's a saving of at least 21% off the cover price. It's quite a bargain! Shipping and handling is just 50¢ per book in the U.S. and 75¢ per book in Canada.* I understand that accepting the 2 free books and gifts places me under no obligation to buy anything. I can always return a shipment and cancel at any time. Even if I never buy another book, the two free books and gifts are mine to keep forever.

102/302 IDN F5CN

Name	(PLEASE PRINT)
Address	Apt. #
City	State/Prov.	Zip/Postal Code

Signature (if under 18, a parent or guardian must sign)

Mail to the **Harlequin® Reader Service:**
IN U.S.A.: P.O. Box 1867, Buffalo, NY 14240-1867
IN CANADA: P.O. Box 609, Fort Erie, Ontario L2A 5X3

Want to try two free books from another series?
Call 1-800-873-8635 or visit www.ReaderService.com.

* Terms and prices subject to change without notice. Prices do not include applicable taxes. Sales tax applicable in N.Y. Canadian residents will be charged applicable taxes. Offer not valid in Quebec. This offer is limited to one order per household. Not valid for current subscribers to Love Inspired Historical books. All orders subject to credit approval. Credit or debit balances in a customer's account(s) may be offset by any other outstanding balance owed by or to the customer. Please allow 4 to 6 weeks for delivery. Offer available while quantities last.

Your Privacy—The Harlequin® Reader Service is committed to protecting your privacy. Our Privacy Policy is available online at www.ReaderService.com or upon request from the Harlequin Reader Service.

We make a portion of our mailing list available to reputable third parties that offer products we believe may interest you. If you prefer that we not exchange your name with third parties, or if you wish to clarify or modify your communication preferences, please visit us at www.ReaderService.com/consumerschoice or write to us at Harlequin Reader Service Preference Service, P.O. Box 9062, Buffalo, NY 14269. Include your complete name and address.

Love Inspired **HISTORICAL**

Love Thy Neighbor?

After years of wandering, Daisy Johnson hopes to settle in
Turnabout, Texas, open a restaurant, perhaps find a husband.
Of course, she'd envisioned a man who actually likes her. Not
someone who offers a marriage of convenience to avoid scandal.

Turnabout is just a temporary stop for newspaper reporter
Everett Fulton. Thanks to one pesky connecting door and a
local gossip, he's suddenly married, but his dreams of leaving
haven't changed. What Daisy wants—home, family, tenderness—
he can't provide. Yet big-city plans are starting to pale beside
small-town warmth….

The Bride Next Door
by

WINNIE GRIGGS

Available June 2013

www.LoveInspiredBooks.com

LIH82967